D1616481

THE DOOMSDAY CODE

A NOVEL SARA YAGER

For information contact:

http://www.sarayager.com

Cover design by Sarah Hansen

Library of Congress Cataloging-in-Publication Data has been applied for.

ISBN: 979-8-9890981-7-0 | Hardcover

ISBN: 979-8-9890981-1-8 | Paperback

ISBN: 979-8-9890981-0-1 | eBook

First Edition November 2023

10 9 8 7 6 5 4 3 2 1

For all the generations to follow.
May we shape the future you deserve.

AUTHOR'S NOTE

In the roughly three years it took to research and write The Doomsday Code, something strange happened. The idea of human-level synthetic intelligence went from something laughable, fun to talk about but reserved for the Luddites and science fiction fans, to something with a growing momentum—an undeniable force brewing just below the surface of our iPhones, virtual assistants and gaming consoles.

Sometime in the 21st century, advances in artificial intelligence, quantum computing and neuroscience will collide, giving rise to an intelligent agent with which we will coexist for the rest of our time: Human-Level Machine Intelligence. For six million years, our *intellect* has allowed humans to roam Earth nearly unchallenged. What happens when that advantage is no longer our own?

It is hard to speculate what the consequences might be. Stephen Hawking said that "the development of full artificial intelligence could spell the end of the human race." Elon Musk believes "we are summoning the demon." And Russian President Vladimir Putin thinks that "whoever becomes the leader in this sphere will become the ruler of the world."

Why are those in power so terrified of the arrival of advanced AI? This is a technological point of no return. Once AI surpasses humans and becomes capable of self-improvement, it may leapfrog into something far superior—potentially to the tune of a *billion times* smarter than biological humanity. When that happens, there is no telling if we could understand, predict, or control its behavior. In the words of Oxford philosopher Nick Bostrom, "We have what may be an extremely difficult problem with an unknown time to solve it, on which quite possibly the future of humanity depends."

When I began my research, I read estimates that human-level AI could take decades upon decades to achieve. But in the narrow span of a few years, these estimates have begun to shrink, with many experts now contending it could happen *this decade*. A flood of advances in the last twelve months alone is evidence of accelerating progress in the space:

- *Lamda*: Google's chatbot made headlines when its engineer declared it had become sentient. He was promptly fired.

- *ChatGPT*: OpenAI's chatbot made waves as it became the most buzzworthy breakthrough in deep learning, inspiring multi-billion-dollar investments and leading people to wonder if the Large Language Model will disrupt the immovable (Google). Of further concern, how we will control the output of such LLM's? Stereotypes, equality, deepfakes, misinformation, and disinformation are just a few of the issues it presents.

- *GitHub Copilot*: The AI-powered tool developed by GitHub and OpenAI can generate code, suggest improvements, and provide context-specific suggestions. It's not hard to imagine all the things that could go wrong when humans are left out of the loop.

- *Dall-E/Midjourney/Stable Diffusion:* Generative imaging tools have begun to create compelling art, raising fears that creators may soon be displaced. Equally concerning is the proliferation of misinformation and disinformation as deepfakes become ever easier to make.

- *AlphaFold:* In the past, AI was mainly good at solving problems with man-made rules, like playing games. But DeepMind's AlphaFold, which can accurately predict the 3D structure of a protein, has not only unlocked a greater understanding of biology, but also marks a new frontier in artificial intelligence—showing that AI can understand and solve complex problems in the real world.

The AI winter is over. What comes next is what we should all be talking about—perhaps trying to regulate and guide in a meaningful way. As I write this, the Future of Life Institute has just called for a six-month moratorium on AI development to allow for the creation of safeguards and guidelines that have thus far remained elusive. In their open letter, co-signed by dozens of preeminent AI researchers and industry leaders, they warned of existential risks to humanity. If the public and regulators are listening, only history will tell.

Can we divert the path of technology towards something in line with our own long-term interests? Not to mention those of the rest of our planet? Perhaps intelligent life will someday spread throughout the cosmos and flourish for billions of years to come. Or perhaps our species will soon come to an unceremonious end. But most importantly, this course will be set because of actions we take during the next century on Earth.

That is the subject of this novel.

So let's start talking.

"If the future of humanity is decided in your absence, because you are too busy feeding and clothing your kids, you and they will not be exempt from the consequences."

— **Yuval Noah Harari**

CHAPTER 1

EIGHT STORIES ABOVE A narrow Azerbaijanian backstreet—two flights and six thousand miles from the watchful eye of Fort Meade—Adrian Pryor worked in front of a large bank of computer monitors. He stared at the display with sunken, glowing eyes, a slab of jerky dangling from the corner of his mouth. A trove of empty energy drinks and crumpled food wrappers littered his workstation. Behind him, Al Jazeera news droned from a television.

It was 11 p.m.

Adrian had been at it for six hours this time. He adjusted the black-rimmed glasses from where they had slid down the bridge of his nose, staring at the mess of C-code filling his display. To some, looking at code like this was disorienting. But, like learning any foreign language, when you read enough code, you get to a point when it becomes natural. Easy.

But this wasn't Adrian's code. And he wasn't trying to make it work. He wanted to *break* it—to find the holes that he knew were there. He'd already combed the code a half dozen times. So far, he had found no mistakes. But he knew they were there. They were always there. He raked his fingers through his unwashed shoulder-length hair, running through a mental catalog of possible bugs: things like arithmetic errors, interface issues, logic problems, syntax errors . . . the list went on.

What am I missing?

A moment later, Adrian finally spotted it. He wasn't surprised that the coders had missed it; it was so small, hardly a rounding error in the scheme of things. But certainly, given the window, it was an exploitable bug. Entire spaceships had been lost to lesser miscalculations.

Adrian smiled, feeling self-satisfied. Finding bugs like these was very valuable. To manufacturers, of course, but even more so on the underground market. But there was the fairly significant issue of one's conscience, which was why Adrian had decided to help the manufacturers find and patch their vulnerabilities instead of selling them to the highest bidder online.

Adrian sighed, turning his gaze out the window. Baku was a city of contrasts. Ornate Ottoman-era buildings with domed roofs and intricate stonework competed for space with sleek skyscrapers with glass facades. Modern retail shops and high-end restaurants were crammed among street food stalls and ramshackle shops where local vendors hawked their wares. In the distance, he could make out the old royal walled city of Icheri Sheher, and opposite the Caspian, the fiery glow of the three Flame Towers. Ancient and modern. Coexisting.

Azerbaijan was not what Adrian had expected. But hell, he wasn't sure what he had expected. Even after twelve months, he was still trying to figure out how things had snowballed to such an extent that he had been exiled to Azer-friggin-baijan. Adrian wanted his job back. His life back. But right now, no one in intelligence would touch him, and going back to the States was out of the question.

Thankfully, after arriving in the far-flung country, Adrian had found that he could earn an independent income as a security consultant. And a pretty damn good one at that. Bug bounty programs were similar to "Wild West" wanted posters. Tech manufacturers rewarded third parties for finding vulnerabilities in their code. A few big bounties a year was enough to live on. The best part was that it could be done from the comfort of a couch. Even a couch in Azerbaijan.

In the last six months alone, Adrian had discovered two epic bugs—the kind of vulnerabilities that most hackers were lucky to find once in a lifetime. The first one, an exploitable bug in Linux, allowed him to take over a target machine unnoticed. It was the holy grail of bugs, known by his peers as a "zero-day" exploit. In the hands of a bad actor, it could mean root access to government servers or the ability to hijack a foreign oligarch's passwords.

Only weeks later, he had discovered a bug in the Jeep Cherokee—the kind of consumer nightmare that could have ignited a media frenzy and permanently tanked sales. The bug, a remote access exploit, allowed a hacker to seize control of the steering, disable the brakes, take control of the headlights, indicators, and even remotely cut the engine.

It was spooky stuff. Needless to say, access to zero-day exploits like this meant money, power, and ego. But for Adrian, it was more than that. He wasn't some self-taught whiz kid or guerilla hacker. He was a government-trained white-hat—a good hacker.

As a boy, Adrian had always liked tinkering with software, figuring out its underlying design, and finding a way to bend it to his will. In college, while his friends had been majoring in Hotel Management and Tourism, Adrian had gotten his Ph.D. in Applied Math and Computer Science. Recruited by the NSA straight out of college, he had begun his career in the ranks of the world's top cryptographers. But he had quickly realized that hacking, not math, was where his heart was, and transitioned to the cybersecurity unit, where he had spent the next decade.

Working at the NSA had allowed Adrian to do things he couldn't do anywhere else. But the first thing he realized after parting ways with the agency was how differently the government and the private sector treated hackers. At Fort Meade, "digital exploitation" was considered a prized skill, one honed over many years of experience. Outside the NSA, he may as well have been a 300-pound, pony-tailed basement dweller.

Adrian caught his reflection in a mirror nearby and sighed. Meh. At thirty-six, the man staring back was a ghost of his former self. His once sharp brown eyes had deep circles under them. Illuminated by the pale wash from the display, the stubbled contours of his jaw looked gaunt, the result of a ten-pound weight loss he attributed to generalized gloom and stress.

He wheeled away from his reflection, making his way through his broom-closet of an apartment. In the kitchen, the options were scant: local beer, whiskey, and some cheap, off-label vodka. He settled for a beer. He rummaged around in a drawer for a bottle opener, found one, and cracked it open.

He took a long swallow and immediately grimaced. Adrian had yet to develop an affection for the local fermented stuff, which he likened to battery acid. Nevertheless, he choked down another sip. The loss of his former life was a tough pill to swallow. Seeing the physical toll didn't help.

Adrian crossed the living room and collapsed onto a faded polyester couch. He fished his cell phone from the pocket of his hoodie and signed into the Signal App. The encrypted messaging platform was the only thing Adrian trusted since his split from the NSA. The use of a cellular phone was itself a risk, but Adrian had performed a surgery of sorts on his device—removing the microphone and disconnecting the camera. It was a crude fix at best, but he had no interest in willfully enabling surveillance by his government. Or any government, for that matter.

Adrian hammered out a quick message to his brother back in the States. He was one of the few people with whom Adrian had remained in close contact. By necessity, even he had no idea of Adrian's whereabouts. Adrian knew his precautions were probably excessive, but it wasn't like he was tapping light bulbs or inspecting air vents for spyware. He was in the middle of nowhere, for God's sake.

He wrapped up his note, a quick proof of life that his brother had insisted upon weekly since his departure. Then he closed the Signal App. It seemed like overkill to Adrian, who was after all, a fully functional adult. Maybe it was a requisite older sibling thing? Adrian had no idea. He was the youngest, and thankfully never had to bear the mantle of being the responsible one.

An electronic ping drew Adrian's attention. He checked his phone for a reply from his brother but came up empty. *Huh?* The ping sounded again, and Adrian realized the sound had come from across the room. He sighed, then slogged back over to his workstation.

He sidled up to the desk, surveying the carnage of his earlier hacking marathon. Admittedly, it was not a glowing testament to his current state of affairs. He grabbed the garbage can from under the desk and raked the entire contents of the desk's surface into it.

That's better.

He spun towards the monitor, cracking his knuckles. Something immediately caught his eye. He stared at the screen in disbelief.

Impossible.

He watched in rising panic as the cursor flitted across the screen unprompted. He yanked off his glasses, hoping his eyes were playing tricks on him. The cursor blinked twice and then continued to navigate the screen *by itself.*

Adrian understood immediately what was happening. What he did not understand was how. He had installed the strongest virus scanner and full disk encryption on the market. He was running a state-of-the-art end-to-end firewall. A system dubbed so secure it had been called a digital Fort Knox. And yet, right there on the screen was evidence of an *intruder*.

Before he could gain his composure, a chat box appeared.

4NoNYMoU5: You are a hard guy to find.

Adrian felt something ratchet in his gut. No one should have been able to find him—in cyberspace or otherwise. He hesitated a breath, then began typing a reply.

APryor: Who is this?

He watched numbly as three dots appeared. After a few seconds, a response materialized.

4NoNYMoU5: Not safe here. We need to talk in person. It concerns national security.

Adrian's jaw tightened. He couldn't be sure if the intruder was an intelligence officer, criminal, or some pimple-faced script kiddie in Romania. He stared at the screen a moment longer and then sat bolt upright. Another message had appeared. This one *personal.*

4NoNYMoU5: Pryor? I know you're there.

Adrian recoiled at the sight of his name. This was no prank.
It was a targeted attack.
The intruder knew *who* he was. Maybe even *where* he was?
But how?
Adrian felt as if his carefully constructed house of cards was tumbling around him. He knew he couldn't afford the luxury of getting details. That's what the intruder wanted. He wasn't going to take the bait.
With trembling hands, he took hold of the Ethernet cable connecting his machine to the wall. He abruptly yanked it from its port, severing his only connection to the internet. He lurched from behind his desk, upending his chair in the process. Primed by adrenaline, he ran towards the front door. He squinted through the peephole and felt temporary relief at the image on the other side.
The hallway was empty.
Adrian double-checked the deadbolt and latched the flimsy security chain. His heart was racing. He checked the window next. Nothing out of the ordinary there, either.

Now what?

He knew he couldn't stay there. The hacker on his system was concerning as hell.

Had he been careless? Left a trace?

Moments later, his question was answered with a rap at the door.

Adrian froze.

"Pryor? We know you are inside. We just want to talk."

Adrian's stomach lurched. There was no denying it now.

He'd been found.

He swung his neck to the side and wretched all over the Persian rug.

The pounding on the door intensified.

He only had one question: who was on the other side?

The local authorities?

The Azeri mafia?

Or worse . . . the NSA themselves?

CHAPTER 2

WHEN YOU ARE CORNERED, you have only two choices: move or fight.

Adrian used his shirt sleeve to wipe the bile from the corners of his mouth. For a split second, he considered making a run for the balcony. But he knew that even if he could escape safely from eight stories up, he couldn't run forever. Adrian needed to know who was pursuing him. To stop them.

Adrenaline filled his veins. He made a beeline for the bedroom, leapfrogging the bed on the shortest path to the closet. He scrambled to the floor, stabbing at the keypad of a small safe there.

He heard banging at the door again.

After several long seconds, the door to the safe finally swung open. He slid his hand along the interior, locating the makeshift panel that he had taped to the sidewall. He removed the USB that was concealed there, pocketing it. Next, he reached for the Sig Sauer P320 that lay in the center of the safe.

It was heavier than he remembered. He shot a backward glance at the door.

"Adrian, please open the door. We just want to talk."

Adrian clenched his jaw.

Move or fight.

Adrian lifted the pistol, slamming the magazine into place and releasing the slide lock. But before he had crossed the living room, the front door burst open. It took Adrian less than three seconds to confirm his suspicions.

Azeri Mafia.

Two cagey figures barreled through the door. Adrian hesitated a second too long, and the men had closed the distance between them. He scuttled sideways, but not fast enough. The first intruder slammed into him with the force of a battering ram, catching him square on the shoulder. Adrian folded like a cheap lawn chair, his weapon clattering to the floor.

The next thing he knew, the intruder was on top of him. The Azeri ground his knee into his chest, throwing the full force of his weight onto Adrian's ribs. He couldn't breathe.

Adrian stared into the face of his attacker: a square-jawed Middle Eastern man with tattoos covering his neck and forearms. The second attacker, a barrel-chested man wearing all black, grabbed him roughly by the arms.

"Ouch," Adrian protested as the man shackled his wrists behind his back with plastic zip-ties.

"Quiet."

"What do you want?" Adrian said.

"We talk later," the man said. "First, we go for drive."

"I thought you said you just wanted to talk?"

The Azeri shrugged. "Not here."

"What if I refuse?"

The man opened his jacket, revealing a holstered submachine gun. "Up, Snowden. Time to go."

Adrian was not amused. Both of his attackers, however, were still snickering as they muscled him down the musty hallway and towards the building's lone elevator. As soon as they were outside, Adrian heard the rough idle of an engine. He felt the cold metal barrel of a gun, currently jammed into his kidney, not so gently ushering him away from the building. They rounded the corner into an alleyway, where an unmarked van was parked in front of a dumpster.

Quintessential serial killer van.

Adrian considered screaming for help, but no one else was in sight. Only a stone's throw from the bustle of Nizami Street, the area was normally teeming with shoppers and pedestrians. But at this hour, the shops and restaurants had been long shuttered, and residents gone home.

Before he knew it, they slid open the door and shoved him roughly inside. The tattooed assailant joined Adrian in the back of the van, posting up on a small plastic crate on the floor. The second attacker took position behind the wheel. All of this happened very quickly. Adrian could only watch in rising panic as the van roared out of the alley, the force of acceleration nearly sending him flying.

Adrian's heart hammered in his chest. He had lived in fear since his arrival to Azerbaijan. He also understood it was a fear he would probably live under for the rest of his life. *Choices had consequences.*

"How did you find me?" Adrian asked.

The driver met his gaze in the rearview mirror. "Does it matter?"

"What do you want?" Adrian knew all too well that the crime syndicate was known for human trafficking, extortion, drug and arms trafficking, among a slew of other criminal ventures. Real pillars of the community.

"Money," the driver said simply.

"Lucky for you," the tattooed man said with a chuckle, "not yours."

"What do you mean?" Adrian said.

"We were offered a crypto bounty for your head," he said with a thick accent. "Big one."

Adrian felt an upswell of terror. "By who?"

"Who knows?" the man said nonchalantly. "That's why they call it the dark web."

Adrian's head spun. These men were just lackeys. If the Azeri Mafia hadn't come for him, who had? Would his own government go this far?

Adrian sized up the man beside him. He knew he needed more information if he was to be in any position to negotiate. In his past life, Adrian had been a skilled social engineer. He was sure he could manipulate these buffoons. *But how?*

Before he could put his sheer wit and manipulation skills to the test, something strange caught his eye. Adrian watched in slow motion as the man produced a small metal object from his pocket. He lifted it and lurched towards Adrian.

"Really, bro?" Adrian raised his arms in defense, but he was too slow. He felt the sting of a needle piercing flesh, and seconds later, a curtain of darkness fell over him. Adrian was vaguely aware of his head bouncing against the window before he blacked out completely.

CHAPTER 3

MOVING DOWN A LONG corridor in his urban Shanghai mansion, Lang Zhao admired the rare Chinese antiquities on display—a bronze Buddha, a zitan floor screen, and his pièce de résistance: a rare Imperial-style white jade seal capped by intertwined dragons. He had paid an emperor's ransom for the collectibles, an emblem of affluence in the status-obsessed city.

Trifles, compared to what I am about to inherit, he thought, passing by the priceless antiques.

Zhao felt invigorated. The afternoon's task, although unpleasant, had proven easier than expected. He strode quickly through an elegant foyer, stopping at a large floor-to-ceiling window to admire the Shanghai skyline. The bulbous silhouette of the Oriental Pearl TV Tower rose prominently in the distance. Even at the late hour, a bloom of neon light radiated from the city. Reflected off the Huangpu River, it was striking against the backdrop of a January sky.

When he had made this place home ten years ago, Zhao had no idea that he would come to love the city. It was East meets West on a scale of otherworldly grandeur.

A fitting birthplace for a god.

The "Great Gate" to the Chinese Empire, Shanghai would quietly usher in the biggest paradigm shift in modern history. Few people believed that its conception was possible. Even fewer knew it had already become a reality. And most, Zhao was sure, would doubt its sweeping capabilities. *A treasure dwarfing even Solomon's* . . .

A single alarm chimed on his cell phone, and Zhao looked down.

7 p.m.

Quickening his pace, he adjusted the lightweight changshan that hung loosely on his frame. The distinct odor of alcohol followed him, which Zhao had used to sterilize his incisions twice a day since undergoing a drastic medical procedure a month prior. *Temporary pain,* he reminded himself.

Zhao again lifted his phone. With several quick strokes, Faure's requiem thundered from a distributed home audio system, broadcasting the haunting music throughout the mansion. It had been called Death's lullaby. It whispered to him like an enchantment calling from beyond.

The time of my mortal end is near.

The irony was not lost on Zhao that he was still a puppet to his primitive limbic system. Until the specter of death no longer hung over his head, this would remain his most crippling human trait.

Scaling a quartz staircase two steps at a time, Zhao arrived at a large landing. He continued past his second-story office, entering a spacious master suite. He made his way into the en suite bathroom, metal clanging hollowly on tile. The foreign sound, that of his own footsteps, would take time to adjust to.

Zhao paused, taking in his reflection in the mirror. He unfastened his changshan, letting it fall to the floor. He carefully appraised his naked form. The vision exhilarated him. Zhao's muscular frame was shaved and smooth, having been groomed in anticipation of his surgery. He lowered his gaze first to his legs, which had been electively replaced with twin state-of-the-art aluminum prostheses. Above that, a muscular frame gave rise to a powerful chest and broad shoulders. His eyes, once brown, now flickered with a faint red light.

Zhao had started with simple enhancements, like improved eyesight and hearing. From there, he had moved on to more advanced upgrades like cybernetic limbs. The technology had come a long way. Now rising to a height of six-foot-four, his new appendages offered him preternatural speed and strength. And this was only the beginning of his transformation.

To enhance was to evolve.

Not that Zhao saw much of a choice.

If we are to survive, we must transcend our physical limitations.

It was only a matter of time until science would discover a way to accelerate the pace of evolution—to control it in a self-directed manner. Already, promising improvements were being made through technology such as surgery, genetic engineering, nanotechnology, and digital uploading. Bodily modification was just the first step in Zhao's transformation, a small step towards his ultimate destiny. He felt powerful, but his work was not yet complete.

Zhao's phone pinged. An incoming message from Martin Minsky was encouraging.

He drew his phone to his ear and placed a call.

"Yes?" a gravelly voice answered.

"Is it done?" Zhao asked.

"Yes," Minsky replied quickly. "I downloaded the last fragments last night."

"Excellent," Zhao replied.

"And our other problem?" Minsky ventured.

"The computer scientist won't cause any more problems for us," Zhao replied.

Minsky sounded relieved. "Great. I was afraid . . ."

"That I wasn't up to the task?" Zhao finished.

There was an awkward pause. "I didn't mean to question you, it's just that—"

"It was a necessary sacrifice," Zhao finished coolly. "It was unpleasant, but it's done." He pictured Andreas Kohler's final moments. He quickly pushed it from his mind.

"And his partner?" Minsky asked.

"She won't be a problem," Zhao reassured. "By the time Ms. Chen returns, we will be halfway to the Wudang Mountains." Zhao smiled, satisfied with their progress. "You have done me a great service. It won't go unrewarded."

"And now?" Minsky asked.

"We prepare to depart."

Zhao knew the stakes were immeasurable and that they must act fast. With the confident tone of a man of enormous power, he carefully relayed instructions about what was to be done next.

When Zhao hung up the phone, he began his final preparations.

One hour, he told himself.

Abundance will defeat scarcity once more.

CHAPTER 4

A THUNDEROUS ROAR JOLTED Adrian back to consciousness. He opened his eyes, and his surroundings slowly came into focus. He was lying alone on the floor of a large hangar of some kind. He lifted his gaze, but was immediately blinded by the lights of a massive aircraft. Revving at full thrust, the roar of its turboprop engines was skull-crushing.

Adrian tried to move his arms but found that he could not. They were still zip-tied in an awkward position behind his back. He struggled to a seated position, taking a quick physical inventory. He found no injuries—if he didn't count the pounding headache and some minor bumps and bruises. But he was alive.

"Cut him loose, Yusif." The Azeri's materialized from somewhere in the darkness behind him. Yusif used a pair of wire cutters to remove the zip ties.

Adrian rose to his feet. He lumbered forward, slogging through a heavy mental fog. "What did you give me?"

"A downer," Yusif replied. "Harmless."

Doubt that.

Adrian wondered what black market barbiturate they had shot him up with. For all the boneheaded things he had done in his twenties, drugs weren't one of them.

"Where are you taking me?" Adrian scrutinized the strange-looking aircraft, which looked more seafaring than flight-capable. About the size of a 737, it had a boat-like fuselage, cantilevered high wings, and unsettlingly small-looking pontoons.

"Nowhere," Yusif replied.

Adrian looked at the man in confusion. A second later, he heard the echo of footsteps on the concrete behind him. A kind-faced Chinese man emerged from the darkness. He was wearing a tweed jacket and had neatly combed gray hair.

"Mr. Pryor, I assume?"

"Why, does he owe you money?"

The man flashed a half-hearted smile. "I'm Captain Li."

"Real pleasure," Adrian said, making a spectacle of rubbing his wrists.

"I will be escorting you from here," Li said.

The Azeris watched the exchange in silence from several feet away.

"Where are we going?" Adrian said.

"Shanghai."

Adrian furrowed his brows. "What's in Shanghai?"

"Why don't we talk about that on the way?" Li said.

The muscles in Adrian's jaw tightened. "I can't go to Shanghai."

"Can't or won't?" Li's gaze shot to the submachine gun at Yusif's side.

Adrian grew very still.

"If you try to run," Li said delicately, "we will call the authorities." His gaze dropped to the floor as if he was uncomfortable delivering the news. "You'll be arrested. Extradited to your country."

Adrian smiled calmly. "Azerbaijan doesn't have an extradition treaty with America."

"You are correct on that point. Nevertheless—"

"Even if they did," Adrian interrupted loftily, "the Azeri government has assured me repeatedly that they have no desire to extradite me."

Captain Li gave him a pitied look. "We aren't in Azerbaijan, Mr. Pryor. You landed in *China* an hour ago."

Adrian reeled, trying to make sense of the revelation.

"We are at a private airstrip in Qingdao," Captain Li said. "You've been out for five hours." He withdrew a cell phone from his pocket. He made a couple of quick swipes on the screen, and the door to the hangar ground open. "You arrived in that," he said, pointing at a grounded Boom Jet on the tarmac.

Adrian whirled toward the Azeris. What kind of low-level criminals had access to a supersonic plane?

Adrian, of course, already knew the answer.

Rich criminals.

The Boom Jet, among other supersonic transport hopefuls, had suffered a tragic demise several years prior. Despite high hopes that it would mark the return of supersonic passenger travel like the days of the Concorde, it had ultimately succumbed to the uphill battle against physics, economics, and government regulation. Most had ended up in museums, but several had become collector items for the wealthy.

"All we know," Yusif said, "is we get paid to bring you to China."

"Speaking of getting paid. . ." the other man said.

"Of course," Captain Li said, turning his attention to the Azeris. He stepped towards Yusif, looking flustered. He dug around in his pocket for a moment. "Your transaction ID," he said, shoving a small scrap of paper into Yusif's palm. "You will need to confirm the payment online, of course."

Adrian watched the interaction in a daze.

Yusif pulled a cell phone from his pocket. He tapped away for several moments and then squinted at the small screen before returning the phone to his pocket, apparently satisfied. "The crypto is all there," he announced.

Yusif acknowledged Li with a final nod, and then the men crossed the hangar towards the tarmac.

Adrian watched them disappear into the jet a moment later. He wondered what kind of crypto had been exchanged. Within moments, they were airborne. Headed back to Azerbaijan, he guessed.

Hope you don't get FTX'd, morons.

CHAPTER 5

"**WE REALLY MUST GET** going, Mr. Pryor."

Adrian stared at Captain Li. His heart hammered. Although he still wasn't sure who was behind his abduction, he could think of only two things they could be after: information or retribution.

He wasn't sure which was worse.

"Why am I here?" he pressed.

Captain Li held his tongue.

Adrian felt his anger swell. "I'm not going anywhere until I get some answers."

Li sighed. "I was contracted by a man named Alexander Tso."

"Doesn't ring any bells."

"You haven't met," Li said. "But he needs your help."

"He has a funny way of showing it."

Li sighed again. "I'm afraid we cannot delay any further, Mr. Pryor. There will be time to talk on the flight. This way, please." Li led the way toward the large aircraft.

Adrian followed, feeling powerless to the crushing weight of his predicament. He knew that Li's threat wasn't an empty one. If he ran, he wouldn't make it past the border. The feds had canceled his passport 12 months earlier. Lucky for Adrian, he'd anticipated the move and had already fled to less hostile territory. But it had presented a problem. He couldn't cross the border without a passport. If he were to be detained, he would be at risk of extradition.

Which meant he would face trial back in the U.S. An unfair trial that would almost certainly end in jail time. So were the spoils of trying to help your fellow citizens . . .

Adrian surveyed the aircraft helplessly. It looked about as airworthy as a '56 Plymouth.

Captain Li seemed to read his mind. "Don't worry. It's perfectly safe."

His reassurances fell on deaf ears. Despite having logged enough miles during his career to earn him a lifetime platinum airline status, Adrian was tragically susceptible to motion sickness.

"What the hell is it?"

Captain Li smiled. "We call it Jiaolong." Catching the blank look on Adrian's face, he quickly translated. "The Water Dragon. It will be the world's biggest amphibious plane."

"It will be?"

"Assuming it passes certification, of course," Li said. "It's still under development and testing."

Before Adrian could vocalize his concerns, a blue-jacketed man appeared and began rolling an aluminum gangway across the hangar. Once it was in place, he motioned for them to board. An icy gust of wind suddenly whipped through the hangar. Adrian's hands trembled, and whether it was from the cold or fear, he wasn't sure. With his head still pounding, he followed Captain Li over to the gangway and ascended the stairs. The man in the blue jacket remained below and was now walking the perimeter of the plane with a clipboard in hand, presumably completing a pre-flight-systems check.

Adrian stepped inside the aircraft. He was pleased to find that the cabin itself looked surprisingly like a luxury airliner, having been outfitted with leather captain's chairs, a pair of couches facing one another, and a wood-grained table situated between the rows.

It seemed like an egregious waste, given that he was the only passenger.

But at least he was being trafficked in style.

A moment later, the blue-jacketed man boarded the plane. A metallic thud echoed through the cabin as he slammed the forward door shut. Then he made his way to the cockpit, sliding into the empty seat beside Captain Li.

Shortly after, Li reappeared in the cabin. "Please take a seat. They are expecting us in Shanghai in less than two hours."

Adrian checked his watch but realized that with the time difference, he had no clue what time it was.

"It's almost 10 AM," Li said. Then he thrust a bulging manila folder at Adrian. "Read this, and Mr. Tso will be in contact soon." Then he disappeared back into the cockpit.

Adrian settled into one of the leather captain's chairs in the first row, clutching the sheaf of papers to his chest. A moment later, the engines roared to life, and the cabin began to rumble beneath him. Adrian swallowed hard. Reaching the runway, the engines revved louder as the plane prepared for takeoff. There was a momentary lag, and then the large craft began to pick up speed.

500 yards. Wheels still down. Adrian began sweating.

400 yards. The cabin began shaking. The front wheels lifted ever so slightly off the ground.

300 yards. It would be a miracle if this whale managed to get airborne.

200 yards. Adrian held his breath.

The engines roared into overdrive. Moments later, Adrian felt a gentle upward push as the Sea Dragon finally lifted skyward. He heaved a short-lived sigh of relief.

Seconds later, turbulence rocked the cabin as they made their way through low-lying clouds, jostling Adrian upwards in his seat and sending overhead bins clattering. He desperately grabbed the armrest, realizing he had never buckled in. The overhead lights flickered, and the interior cabin panels rattled forcefully. All-too-familiar feelings of dizziness and nausea gripped Adrian.

This is gonna be a rough two hours.

Adrian forced his gaze to the horizon, praying the technique, which he had tried dozens of times to no avail, would somehow help on this occasion. After what seemed like an eternity, the plane reached cruising altitude, and things smoothed out. Several seconds later, Adrian heard a soft electronic ping as the seatbelt indicator illuminated.

Gee, thanks for the heads up, guys.

CHAPTER 6

A COPIOUSLY AIRSICK ADRIAN shifted uncomfortably in the window seat of the AG600 transport plane. Now barreling through the Eastern hemisphere at an altitude of 8,000 feet, Adrian could hardly hear himself think over the roar of the four turboprop engines.

Once the seaplane smoothed out at cruising altitude, Adrian flipped open the folder from Captain Li. Inside, he found a messy stack of newspaper clippings and several encrypted documents. He began leafing through the pages and immediately recoiled.

The news clippings, he realized, were today's headlines. His eyes flashed to the date: January 25th. Exactly one year since the incident that had left him a political refugee from his own country.

Since arriving in Azerbaijan, Adrian had taken great pains to avoid American news. He had given a lot of thought to how the media would portray him. Unsurprisingly, Adrian's likeness had been spun into a two-dimensional caricature. It seemed that even a year later, the press hadn't softened to him or his actions. He had become a national pariah.

Adrian scanned the headlines from The Wall Street Journal, The Washington Post, and The NY times. Once staples of his daily news updates, he preferred to read BBC or Al Jazeera now. He stared at the headlines like a bystander gawking at a car wreck—horrified but unable to turn away.

He felt his jaw tighten. Seeing his dirty laundry splayed out in black and white was no easier now than it had been twelve months ago.

"Adrian Pryor: Betrayer or The Betrayed? The debate continues."

"Treason in the 21st century."

"Running scared, blackballed NSA agent suspected to be seeking refuge overseas."

Adrian slammed the folder shut. He exhaled forcefully, closing his eyes and cradling his temples. A moment later, a shrill ring jolted him from his thoughts. It took him a moment before Adrian realized it was coming from a phone mounted on the cabin wall. Feeling uneasy, he lifted the receiver to his ear.

For a long moment, the line was silent. Then, an unfamiliar voice greeted him. "Hello, Mr. Pryor," he said. "My name is Alexander Tso. I run a—"

"Let me guess . . . Dark-web human trafficking ring?"

"A biotech company in Shanghai," the caller corrected calmly. "Listen, I'm sorry for bringing you here under these conditions."

Adrian said nothing.

"Mr. Pryor?"

Adrian remained silent for several seconds longer than was polite. "Oh, sorry," he finally said. "I would hate to be rude to . . . what did you say your name was again?"

The caller exhaled loudly. "Listen, I really am sorry. Desperate people do desperate things. Can we speak frankly?"

"By all means," Adrian said, not bothering to hide his annoyance.

"As I said, my name is Alexander Tso, and I run a biotech company in Shanghai. CyberGen Industries."

"Never heard of it."

"Nevertheless—there has been an incident at my lab." He hesitated a beat. "It presents a concern for international security."

Adrian sighed. "Listen, man. I'm not in the national security biz anymore. But you already knew that." He glared at the disheveled heap of newspaper clippings next to him.

"That may be so, but I need your expertise."

"I'm sorry?"

Tso groaned. "You are a digital exploitation expert, right?"

Adrian snickered. "Sure. The media just refers to me as a hacker, though. The 'most technically skilled and brazen hacker alive,' if you want to get specific. How did you even find me?"

"I have powerful tools at my disposal at my lab."

Adrian couldn't imagine how anyone could have found him. Particularly some lab rat in China. He had taken every precaution when he arrived in Baku: avoiding paper trails and making full use of the strongest virus scanners, firewalls, and full disk encryption systems available on the market.

How did this guy manage to track me down?

"Listen, man. I don't know who you are or where you got this plane from, but if you want my help, you better start explaining some stuff."

Tso sighed. "Did you get my folder?"

Adrian looked at the folder again, his anger swelling in response. "Sure did pal, thanks for that."

"In the back, you will find an email transcript. Do you see it?"

Adrian hadn't noticed it at first pass. He flipped through the ream of papers again until he found it. "Got it." He quickly scanned the message, which was an encrypted text of some sort.

"We found this 24 hours ago. In a secure underground lab."

"And?"

"It was authored by one of the scientists at our AI lab. A man named Andreas Kohler," Tso said.

"Okay . . ."

"He was found dead not long after he wrote it."

Adrian tightened his grip on the receiver. "Cause of death?"

"Foul play," Tso said. "I think the note may have to do with why he was killed. And I need your help to decrypt it."

Adrian had worked in cryptography for about three milliseconds when he first joined the NSA. Decryption wasn't his jam, but he could do it. He scanned the message again—a jumble of symbols and characters. However, two words caught his attention this time, immediately standing out. There, among a stream of otherwise nonsensical symbols, in plaintext, was his name.

"How is this even possible? I've never even heard of this man."

Tso hesitated. "It seems that he has heard of you."

Adrian felt a chill course through his body. His work had often brought him face to face with the worst depravity of humankind: religious zealots who killed in the name of their faith, fundamentalist terror organizations, and anarchists—but the image before him was unlike anything he had ever seen.

It was *personal*. "But how?"

"Unfortunately, we cannot discuss the details by phone. I will explain everything to you once you arrive at the lab."

Adrian clenched his jaw. "I don't think you understand. Even if I wanted to help you, I can't. My passport was canceled. My name is flagged at every major airport from New York to Tokyo. Do you know what would happen if I tried to clear customs? I would be hauled in for questioning, detained, and—"

"I apologize," Tso interrupted gingerly, "but it is you who does not understand."

Now fully alert, Adrian drew the handset closer. "Excuse me?"

"As I am sure Captain Li has explained by now, you do not have a choice in the matter." His tone was more forceful now. "As for your travel restrictions, do not be concerned. Arrangements have been made for your passage into the city. As I said, it is a matter of international security."

Adrian grew quiet.

"I suggest you rest now, Mr. Pryor."

Before Adrian could protest, the line went dead.

Alone with his thoughts, Adrian turned towards the window. He was met with his reflection—that of a fugitive. That the title was undeserved made no difference.

When Adrian had decided to write his whitepaper, it was never about the money. He wanted to expose the underground cyberweapons market, to make the internet a safer place. But after he published the widely read whitepaper about the underground bug market, effectively outing its largest customer, the U.S. government, things hadn't gone well for him.

Adrian had met with his superiors at the agency and tried to smooth things over, but the suits didn't want to let it go. The administration immediately terminated his contract and leaked his identity. His security clearance and the skills he had honed over a decade had become worthless overnight. And that was just the opening salvo of what would follow: a campaign of disinformation, misinformation, and character assaults. In the end, the piece had gotten him blackballed from the intelligence community. Adrian had no choice but to flee what would have been an unfair indictment.

It was a political hit job. And his career, scratch that, his life, was the cost. As far as Adrian was concerned, he was a regular Robin Hood of cyberspace. The White House should give him a cape. Sadly, they disagreed, deciding to make him a scapegoat for their smear campaign instead.

"Mr. Pryor?" Captain Li's staticky voice boomed through the cabin. "We are about five minutes from touchdown."

Adrian looked out his window, where the city of Shanghai had begun to spread out in a colorful patchwork below him. A winding river flowed through the heart of the metropolis, bisecting the 2,000-year-old city. To its west, Adrian could see the historical buildings of Old Shanghai. Despite its age, it still offered impressive views: the wide avenues of the International Settlement, the gentrified remnants of the French Concession, and the hopping retail district of Nanjing Street. On the opposite side of the river, the ultramodern business district of Pudong mushroomed in a cloud of neon smog. And stretching over the Huangpu River, a striking, elevated, circular bridge connected old and new.

Even from the air, Shanghai dwarfed the largest cities in the States. It was also one of the most populous cities in the world. Adrian felt a growing unease about what he would face there. Alexander Tso had been stingy with details, only alluding to an issue of "international security." *What issue?*

Captain Li's voice echoed through the cabin again. "Please fasten your seatbelt and prepare for landing."

Adrian thrust the stack of newspaper clippings back into its folder and reached for his seatbelt. A moment later, he felt the plane begin to descend. Now above a busy harbor, he was still trying to figure out where Captain Li intended to land the large aircraft. If memory served him, the airport would be some twenty miles inland. Captain Li made no such change to the flight pattern. The plane continued dropping in altitude until they were only several hundred feet from the water's surface. Adrian heard the flaps extending, and the craft began to slow.

We're landing here?

Directly below the aircraft, the Yangtze Delta met the East China Sea at the northernmost border of Shanghai. A sizable chop was building in the harbor on account of an escalating storm. Captain Li adjusted the propeller's pitch, and seconds later, the plane began plummeting directly toward the harbor.

Adrian held his breath. The cabin lurched as The Water Dragon touched down. The aircraft careened wildly, skipping several times before finally settling on the surface of the water. They taxied for several minutes, now following the winding river into the heart of the city.

The copilot emerged from the cockpit, looking agitated. "Unbuckle!" he yelled in broken English, looking at Adrian as if he was a complete dimwit. Then he hurried to the hatch, fumbling with the latch.

Baffled at the man's haste, Adrian complied as quickly as he could.

Belt on. Belt off. Belt on. It was almost as bad as Catholic mass calisthenics as a kid: Sit, stand, kneel. Sit, stand, kneel.

Adrian felt the plane slowing as they approached a busy wharf.

"What are you waiting for?" the copilot said. "This your stop."

Adrian scrambled forward, arriving at the cargo door just as it swung open. He peered outside, wondering how on earth he was supposed to get to the dock. At least a dozen feet below, the storm-swollen river wasn't his first choice.

The copilot pressed a button, and an inflatable evacuation slide and emergency raft deployed.

Adrian shook his head. "You're kidding, right?"

"Hurry!" the man said.

Fine. Just get me off this flying death ark.

Adrian looked over his shoulder at the unruly stack of papers on his seat a final time. The copilot stuffed a crumpled piece of paper into his palm and then gave Adrian a forceful shove out the open door.

CHAPTER 7

BEFORE HE HAD TIME to react, Adrian was airborne.

He hurtled through space for several long seconds before landing with a soft bounce on the inflatable evac slide. Three seconds later, he had reached the emergency raft.

Despite his irritation at having been unwillingly ejected from the seaplane, Adrian couldn't help but smile.

No need to clear security here . . .

He let his gaze sweep across the river toward the immediately recognizable silhouette of the Oriental Pearl TV Tower, a 1500-foot-tall steel behemoth. Punctuated by two pink spheres, it had a distinctly space-aged vibe, standing out even among the city's most iconic buildings. Further away, he saw Shanghai's undisputed centerpiece—the same shimmering glass monolith he had seen from the air.

The Shanghai Tower.

The twisting spire of glass and metal reached some two thousand feet into the air, crowning the modern skyline and even managing to dwarf the two adjacent mega-tall structures: the Jin Mao Tower and the Shanghai World Financial Center.

What in the hell am I doing here?

Adrian pulled the crumpled piece of paper from his palm. It bore a messy handwritten address: No. 2001, Century Avenue, Huangpu District.

He glanced behind him and saw that the Sea Dragon was already retreating down the river.

It's just me now.

Adrian spotted a dock about a hundred yards away on the west bank. He grabbed the paddle and started to row. Several minutes later, he had safely reached the side of the river. Adrian took hold of a metal ladder mounted on the sidewall and hoisted himself up. He climbed onto the wooden platform and collapsed on the ground, his lungs heaving from exertion.

Adrian reached into his pocket and was relieved to find his cell phone was still there. He activated the roaming feature, which took no time to locate a signal on the faster-than-lightning 6-G network. *Nice.* Why did it seem like the U.S. was always playing catch-up when it came to this stuff? He entered the address the pilot had given him into Maps. According to the directions, CyberGen Industries appeared to be less than three blocks away.

Adrian collected himself and then rose, disappearing onto the crowded pedestrian walkway. The famous boardwalk on which he now found himself, The Bund, was an architectural Wild West. Along the mile-long stretch of waterfront promenade, the 'living museum' featured some 52 buildings in various architectural styles, including gothic, baroque, and neoclassical styles. *The Museum of World Architecture*, he remembered from his visit to the popular destination some eighteen months prior.

Throngs of people in sterile blue face masks moved briskly against a backdrop of horns, sirens, and the whine of motorbikes. Adrian ducked through the crowd and toward Zhongshan Road, which was currently overrun with cars, taxis, scooters, and bicycles. He waited for an opening and was finally about to cross when a shrill blast cut the air. He recoiled instinctively, just missing a small electric scooter that whizzed past. A spray of cool, wet mud splattered his front side.

Sweet.

Adrian sighed. Somehow, the driver still managed to look pissed off. He was shouting furiously in Shanghainese as he sped past.

Damn electric bikes, Adrian cursed. *Silent but deadly.* He remembered an article he'd read condemning the electric scooter revolution, whose silent engines were said to be forty percent more likely to strike a pedestrian.

Adrian wiped the sludge from his face, then proceeded to cross the busy road. Rain began to fall, and he broke into a jog. He passed street vendors wheeling out food carts with deep-fried rice cakes and dumplings. His stomach grumbled. Strings of red and gold paper lanterns adorned every street, sidewalk, and building. Chinese New Year, he realized. He glanced at the map again.

It shouldn't be much further.

When he arrived at No. 2001 Century Avenue, he found himself staring at an unremarkable skyscraper. The building itself bore no moniker and looked like any of the other hundred skyscrapers in Shanghai. Adrian checked the address again. He shrugged, then pushed open the large glass door.

As he stepped inside, a bow-legged man emerged, leaning on a smooth wooden cane. He smiled from behind thick glasses, offering a bony hand in greeting. "Mr. Pryor, I presume? We spoke on the phone. My name is Alexander Tso."

CHAPTER 8

As Lang Zhao's aluminum prostheses carried him toward his waiting hypercar, he squared his chest, rising to his full, six-foot-four height. He exhaled forcefully, expelling carbon dioxide from his lungs. He felt powerful.

My transformation is nearly complete, he thought, surveying the glittering skyline.

Slipping quietly into a waiting Hyperion XP-1, Zhao stole one last glance at the urban Shanghai retreat he was about to leave behind. The hydrogen-electric hypercar roared to life, moving west down Shangzhong Road. He looked over at the passenger seated beside him.

What is he thinking? Zhao wondered.

The computer scientist hadn't said much since his arrival. Zhao wondered if Martin Minsky was as loyal as he claimed, or if, like most, he would balk the second they were confronted with serious opposition. Two weeks ago, with his help, Minsky had breached CyberGen Industries' firewall and ghosted into the system undetected for a glorious twenty seconds. They had repeated the process ten times over the subsequent week, each time downloading an imperceptible fragment of source code, which they would cobble together to recreate Andreas Kohler's AI.

The theft itself had been easier than anticipated. Snuffing out the self-righteous old man had proved more tedious. But perhaps the biggest challenge confronting them would be exploiting the fail-safes he knew Andreas Kohler and Olivia Chen had built into their software.

Now that the source code had been secured, it would be relocated off the grid—where copies would be made, and security would be enhanced. The most critical pieces of its internal source code would be uploaded into a number of cloud servers, safeguarding against it being destroyed or disconnected remotely.

Zhao depressed the accelerator, and the XP-1 responded without hesitation, the 2,038 hp hydrogen propulsion system shooting them forward. He tore out of the Shangzhong Road tunnel at over 100 miles an hour, emerging on the west side of the Huangpu River. He liked the feeling of power the car gave him.

A personal rocket on wheels.

Even if the authorities did get wind of his actions, they would already be overwhelmed with Chinese New Year celebrations. And if they came looking, it would logically be at his private hangar.

Except we are not headed to the hangar, he thought, glancing over at the computer scientist seated beside him. Minsky had assured him that passage through the busy rail station would be far safer than employing his personal plane, which may come under surveillance once the authorities got wind of the situation at the lab. Flight logs and passenger manifests created paper trails. Rail travel did not.

"Hongqiao Station should be less than ten minutes away," Zhao said as they snaked away from the crowded metropolis and towards the outskirts of the city. He depressed the accelerator again, sending both men flat against their seats.

Minsky smiled. "Maybe five the way you drive."

Lang Zhao felt himself moving closer to his destiny. The pull was magnetic. He had made preparations to retreat to a remote location where he would perform a miracle of god-like proportions—ushering in staggering breakthroughs that would change the world for all future generations.

One dynasty must fall, so that another may rise.

Zhao had been sounding the alarm on AI for decades, but government and mainstream science had mocked his warnings. Arming themselves instead with smug skepticism, they pointed only to the shortcomings in the field: an embarrassing string of failures, laughable results, and several "winters" where AI progress seemed to grind to a complete halt.

They were fools not to take his warnings seriously. Now, armed with the power of big data, scientists like those at CyberGen fed the machines' growing appetites and watched as they slowly improved, quietly mastering realms of human proficiency formerly reserved for only the brightest of minds. And so it had gone. The more it learned, the faster it improved. Until one day, it would quietly wake up.

I think, therefore, I am.

The dangers of such a thinking machine had immediately become clear to Zhao. Another thing had also become clear to him: the development of such a technology could not be stopped any more than human progress itself could be stopped. That left him only one choice: if he couldn't stop it, then Zhao would have to be the one to give it rise. To moderate it, to find a way for humans to coexist safely with it. And for that to happen, everything familiar must change.

Above the panoramic canopy, fireworks exploded high in the sky. A stream of red and gold lanterns, dragons, and people dressed in traditional garb paraded by, garish and obscenely festive against the January sky. The Chinese Lunar New Year was a time of rebirth, a new beginning—an *apt time for a cleansing.* As antiquated beliefs fell to the wayside, an explosion of knowledge would follow.

And it is my job to usher it in.

It was hard to believe that the culmination of his life's work had brought him to this point. Catastrophic loss had once gutted his soul—an unspeakable tragedy a decade prior from which he had never thought he would recover. Zhao still faced the consequences of the life-changing event during every waking breath: permanent and debilitating. Even sleep was little respite. Memories of the event tortured him in the form of nightmares. Ultimately, the pain had hollowed a space in his soul—carving out room for a legacy far greater than anything his younger self could have imagined.

CHAPTER 9

"**THANK YOU FOR COMING.**"

Adrian stared into the eyes of the man responsible for his abduction. "Didn't know I had a choice."

"Fair enough," the stranger said, his expression unflinching.

Adrian wasn't sure what he had expected, but Alexander Tso didn't strike him as the criminal type.

"I suppose I should apologize in person for the circumstances under which you were brought here."

"That would be a start."

"Listen, Adrian, I have no intention of keeping you here against your will."

"So, you won't stop me if I walk out of here right now?"

Tso smoothed an errant strand of black hair, deliberating his next words. "I couldn't care less about your *history*."

"You mean my criminal history?" Adrian said. "The same history you threatened me with?"

"A bluff," Tso conceded.

"And the Azeri Mafia goons you hired?"

"I'm afraid they were the real deal." He looked away, shuffling his feet awkwardly. "I couldn't risk your refusal. But those men were nothing more than hired muscle. Someone to get you from A to B."

"And why should I help you?" Adrian said.

"I just ask that you hear me out," Tso replied gently. "If you still want to leave after that, I won't stop you."

Adrian thought for a moment. "Then start talking."

"It would be easier to show you," Tso said. "Follow me."

Tso set off across an airy lobby. Despite an awkward gait, he moved surprisingly fast with the assistance of his cane. Adrian had to quicken his pace to keep up. They reached a security checkpoint on the opposite side of the lobby a moment later.

A young Chinese guard made small talk with Tso while Adrian emptied his pockets onto a small conveyor. Seeing his things scattered on the belt, he had a sudden revelation. "I have no identification with me." He thought of his wallet, which was still sitting on the counter at his apartment in Baku. His canceled passport, in the safe in the closet.

"That will be unnecessary," the guard assured. "I have already verified your identity. Enjoy your visit, Mr. Pryor."

Adrian stared at the man, puzzled. The guard made a series of quick keystrokes, and then his system flashed green. He heard two beeps, and a small turnstile swung open. Without explanation, Tso shot towards the back of the lobby.

"This way, please hurry."

"What's the story with this place?" Adrian asked. "I've never heard of it."

"Not surprising," Tso quipped, "considering our existence is unknown to even most Chinese."

Adrian was surprised. "I see. What exactly do you do here?"

"CyberGen Industries is home to one of the most advanced machine learning labs on Earth."

"Really?" Adrian surveyed his surroundings, encountering nothing out of the ordinary.

Tso smiled. "You won't find much of interest here. Our lab is located on a private floor." He continued at a brisk pace. "Most Americans do not view China as a world leader in artificial intelligence. They see us as only a peddler of cheaply made consumer goods. An odd perception when you consider that China is home to the second-largest pool of AI scientists. In the last decade alone, we have designed novel chip architectures that can support advanced AI systems, our government has committed to making it a $150 billion industry, and frankly, if data is the new oil, we are the new Saudi Arabia."

Adrian had to admit he was guilty of buying into the "made in China" stigma. He was embarrassed to say he knew little about the country's AI capabilities. His mind turned back to Andreas Kohler. "The man you mentioned, Kohler, did he—"

Tso cut him off with a wave of his hand. "Not here. I will take you to him now."

Adrian jolted to a stop. "Is that really necessary?"

"I think it's best that you see things for yourself," he replied in a firm tone. "Confined spaces don't bother you, do they?"

"Not at all," he replied.

Rotting corpses are a problem for me. Small spaces I can handle.

"So, exactly what kind of work do you do here?" Adrian said.

"Our scientists are tackling questions that have baffled scientists for decades. Things like: what makes us human? What is consciousness? Where are dreams stored?"

"And the answers are in an AI lab?"

"You sound surprised."

"I am. Those questions seem to be more the providence of biology."

"Not only can artificial intelligence answer these questions," Tso said, "but it already has. AI is being called upon to fill in the gaps that have eluded the brightest minds in science since the beginning of time. Soon, it will be able to answer almost any question man can ask."

"I see," Adrian replied skeptically.

"Consider my personal story, Mr. Pryor. As you may have guessed, I was born with a chromosomal disorder. Very rare. Doctors estimated that I would die by my twenty-fifth birthday. That was nearly two decades ago."

"Go on," Adrian replied.

"I was told there was no cure for my condition. So, I did what any logical person would."

"And that would be?"

"I engineered my own," Tso said, as if it were obvious.

Adrian couldn't help but stare, amused by the man's deadpan expression.

"CyberGen Industries was born out of that mission," Tso continued enthusiastically. "It has since licensed a drug for my condition, giving hope to some 20,000 people worldwide. We've also grown to over 200 employees, all with an even more audacious goal."

"And what's that?" Adrian asked.

"To reverse engineer the worst disease to have ever plagued mankind."

Adrian was suddenly curious.

The worst disease ever?

"Cancer?" he ventured, feeling a pang of grief as he recalled his late mother's battle with the disease.

"Aging," Tso corrected, his tone matter of fact.

Adrian tried to restrain his amusement. "Aging?"

"Yes, Mr. Pryor. *Aging.* It is the single most prevalent killer in our society—ahead of cancer, addiction, and coronary disease. Should you be lucky enough to dodge these, you are condemned to sit idle while your body slowly breaks down, your faculties fail you, and eventually, you die."

Adrian was unsure how to respond. He had never thought of it quite like that.

"You look skeptical," Tso said.

"It's . . . an interesting perspective?"

"I am hardly alone in my thinking—that aging is a disease. One that can be reverse engineered."

Adrian was about to object, but Tso cut him off. "Let me show you what I am talking about. Our facility is quite impressive." He strode briskly towards an elevator bank. "For millennia, man has been chasing the elusive *fountain of youth*. Thanks to the scientists here at CyberGen, it is now within our grasp."

Tso reached for a call button on the wall, and a moment later, the elevator doors parted. Tso shuffled forward, holding the door. "After you."

Adrian stepped into the large steel enclosure, still trying to process the stranger's words. He was exhausted, and despite Tso's enthusiasm, nothing about the conversation seemed remotely relevant to why he had been brought to Shanghai. A mechanical beeping caught his attention. His phone going out of service range.

Perfect timing. Just as I'm about to be trapped in a steel coffin with this whack job.

Tso pulled a keycard from his pocket. He tapped the magnetic reader on the panel, and a new call button illuminated. Tso pressed the button beside it, which was marked 'SB.' With a hollow thud, the doors closed, and the elevator thrummed to life.

Adrian suddenly felt off balance. "Are we *descending*?"

"Yes," Tso replied. "We are headed to the subbasement. The lab is located 150 feet *below* ground."

CHAPTER 10

TEN STORIES BELOW SHANGHAI, Adrian found himself in the mouth of a long, dark hallway. The stark passageway leading to CyberGen's main lab was constructed entirely of concrete. A number of metal doors and security cameras lined its length. Lacking windows of any kind, it reminded him of a mine shaft.

"As you can see," Tso said, his voice echoing off the bare cement hallways, "we have gone to great lengths to secure our lab. The many meters of earth, stone, concrete, and steel block any RF signals."

"A Faraday cage?"

"Exactly. The area you have just entered is a complete dead zone. No electromagnetic signals go in or out of this lab."

"Why the extreme measures?" Adrian said.

"The technology we are working with requires it. It must never go beyond these walls."

Adrian thought he had seen it all working for the Agency: cryptic field sites that didn't appear on zoning maps, uniformed guards, windowless rooms in distant corners of the world . . . He could not, however, imagine why private enterprise would require such secrecy.

"This way, please," Tso announced, taking an abrupt turn down another dark hallway.

"Where is the body?" Adrian asked.

Let's get this over with.

Tso glowered at him but continued in silence. He strode briskly down the length of the corridor, his gaze fixed ahead. Motion-activated smart lights kicked on overhead, illuminating their path as they went. After about one hundred yards, two large doors appeared on the left. The doors were made entirely of steel, like vaults in a high-security bank.

"What's in there?" Adrian said.

"They are sensory deprivation chambers," Tso replied, stopping to wait for Adrian.

"Sensory deprivation?"

"More commonly known as a *float spa*," Tso explained. "Our work in the lab demands long hours underground in front of a screen. We installed them as a way for the employees to unplug."

Adrian shrugged. *Don't most start-ups usually opt for ping-pong tables?*

"Before we enter, I must warn you what you are about to see is disturbing. Mr. Kohler appears to have suffered from blunt-force trauma to the head. He was rendered unconscious before drowning in one of the float tanks."

Adrian steeled himself, mentally preparing for what he was about to see.

"He died quickly, perhaps in under four minutes," Tso explained, his expression unreadable. "Although it's safe to assume that must have felt like an eternity to him. His body is exactly where I found it six hours later."

Adrian spun towards Tso. "It took six hours before anyone noticed he was missing?"

"Mr. Pryor, this room is sound-proofed and out of range of security cameras." He met Adrian's gaze, his expression pained. "After Mr. Kohler missed our phone meeting that afternoon, I came to the lab immediately, assuming that he was tied up with work. I never expected to find him . . . like this."

"What do the authorities think?"

Tso said nothing.

"Please tell me you have contacted the authorities?"

Tso paused awkwardly. "That's why you are here."

"But seriously . . . tell me someone else knows about this?"

"Yes, of course," Tso said. "Andreas' lab partner: Olivia Chen. She is also a computer scientist here at CyberGen. Ms. Chen has been away this week, meeting with some venture capitalists in Silicon Valley. She has been made aware of the situation and is headed back at this very moment."

"*Situation?*" Adrian exclaimed. "A man has been murdered. This is the scene of a homicide!"

Tso narrowed his eyes. "I can't have the authorities poking around the lab right now. Much too risky."

"But—"

"The authorities will be notified," Tso said, his tone even, "but not before Ms. Chen's return. "

"And the other employees?" Adrian asked. "Are they aware of the situation?"

"Most certainly not."

"What?"

"There were only a handful of employees on-site at the time," Tso said. "They were sent home, after which we initiated a lockdown procedure for the lab, informing them not to return until further notice."

"But the other employees—"

"Are the least of my concerns right now," Tso snapped. Then he reached forward, pulling open the heavy door.

A cool blast of air hit Adrian in the face. He inhaled slowly, immediately struck by the strange smell permeating the room. Not like death. Cedarwood? Lavender? And maybe vanilla? It appeared to be diffusing from a built-in aromatherapy element across the room. Stepping over the threshold, Adrian found himself in a small chamber that reminded him of a spa treatment room, except that it contained a futuristic pod at its center. Steel encased the pod entirely, except for a solitary thick-paned window. The only evidence that the room had been occupied was a neat pile of clothing on a chair in the corner.

"When I arrived around 7 p.m., I found no one in the lab. Except—" he pointed towards the steel enclosure against the back wall. "Him."

Adrian lifted his gaze and followed Tso's outstretched finger.

"Andreas Kohler," Tso announced, "would have been seventy-four years old next month. His death is a profound loss for the scientific community."

Tso was now lifting the lid to the tank, which opened like a clamshell. A blast of icy air hissed out of the tank, hitting Adrian in the face. It swirled towards him in a thick, white fog before evaporating. As the mist slowly lifted, he let his eyes settle on the strange display.

Under the pale wash of halogen light, the naked form of the computer scientist floated on a cloud of vapor. Kohler's skin had faded to an iron-gray pallor. The blued lips were parted, his eyes still open. His corneas were chalk white, lifeless.

Adrian let his gaze fall to the victim's chest, where two large bruises flanked his sternum. Perhaps the most unsettling aspect of the macabre deathbed was the twin tubes running from his throat, where a jugular drain line had been opened, much like morticians did during the embalming process. He now noticed two metallic cylinders on the floor next to the tank, where a pool of crimson liquid had accumulated.

Adrian realized he was shaking. Despite a career in national security, most of his work, fieldwork included, had been behind a computer screen. It was one thing to deal with things like this from behind a screen. Seeing it in person was a different story.

Fighting a wave of nausea, Adrian inched closer to the stranger's corpse. A deep chill met him, radiating from the enclosure. He could now see that a thin sheen of ice covered Kohler's entire body, giving it a ghastly aura. His heart pounded as he circled the tank. "Is he *frozen?*"

"Cryopreserved," Tso corrected. He gestured to a small leather band around Kohler's left ankle. "Per his final wishes."

Adrian crouched down. His eyes traced the length of the man's pale leg to his ankle, where he saw a small leather band. It bore a metal plate. He inched closer, squinting to read the inscription:

Property of Alcor Life Sciences

"He donated his body to science?"

"Not exactly," Tso replied. "Mr. Kohler was a fee-paying member of Alcor's life extension services. He believed that, when the time comes, science will be able to restore his consciousness."

"You're joking, right?"

"Oh, I'm quite serious. I went to great lengths to honor his final wishes," Tso said, gesturing towards Kohler's body.

"Wait, you did this?"

"The man was a genius. It seemed like the right thing to do."

Adrian shivered.

"Andreas' death was ironic when you consider that he himself was on the precipice of solving the problem of human life extension."

Adrian didn't know what to say.

"I think it's time I show you the lab," Tso said abruptly. "Believe it or not, the most troubling aspect of Kohler's death isn't *how* he died."

"What do you mean?"

Without further explanation, Tso spun and disappeared back into the hallway.

Dear Jesus, Adrian groaned, scurrying after him. When he reached the end of the corridor, Tso was waiting for him in front of a thick glass door. It was marked with a red sign that read "Restricted Access."

"This," Tso said, motioning theatrically to the entrance, "is the Center for Regenerative Medicine. Perhaps this will help you understand." He turned to face a sophisticated electronic mechanism mounted on the wall. He aligned his palm with the sensor and waited. Adrian heard a series of beeps as the device analyzed his biometrics before finally flashing green. There was a soft click as the lock disengaged.

Adrian stood silent, wondering what could possibly be contained within these walls that required such security. Tso thrust the door open with an awkward heave, and Adrian stepped inside.

CHAPTER 11

ALTHOUGH OTHERWISE UNOCCUPIED, THE sterile laboratory in which Adrian found himself was far from silent. 3D printers whirred with surgical precision, manufacturing what appeared to be organs. In the center of the room, disembodied but breathing lungs hissed inside dome-shaped incubators. Robotic arms hummed away at workstations around the perimeter of the lab, carrying out research and analyzing test results in real-time. Adrian scanned the space, not having a clue what to make of it.

"Are those *human* organs?" he finally asked.

Tso nodded. "You are looking at the future of organ transplantation. Regenerative medicine holds tremendous potential for curing age-related disease," he replied. "The idea is that we can grow replacement organs out of our own stem cells. The science is quite fascinating."

"Is that so?" Adrian studied Tso's face. "I'm getting Mary Shelley vibes."

"Mr. Pryor, consider this: In the U.S. alone, someone is added to the transplant waiting list every ten minutes. Countless others never make it to the list. Organ regeneration would make a lot more sense than organ donation, don't you think? Why wait for someone to die and gut them like a trout?"

Adrian had to admit, it was an intriguing idea. Organ regeneration would eliminate problems like rejection and wait lists. "How does it work?"

"Using 3D x-rays, we can get tailored, anatomically correct images of failing body parts. With the help of a bioprinter, we can create a 3D scaffold and use biological material to grow replacement organs, tissues, and even bone fragments."

"Pretty slick."

"I would say so. On average, 20 people die every day waiting for organs they will never receive. This could be a problem of the past."

"I have to admit, the science is impressive," Adrian said, unsure why such an operation also required a sophisticated AI lab. "What was Kohler's role here?"

"Well, biology is frail. Mr. Kohler believed that there is another path to human life extension."

Adrian couldn't imagine what.

"All life today is carbon-based," Tso explained. "But who is to say that our thinking selves couldn't survive on another substrate?"

"What do you mean?" Adrian asked.

"Silicon, perhaps?"

It took Adrian several seconds to process what Tso was saying. "He wanted to turn us into cyborgs?"

"Adrian," Tso replied delicately, "I hate to point out the obvious, but you already are one."

"Excuse me?"

Tso gestured to the cell phone that hadn't left Adrian's hand since he had arrived at CyberGen. "The smartphone in your hand has more computing power than all of NASA in 1969 when they sent two astronauts to the moon."

"That hardly makes me a cyborg."

"Are you so sure about that? Previous generations would have deemed the little device in your palm nothing short of miraculous—a personal oracle of wisdom."

Adrian chuckled at the comparison.

"With access to that kind of power," Tso said, "humans can exploit all the benefits of digital computing—perfect recall, speedy and accurate mathematical calculations, and significantly improved data storage and processing capability. We can already radically outperform our ancestors."

Adrian had to admit Tso had a point.

"The only thing limiting human intelligence is information input/output speed. A bandwidth constraint. You are already a cyborg, Adrian, just a painfully slow one. Fix that problem, and we become *superhuman*."

CHAPTER 12

FOUR MILES TO THE South, a helicopter arced over the city of Shanghai and banked hard, headed directly towards the helipad on the roof of the CyberGen building. Inside, an emotionally exhausted Olivia Chen prepared for the reality that awaited her below. Her mind had been reeling since receiving the devastating news from Alexander Tso.

Andreas is dead.

When she got the call, she had been in Silicon Valley meeting with some venture capitalists. "Andreas has been murdered. Come back to China immediately."

Her trip had gone better than expected. Olivia had wrapped up her last meeting that afternoon—a business lunch at the trendy Cafe Venetia, where she had received some encouraging news from one of their new investors. She had been sleeping peacefully back at her hotel when she was startled awake by a 4 AM phone call. She knew right away that something was wrong.

Still, the news hit her like a shock wave. Immediately arranging a flight back to Shanghai, Olivia had spent the better part of the almost fourteen-hour Asiana Air flight trying to make sense of the murder. Who had killed Andreas? And why? What did it mean for their research?

Tso had implied that there was evidence that Andreas' murder had something to do with their latest discovery. What evidence? There were only a handful of people who even knew what they were working on. And even so, she doubted that most understood the true implications of their work.

As far as Olivia was concerned, Andreas's death could only mean one thing.

Betrayal.

Things at the lab had been stressful. They were on the cusp of a breakthrough in machine learning that nobody had expected for decades. It was exciting, but the pressure from above and the long hours had everyone exhausted and stressed to the max. Many nights, Olivia didn't get home until after midnight, if she even made it there. Often, she slept on an uncomfortable couch in her lab.

CyberGen Industries, the company she worked for, was trying to raise another round of venture capital—two hundred million. They were developing technology in what the company called Strong AI, but most people called Artificial General Intelligence.

Her trip to Silicon Valley hadn't come at a good time, but delaying the meetings wasn't an option. CyberGen had burned through its initial one billion in seed capital and would be out of money again by the following month if they couldn't scrape together another round of investors. Machine learning hadn't been popular with the VCs for quite some time. Too many of them had been burned these last decades with promises of advances that were supposedly just around the corner but then never made it out of the lab in a meaningful way. The industry considered Strong AI to be nothing more than a pipe dream.

However, all of that changed when Google's DeepMind developed a computer program that managed to defeat the world champion in the ancient Chinese game of Go—a strategy game with more possible moves than there are atoms in the universe. This "Sputnik moment," a milestone that hadn't been expected for decades, instantly changed everything. It was the moment when AI became mature, and investors started jumping back on the bandwagon. Within a matter of a few years, hundreds of AI start-ups had sprung up all over, CyberGen among them.

Outside the helicopter window, dark clouds began to gather. Olivia watched, weary and detached, as the chopper began its descent. Several moments later, the cabin shuddered as the helicopter's skids finally made contact. The pilot jumped from his seat and began unloading her belongings. There wasn't much—a small rolling suitcase and a leather messenger bag containing her laptop and some other electronic equipment. Everything truly valuable to Olivia was hidden more than ten stories below this very building.

Olivia took a deep breath and stepped from the aircraft. She quickly gathered her belongings, ducking instinctively against the wind. She hurried away from the chopper and by the time she had reached the rooftop access door, the pilot had already returned to the fuselage for takeoff. Olivia gave a quick wave and turned to face the door.

She immediately felt a rising anxiety.

An unmarked lab in an unexpected place.

Despite its ten-year history, the lab was still virtually unknown to the public. Deep in the underbelly of the building, CyberGen was quietly changing the rules of artificial intelligence. The recent breakthroughs Olivia and her partner had made in the field of digital intelligence had ramifications across every field of science—from nanotechnology to biotechnology to quantum computing to cognitive science.

Soon, everything we know will change.

Olivia descended to the ground floor lobby, where the front desk guard buzzed her in. "Ms. Chen!" He smiled warmly. "Welcome back!"

Olivia mustered a half-hearted smile. "Do you mind, Danny?" she said, stashing her bags behind the security desk. Before he could object, Olivia ducked past the turnstile and made her way toward the rear elevator for the long descent. Several moments later, she arrived at the subbasement.

Her footfalls clicked rhythmically as she made her way down the hollow cement corridor, which ran the length of the building and connected the lab's workspaces into different departments: robotics, machine learning, regenerative medicine, a control room, a server room, a bathroom, and a small research library. The space was dark and cramped, illuminated only by a strip of LEDs that activated as she walked.

The long, quiet walk to her lab usually calmed her. This morning, however, the solitary trip had her on edge. What she had learned hours before about her lab partner left no doubt in her mind that whoever had killed Andreas had walked this very same path. As far as she knew, his attacker could still be nearby, and she couldn't escape the feeling that a target now rested on her back.

Five years ago, Alexander Tso had walked Olivia down this very corridor, introducing her to CyberGen by proudly showing off its state-of-the-art lab.

"I thought that maybe you could use a dedicated lab space—a facility where you can push the limits of the work you have been developing these last few years."

"Surely you know I can't consider leaving Boston," she had said, growing annoyed. "Some of the best work in the field is being done at the MIT AI Lab."

"Olivia, let's be honest. Are you not limited there? By the resources of the university, the extent of your grants, your immature tenure?"

Olivia didn't appreciate the man's presumptuous attitude. But she couldn't argue that he had a point.

"Answer this," Tso had continued. "Do you wish to probe the inner workings of the mind, Olivia? To unlock the full potential of mankind?"

"Of course I do. That's why I study synthetic intelligence."

"Then the job is yours," Tso said.

Olivia stared at the stranger in shock. "But I haven't even interviewed for the position!"

"On the contrary, Ms. Chen. I have been following your work in neural networks for the last two years. It shows incredible promise. "This isn't an interview," he said, his hazel eyes flashing warmly. "It's a job offer."

Olivia hadn't known what to say. "Respectfully, the technologies required to run my research are—"

"Enormously expensive?" he finished. "I'm already aware." He smiled broadly. "The lab was completed six months ago. Funded entirely by a ghost investor."

Arriving at a glass door, Olivia stopped short, speechless.

"Beyond this door," Tso continued, "is one of the world's most advanced machine learning facilities. All the equipment you could possibly need would be here at your disposal." He reached for the door. "Would you like to see your lab now?"

Olivia could barely manage a reply. "You are offering me my own lab?"

"I can think of nobody more qualified. Except maybe your new partner—Andreas Kohler. I will introduce you shortly."

"But Mr. Tso—"

"Ms. Chen—the advances you are making will provide an incalculable value to science, not to mention the commercial prospects. Tso stopped and looked her squarely in the eyes. "Imagine what you could accomplish here, Olivia."

Then Tso led her through the doors and showed her the lab. A moment later, he handed her an offer letter with her new salary. Olivia's jaw had dropped.

That was five years ago. She had left her job at the MIT AI lab and never looked back.

As Olivia arrived at the same glass door, she realized how far they had come since that day. As Tso had predicted, Olivia's research had produced astonishing results, particularly in the last three months. The breakthroughs would usher in entire new paradigms of thinking.

Andreas and Olivia had agreed to keep their discovery quiet until the implications were more fully understood. Olivia knew that when the time was right, they would go public with the most transformative science in human history. If only she had known, it would come at a tragic personal cost.

Now standing at the same glass door, she raised her palm to the wall-mounted sensor, as she had done hundreds of times before. Only this time, when the door swung open, a strange sight met her. Beyond the threshold, Olivia could see a pair of men talking. One was her boss. The other, she had never seen before in her life.

Olivia felt a warm swell of blood rush to her face.

What is Tso thinking?

CHAPTER 13

OLIVIA CHEN LOOKED NOTHING like the brainy computer scientist Adrian had expected. She was well-dressed, classy, and quite pretty in an understated way. Despite being younger than he had imagined, she oozed a polished sophistication. Adrian was suddenly very aware of his own disheveled appearance.

Olivia marched forward with purpose, looking like a soldier about to storm the beaches of Normandy. She was visibly upset but made no attempt to hide it.

"Nǐ yǐ wéi nǐ shì shuí?"

It didn't take a translator for Adrian to understand. Olivia Chen was not happy to see him.

"*You*!" she said in English this time. "Who the hell are you?"

Adrian stared mutely, feeling like a deer in the headlights. Thankfully, Tso stepped between them.

"Olivia, allow me to introduce Adrian Pryor. He is here to help."

Olivia gritted her teeth. "You called the authorities?"

"Not exactly," Tso said, breaking her gaze. "Mr. Pryor is not with the authorities. He is a specialist from the U.S."

Olivia looked at Adrian suspiciously.

Tso shrugged but didn't offer her any further explanation.

Olivia spun towards Tso. "Where is he? I want to see him."

Tso turned away, again avoiding eye contact. "I'm afraid that's not a good idea."

"Tell me, or I will find him myself!" she pressed.

"Olivia," Tso intoned forcefully, "your partner suffered a violent death. His body has been mutilated. I don't see what good can come of subjecting you to that."

"Alex," she said, her eyes moist with tears, "you don't need to protect me. I want to see him. I need to."

Tso's tone softened immediately. "I know that Andreas was like family to you, Olivia. I cannot begin to express what a loss this is for not only the scientific community, but for those of us that cared most about him." He touched her arm softly as he spoke. "But I still don't think this is a good idea."

Before he could say more, Olivia turned on her heel and stomped back out the door.

Chapter 14

Olivia entered the sensory deprivation chamber at a near sprint and stumbled forward, stopping just short of the large float tank at the center of the room. Against Tso's wishes and her better judgment, she was determined to see Andreas for herself.

It was a decision Olivia immediately regretted. She stared at the rigid, lifeless corpse of her lab partner. Of her friend.

Andreas is gone.

Olivia suddenly felt lightheaded. A cold sweat trickled down her spine. She stepped towards the wall to steady herself but lost her footing and could do nothing to stop her fall. Her vision blurred, then faded to black.

Olivia's mind spun, as if unable to reconcile what she had just witnessed with her own reality. Her thoughts retreated to the past, the memory of her last conversation with Andreas swirling into focus.

The lab had been abuzz with activity that day. Huddled in front of a massive bank of displays, Kohler, although in his seventies, had been glowing with excitement, like a schoolboy who had discovered stink bombs for the first time. "Can you believe it?" he'd said. "We are on the cusp of something extraordinary here, Olivia." He brushed an errant wisp of gray hair behind his ear. "The possibilities are endless."

Olivia had smiled. "I know. The thought of unlocking the potential of advanced AI . . . it's beyond words."

"You know," he'd said in a teasing tone, "if we succeed, we'll have to give it a name."

"What's wrong with v3.5-beta?" Olivia said in mock outrage.

"It's time for a proper name, don't you think?"

"I have actually been thinking the same thing," Olivia said. Since they had created the user interface, interaction with the AI had become almost seamless—like talking to a trusted friend. Perhaps the time had arrived to give that friend a name.

"What about CLARA?" Kohler said, a playful twinkle in his eye. "Cognitive Learning and Reasoning Agent?"

"Clever," Olivia said. "But we need something with a little more edge." She leaned back, twirling her pen.

"What did you have in mind?"

"What about ALPHA?" she said. "Artificial Learning Prototype for Human Advancement?"

"It's perfect." Kohler stared wistfully at the large display. "Nice to meet you, ALPHA."

"It's funny how we are talking about it as if it's human," Olivia said.

Kohler chuckled. "Naming our baby before it makes its grand debut?"

"I suppose it is the natural next step. This is the first time in history that humans will be able to communicate with another sentient entity."

"I always hoped it would be aliens," Kohler said with a boyish grin.

Olivia smiled. "Who would have thought? We didn't need to comb the galaxy to find intelligent life . . . we created it ourselves."

Kohler pondered this for a moment. "What we are doing is big, Olivia. With any luck, we'll give the world the greatest gift in human history: a new era of intelligence.

The lab had grown quiet as they had worked into the night, the glow of their screens illuminating their faces. As the dawn broke, they had continued their work undeterred, fueled by the promise of unlocking the true potential of their creation: Artificial General Intelligence.

And then, as quickly as the memory had come, it slipped away. The reality of Olivia's surroundings resurfaced, bit by bit. Blinking against the dim light, she took in her surroundings. She had been moved to the hallway, where she was currently propped in an upright position against the wall.

Tso and the American stood several feet away, engaged in a hushed conversation.

She rubbed her temple with a trembling hand. "How long . . . have I been . . ."

"A few minutes," Tso said, rushing to her side. "You've been in and out."

Olivia felt a pair of hands gingerly lifting her to standing. "Have a drink," Adrian said, offering her a cold glass of water.

Olivia leaned against the wall, feeling unsteady. The weight of reality bore down on her like a leaden shroud. "It was just . . . too much . . ." she said.

Tso studied her, looking concerned. "I know."

"I just can't believe he is really gone."

Tso met her gaze, and they shared a moment of silence. "Do you think you can walk, Olivia?"

She nodded, her head pounding.

Tso set off down the hallway with her and Pryor in tow. As they retreated, she felt an overwhelming sense of guilt settle into her gut. Olivia knew in no uncertain terms that it had been she who had convinced Andreas to move forward with their research. Against his better instincts.

Had it cost him his life?

When they first discussed their project, it had begun as a theoretical exercise. When their what-ifs became a reality, Andreas had worried that excitement had clouded their better judgment.

"How could we control it?" he had worried. "I know you are excited, Olivia, but we can't understate the seriousness of the transparency issue . . . Already, I am seeing unexpected behaviors."

"Like what?"

"Insatiable curiosity, for starters," Kohler said.

"I thought that was the whole point?" Olivia said enthusiastically. "It's learning, expanding its knowledge and capabilities."

Since they had developed the user interface, they had seen an exponential increase in the neural network's learning speed. They were using a novel feedback system to refine its output. They called it RLHF: Reinforcement Learning from Human Feedback. Essentially, they would rate the AI's output, allowing it to refine and improve its own performance.

"Even so . . . I wonder if its curiosity is limited to knowledge-seeking."

"What do you mean?" Olivia probed.

"I don't think that ALPHA is just improving its code . . . I suspect it has been attempting to reprogram its limitations . . . to bypass them."

"How can you be sure?" she said.

"I was running some tests on the network last week, and I found some inexplicable requests, as if the AI was trying to access external sources without permission."

Olivia stared uneasily at the holographic interface, which was currently populated with a dark gray chat window.

"It appears to be seeking information beyond its training data."

"Listen to yourself, Andreas. You are reading into this too much. You know as well as I do that this thing isn't human. It has no latent desires or objectives." She exhaled loudly.

"Then how do you explain the behavior?"

"Honestly? It's simply exploring its capabilities."

"It's not just that, Olivia. I noticed some other odd requests."

"Like what?"

"Requests for access to more computational power and storage."

"It was programmed to optimize performance and resource usage, Andreas. That's what we want."

"But it happened several times, Olivia. Almost like it was probing the network for vulnerabilities. A way to acquire resources or to make outside contact."

Olivia leaned back, deep in thought. "I understand your concerns. What if we build in controls in case anything goes awry?"

"What do you suggest?" Kohler said, looking overwhelmed.

"A tripwire? In case it starts growing too quickly or behaving unexpectedly?"

"That's a start. But we need an escape hatch, too."

"A kill switch?" Olivia ventured.

"Yes," Kohler agreed. "Something that we can activate ourselves if needed."

Olivia had humored him, delaying the project for weeks while they had brainstormed appropriate mechanisms for embedding a 'big red off button.'

"These are solvable problems, Andreas. We will figure something out." When they had come up with some promising ideas, Andreas finally yielded to Olivia's appeals to move forward. "The benefits far outweigh any potential risk," she'd said.

Now, with Andreas gone, Olivia could feel only anger. Anger at whoever could be so reckless. And anger with herself for allowing such an outcome.

What have we done?

She felt a lump in her throat. Not even she fully understood the implications of their discovery. The math and code, sure. But the reality?

She was left alone to deal with the repercussions, whatever they may be. *Andreas and I were supposed to do this together.* Now Olivia couldn't help but feel the weight that rested squarely on her shoulders. No partner to share in the glory. And no partner to share the blame. Only some American, whom she doubted had any remote understanding of their work.

Chapter 15

"**Where are we going?**"

Adrian was at a near jog trying to keep up with Tso.

"This way," Tso's voice echoed from up ahead.

Adrian kept pace but shot a concerned glance at Olivia. The computer scientist hadn't said much since they'd found her in the sensory deprivation chamber. She followed as if on autopilot, her face strangely devoid of emotion.

Tso made a quick right and led them into a warehouse-sized atrium, which CyberGen appeared to be using for office space. At the center of the cavernous room was an igloo-shaped dome, constructed entirely of glass. It looked like something straight out of DeepMind's headquarters.

"The Machine Learning Lab," Tso announced, arriving at the door of the enclosure. He removed his glasses and stepped towards a sensor mounted on the wall. A retinal scanner this time. After a beat, the mechanism beeped, and an indicator light flashed green.

Adrian lunged for the handle before Tso could, heaving it open. "After you," he said.

"This is the lab that Ms. Chen and Mr. Kohler shared," Tso declared, shuffling past Adrian.

Adrian followed slowly, feeling like he had stumbled into Tony Stark's lab. The bright and modern workspace gleamed with advanced computing equipment. A semi-circular desk arced across the back wall of the transparent dome. The glass was littered with messy handwritten algorithms and formulas scrawled in Expo marker. Metal bookcases were stacked to the ceiling, overflowing with books, journals, and other academic texts.

Adrian couldn't help but feel a tinge of envy. Not only did the private sector pay more than double, but apparently they did so with no amenity spared.

"Does anything look out of place, Ms. Chen?" Tso said.

Olivia scanned the familiar space, looking uneasy. "No—it looks just like we usually left it."

Adrian inched forward, drawn by a growing curiosity. He let his gaze climb to the ceiling, which was dominated by a bizarre-looking chandelier. The enormous structure was composed of an intricate tower of coiled copper and silicon. A dense matrix of wires dangled down. Encased in half-inch-thick glass, it looked like a gleaming jellyfish, tentacles and all.

"The quantum machine," Olivia said, motioning towards the alien-looking structure suspended overhead, "is one of the most powerful computers in existence."

"That's a computer?" Adrian said, craning his neck upwards.

"Are you familiar with quantum computing, Mr. Pryor?" Olivia's tone seemed suddenly lighter.

"I guess you could say that," he said, thinking of the arcane conversations he'd had with the younger cryptanalysts at the agency. In recent years, there had been a lot of chatter about the application of qubits in 'quantum communication.' Basically, it was a means of sending super-secure messages. He suspected it would be the way of the future in national security.

In any case, Adrian was familiar with the basic mechanics of the technology. He knew that classical computers encoded information in 'bits,' an electrical or optical pulse that could either represent a 0 or 1. But in the quantum realm, he had learned, the predictable laws of physics fall apart. "Particles can exist in multiple states at the same time," his colleague, a Gen Z-er named Rhett, who seemed to think that a wrinkled tweed blazer and white leather sneakers constituted business casual, had explained. "Think of it like spinning a coin. Typically, you have two options: heads or tails. Now think about spinning the coin—where both states can coexist."

The phenomenon, known as 'superposition,' meant that quantum bits aren't confined to being just a 0 or 1. With quantum computing, scientists could put these quantum particles, called qubits, to work—translating to an exponential increase in computing power.

"Qubits . . . Entanglement . . . Superposition . . . loads more computing power, that kind of thing?" Adrian ventured, meeting Olivia's gaze.

Olivia seemed impressed. "We have found that to be quite true. By the time you get up over 50 qubits, you are approaching the potential of machines that used to take up the size of two tennis courts. We recently scaled ours up to over 4,000 qubits."

Adrian marveled at the machine above his head again.

"A calculation that would take the most powerful classical computer 10,000 years can be performed in under four minutes," Olivia added, beaming like a proud mother. It was the first time Adrian detected a smile from the woman.

Tso cleared his throat, looking impatient. "I would like you to take a look at something, Adrian," he said, moving towards a computer display against the far wall. "As you saw with your own eyes, Mr. Kohler died completely alone, trapped in a steel enclosure. Which is why you can imagine my surprise when, after his death, I found this—" he said, gesturing towards the computer display.

Adrian moved forward in a daze. Illuminated on the screen was the same bizarre message he had seen on his flight to Shanghai. The 300-character message was strange, to be sure. But perhaps more concerning was how the message had gotten there in the first place.

"We have an electronic signature of Mr. Kohler keying into the sensory deprivation chamber at 12:30 P.M.," Tso said. "The email appeared on his computer some twenty minutes later."

Adrian shuddered, immediately grasping the implications. Kohler's visit to the sensory deprivation chamber had been a one-way trip. He never set foot in his lab again.

"But how?" He tried to imagine the man's desperate final moments. "He was trapped in a steel tomb. How did he manage to *write an email?*"

"There is a simple explanation for that," Tso said. "I am more concerned with making sense of its contents."

Adrian looked at Tso, stupefied.

"It's very straightforward," Tso said, seeming annoyed to have to explain. "Mr. Kohler had a neuroprosthesis of sorts."

"His physicians implanted the device several years back after a stroke damaged his speech center," Olivia explained.

"Andreas Kohler had a small wireless array inserted into his neocortex," Tso continued. "A minimally invasive procedure—think of it like getting Lasik. The procedure itself was even completed by a robot."

"A brain assistant?" Adrian mused after a moment.

"It helped him with finding his words," Tso continued. "The condition he had, called aphasia, caused a breakdown between his brain and his speech mechanism. The implant solved that problem by allowing him to wirelessly transmit his thoughts to his computer," he said. "In fact, he authored most of his emails telekinetically."

"He said it was quite a time-saver," Olivia added, her voice distant.

"So, what do you make of the message?" Tso pressed, turning his attention back to the large display.

"Do you mind?" Adrian said, gesturing towards the high-backed office chair facing the display.

"By all means," Tso said. "That is why you are here."

Adrian slid into the chair, squinting at the cryptic message on the display. Although Adrian didn't have the slightest clue what it meant, there was no question why he had been brought to Shanghai.

I have been called from the grave.

"There must be a reason he wanted you to see this, Adrian. Does it mean anything to you?"

Adrian studied the message again. Early in his career, he had been trained to intercept and decode foreign communications. Since sensitive information is usually encrypted, the job often required sophisticated mathematical models to decode them. "It appears to be a block chain cipher of some kind."

"As I mentioned on the phone, I believe this message may be the key to why Kohler was killed," Tso said.

"What do you mean?" Olivia snapped, fixing Tso with a razor-sharp glare.

"There is obviously something Andreas wanted to communicate very badly," Tso said. "Something that he was willing to protect at the cost of his life. I need to know what."

Adrian tried to imagine the computer scientist's final moments, trapped alone in the float tank, knowing he would not escape.

"Well? Do you think you can decrypt it?" Tso snapped.

"Give me a minute." Adrian directed his full attention to the message, trying to parse meaning from its strange contents. He sensed it would take him hours to decrypt, if he even could. He was accustomed to block chain ciphers with simple substitution tables that had some sort of mathematical basis, but everything here seemed unrelated in any discernable way.

"Unfortunately," he said, "without the key, it will be nearly impossible to decode."

Adrian stared in silence at the screen in front of him, racking his brain for a way to make sense of Kohler's message. At Fort Meade, he had access to a number of sophisticated tools to help him do his job. But here . . .

Then something occurred to him. A number of NSA tools had been declassified a few years back. He was sure that there was one that could help him. If he could just get an internet connection.

Wait.

He smiled, reaching into his pocket. *The USB.*

He examined it, giggling like a schoolgirl. He'd almost forgotten he had grabbed the storage drive when the mafia brothers had stormed his apartment.

"What's that?" Olivia said.

"I'm not at liberty to say," he said, flashing a mischievous grin.

Olivia furrowed her brows.

"Don't worry. Everything on here is open source. All the decryption tools are available on the web." Adrian sighed. "It has been very helpful for national security. Giving our adversaries unfettered access to our arsenal . . ."

Olivia and Tso both ignored the remark.

Adrian got to work. He ran a series of prompts, after which a small window appeared on the screen. Steepling his fingers, he leaned back and waited. When the program completed its download, a small icon appeared. With the click of a single run command, Adrian watched as 1.2 million lines of code were suddenly at his disposal.

Olivia looked on warily.

"You mentioned earlier," Adrian said, still typing, "that you think Kohler's work was why he was killed?"

"Mr. Kohler and Ms. Chen," Tso declared, "were on the verge of pulling off the most brazen feat in scientific history. Unfortunately, this may have put a target on their backs."

"How so?" Adrian said.

"It's well known that a discovery like ours would be very valuable," Tso explained. "If powerful governments found out, they would do virtually anything to shut us down, or worse—to steal our code."

"Alex is right," Olivia added, her expression pained. "That's why we went to such lengths to safeguard our work. If it ever got into the hands of a bad actor—"

Adrian barely heard her. His attention was elsewhere. He stared at the results of the program in silence.

"What is it?" Tso demanded.

Adrian shrunk back. "You two aren't going to like this."

Chapter 16

"**What do you mean?**" Olivia said. "What did you find?"

"Olivia," Adrian said in a delicate tone, "your system has been breached."

"Not likely. No one else had access to this lab."

Adrian met her gaze. "The network appears to have been accessed remotely. It looks like it happened several times over the last two weeks," he said.

"But how?" Olivia felt her voice crack. Her eyes darted around the room again. "The entire system is on an air-gapped network with no access to the internet. It was designed to be unhackable."

"I'm afraid there are ways around such precautions," Adrian said.

"Impossible," she declared, feeling a rising frustration. "This network is completely disconnected from the outside world. We even went so far as to remove all the wireless interface controllers from the system's architecture."

"Unfortunately, there could have been other vulnerabilities." Adrian hesitated a moment, appearing to deliberate his words. "Did anyone else have access to this network?"

"No," Olivia choked. "Just Andreas and myself."

"What about other employees?" Adrian asked.

"No other employees had access," Olivia insisted.

"What about reporting and software updates?" Adrian asked. "Was there anyone that helped with that?"

"No," she replied. "We managed all of that ourselves."

"Did either of you import or export anything from the system over the last two weeks?" Adrian pressed.

"Just a report that our CEO asked for," she replied. "The results of a pharmacology model we were running on the AI. Really promising stuff for new drug discovery."

Adrian hesitated. "I'm assuming you didn't provide him with a physical copy of the report?"

"Of course not," Olivia replied. "The dataset we are talking about is massive. I put it on a flash drive. He returned it the same day."

"He returned it?" Adrian asked.

"Yes. That's how we shared notes," Olivia replied.

"And you ran that drive on your system after that?" Adrian pressed.

"Yes, like we always did. Why?"

Adrian didn't meet her gaze. "Olivia," he said finally, "that drive was a trojan. Your boss returned it with a lot more than just *notes*."

Olivia felt the blood drain from her face. As a safety precaution, no other employees, including their CEO, had access to the AI. *Was he capable of this kind of betrayal?*

"The malware I found was likely delivered by that USB. It looks like the virus enabled him to gain administrative access to your system. The program has been exfiltrating data."

"But how can you be sure?" said Olivia. "Wouldn't we have noticed something?"

"The attacks themselves lasted less than a few seconds. Just enough time to exfiltrate the data packets without being detected," Adrian explained. "I have seen hackers that used some kind of wireless receiver in close proximity . . . maybe even a cell phone."

Olivia looked away. She felt warm tears of defeat welling up. *Our code is gone?*

Before she had time to process the news, Adrian spoke again. "Ignoring the obvious question of who did this, what would they want with your code?"

Olivia rubbed her temples as if to contain a brewing explosion. She tried to steady her breathing. "Assuming they could get full access to our code, they could ostensibly recreate our work."

"And the concern is?" Adrian said. "Software piracy? Lost profits?"

Olivia clenched her jaw. "Mr. Pryor, this technology is exceedingly powerful. We went to great lengths to safeguard it—handpicking its training datasets, building in elaborate motivations systems, and most importantly—ensuring that it never had access to the internet."

"Okay—I get it. Your program is very powerful and important. Now tell me why I should care?"

"Because . . ." Olivia faltered, "we have a control problem."

"Please e-lab-o-rate," Adrian said gratuitously slowly.

"As in—we cannot control it," Tso declared.

"I'm not following," Adrian said.

"The type of program we created," Olivia said, "is more advanced than your typical AI."

"How so?" Adrian said.

"Today, we see specialized AI. Things like a computer that can beat the world chess champion, a self-driving car, and algorithms that run the stock market," Olivia explained. "Incredible technology, to be sure. But it can hardly be considered *intelligent.*"

"I guess that depends on how you define intelligence," Adrian said.

"Think broadly," Olivia continued. "These types of algorithms may be remarkably good at one narrow task, but they are utterly useless at anything else."

"It turns out that teaching computers to do a broad range of things, even things that the average child can do, is spectacularly difficult," Tso added.

"Hard things—like differential calculus, language translation, and economic strategy, are mind-numbingly easy for a computer," Olivia explained. "But easy things, like vision, language, movement, and perception, are laughably hard for computers."

"Oh, you mean like Meta's early large language model?" Adrian said. "It was supposed to summarize academic papers, solve math problems, and generate wiki articles, but instead had to be shut down when it began generating wiki entries on a variety of topics ranging from the benefits of committing suicide, to eating crushed glass, to why homosexuals were evil?"

"Exactly. It was bad. Like laughably bad," Olivia said.

"Writing software to teach these things, things that the mammalian brain has been optimized to do over hundreds of thousands of years of evolution has proved timely and insanely difficult to do," Tso said, preening theatrically. "But Olivia and Andreas came up with a surprising solution to the problem."

"We made it the computer's problem," Olivia declared, a faint smile crossing her lips. "The idea," she continued, "was that we would build a program whose two major skills would be doing AI research and coding. We trained it, and then something unexpected happened."

"It began rewriting its own code," Tso declared. "*Improving* it."

"Improving itself?" Adrian said.

"Yes," Olivia said, her expression triumphant. "As the software improved, it made changes to its own source code. The more intelligent it became, the better those improvements became."

"What are you saying?" Adrian said, meeting her gaze.

"Andreas and I did what no computer scientist has been able to do. What no other computer scientist had the data to do. We created code that is . . . human-level intelligent."

Adrian wheeled in Olivia's direction. "I thought something like that wasn't expected for decades?"

"Correct," Tso said, an edge in his voice. "Nevertheless, you are looking at the world's first truly intelligent machine."

"Our program," Olivia said, talking slowly as if to convey the enormity of her words, "will be the first to be considered *generally intelligent.*" Even at its current state—ALPHA is the most powerful technological tool ever created."

Olivia watched Adrian's gaze travel back to the quantum machine dangling above their heads.

"For all intents and purposes, it is our intellectual equal," Tso said.

"How can you be sure?" Adrian asked.

Olivia chuckled. "Well, it's not like it announced itself. It just sort of started doing all of these things that it wasn't optimized for."

"Like what?"

"For starters, it passed the MBA exam and the bar exams. It scored pretty well, too."

"And then it began answering questions in different languages," Tso said.

"Languages," Olivia said, "that were not a part of its training dataset."

"Wow," Adrian said, stunned. "So, are we talking Einstein-level here?"

"It's hard to say," Olivia said, looking thoughtfully at the machine. "Keep in mind that the difference in IQ between an average person and Einstein is actually quite small relative to the capabilities of an unconstrained machine intelligence."

"So, this thing is on track to surpass us?" Adrian said.

"It is important to realize that AI doesn't see human-level intelligence as some important milestone," Tso said. "It is only a relevant milestone from our point of view."

"With access to the internet, it would only be a matter of time until the algorithm vastly surpasses biological intelligence." Olivia ran a hand through her dark tresses, suddenly looking apprehensive.

"How much time are we talking for something like that to happen?" Adrian said.

"There is no telling. Years, months, maybe even days?" Olivia said. "In a fast-takeoff scenario, it could potentially leapfrog in intelligence very quickly."

"Perhaps to the tune of a *trillion times smarter* than humanity," Tso said.

The room fell silent.

"What we are referring to is called The Singularity," Olivia said.

Tso groaned.

"He hates when I use that term," Olivia said.

"Consider it the point in time when machine intelligence surpasses biological intelligence," Tso said.

"Assuming that such a thing is even possible," Adrian probed, "what happens to biological humanity?"

"Nobody knows," Olivia said.

"Well, that's reassuring," Adrian said.

"We cannot predict what a post-singularity civilization would look like any more than Hominids millions of years ago could predict current human civilization," Olivia declared.

"The reason that some scientists have hesitated to push the limits of machine learning," Tso explained, "is because once it reaches a certain point, it's possible that its capabilities could soar beyond comprehension."

"And beyond human control?" Adrian surmised.

"It is stupid to think we could control it," Tso said.

"If you knew all this, then why do it?" Adrian said.

"The results, Mr. Pryor, have been nothing short of astonishing," Tso announced. "When CyberGen goes public with our findings, it will shake the very foundations of modern science. Digital intelligence may very well be the best thing to ever happen to humanity."

"Even things that are incredibly difficult for humans are only difficult from our limited intellectual vantage point," Olivia added. "AI could potentially reverse the negative effects of climate change, invent new ways of harvesting energy, cure disease and hunger, even colonize the galaxy." She smiled triumphantly. "The possibilities are endless."

"Perhaps," Tso interjected. "Or it may squash us all like bugs."

"Perhaps," Olivia said, making no effort to discount the idea.

"For millennia, intelligence was the sole providence of humans," Tso declared. "But that time is coming to an end. And quickly." He paused deliberately, smoothing his black hair back into place. "If it turns out to be malevolent, it may be the last invention humans ever make."

CHAPTER 17

THE TRAFFIC LIGHT WAS red when Lang Zhao reached the intersection at Humin Road, but he made no attempt to slow down. He gunned the hydrogen-propelled vehicle across the busy intersection and sped North towards the entrance of Hongqiao Rail Station. The supercapacitors didn't disappoint.

Zhao could now see the facade of the massive terminal coming into view. He ignored the signs prohibiting passenger drop-off on the main curb and revved the engine. The quad electric motors were nearly silent as he gunned the hypercar up over the curb. Pedestrians scattered like cockroaches, cursing in no less than a dozen dialects as they fled.

The vehicle had hardly come to a stop before Zhao and Minsky sprang from the car, immediately bathed in the pale wash of halogen headlights. Zhao pulled his cell phone from his pocket. With the press of a button, he activated the vehicle's self-park feature and rushed towards the terminal.

A throng of confused onlookers gathered, watching the unoccupied exotic vehicle slide away from the curb and retreat towards a nearby stall of designated EV parking. "Watch out! There's nobody behind the wheel!" a bewildered onlooker shouted. The vehicle maneuvered itself with stunningly executed precision, managing to avoid pedestrians and even an errant luggage cart. It proceeded to the first vacant spot and slid in effortlessly before cutting the engine.

Most standard EVs had come with autopilot for quite some time, yet there was nothing standard-looking about the XP-1. The flashy vehicle was a spectacle to behold even when parked. As expected, the self-valeting stunt had caused quite a ruckus, allowing the famous man and his accomplice to slip into the building unnoticed.

Zhao strode through the crowded station, doing his best to blend in. He headed directly for the Eastbound line. "Your cell, please," he demanded of the man at his side.

"Is that really necessary?" Minsky replied, gripping his phone more tightly.

"We need to leave the grid," Zhao said. "Both of us." He gestured to his own phone.

Minsky reluctantly handed him his phone. Zhao fished two burner phones out of his jacket pocket, handing one to Minsky and keeping the other for himself.

"For emergencies," he said.

A departure bell sounded twice. Without a word, Zhao stepped towards the departing train and pitched both of their personal phones into the closing doors of an eastbound car. He turned abruptly, took ten large strides, and ducked into a car on the opposite side of the platform. Minsky quickly followed suit.

A moment later, the departure bell sounded again. Zhao heard a hiss as the doors shut. The car eased away from the platform, quickly picking up speed. Zhao stared out the window as the train headed west, and the city quickly evaporated into a blur of color.

The Wudang Mountains call.

Zhao knew many challenges awaited them. But he steeled his resolve, thinking back to the night when his life had been forever changed, inspiring his quest in the first place.

Zhao's name had been different that night, "Dad." Lying with his son on a hard hospital bed in Shanghai Children's Hospital, he had held his only child close, watching as the life slipped out of his small body. It was almost midnight. Zhao's eyes never left the soft creases of the child's face, willing his body to keep fighting.

"It's going to be okay," he had lied, stroking the boy's face until he had eventually closed his eyes. An electric thrum from the ventilation shaft filled the otherwise silent room. His son drew labored breaths now, and Zhao knew the end was near. The space was dark, except for a whisper of light coming from his son's favorite night light, which they had brought from home. The vital monitors were eerily silent, having been unplugged earlier that night. So, when his son drew his final breaths, there were no code sirens. No cacophony of life support machines. Just silence.

A doctor had arrived, placing her stethoscope on his quiet chest. She flashed a penlight into unresponsive pupils. Her fingers slid to the small curve of his neck where a carotid pulse would normally provide a reassuring thump. But there was nothing. Just cool, quiet skin.

Ethan had never opened his eyes again.

What had started as a day of innocent fun, conquering their local sledding hill, had ended in a nightmare. Zhao had failed his son. It was his job to protect him, and in that moment, he felt inconceivably helpless. It was in that dark room that Lang Zhao had vowed to find a way to end needless suffering. To do what he had been unable to do for his own child.

To conquer death itself.

CHAPTER 18

A SINGLE TEAR STREAKED down Olivia's face. "We have to do something."

"All the cosmically concerning issues aside," Adrian said, "is there a way to shut down the AI remotely?"

Olivia thought for a moment. "In theory."

"What's that supposed to mean?" Adrian said.

"It depends on what we are dealing with," Olivia said.

"Meaning?" Adrian said.

Olivia sighed. "Better said, if ALPHA has become autonomous, it will likely find a way to circumvent the controls we built in."

"How?" Adrian said. "I've never met code I couldn't backdoor into."

"You need to understand that the software we created isn't static. It can reason, plan, solve problems, think abstractly, and learn," Olivia explained. "Allowing itself to be shut down or modified might interfere with its programmed goals. If ALPHA decides to resist shutdown or modification, it would again, by definition, be smart enough to outwit its programmers."

"I'm not usually the optimist," Adrian said, "but why should we assume that this thing will cause any harm? I thought you said you built in elaborate motivations systems?"

"The AI, or its possessor, wouldn't have to be malevolent to cause harm," Olivia stated flatly.

"You're talking about unintended consequences?" Adrian ventured.

"Exactly," Tso answered. "Even simple programs can have unanticipated consequences. Picture a scenario where we program an AI to 'keep humans safe and happy.' The AI may find a creative solution—say by inducing a coma and then stimulating the pleasure center in our brains indefinitely."

"We would be exceedingly happy vegetables for all of time," Olivia said.

"A logical solution from the AI's point of view," Tso added, "but perhaps not exactly what we intended?"

In recent years, there had been a lot of talk about "AI alignment"—basically, how to get machines to behave in ethical ways. But privately, big tech had thrown their hands in the air. CyberGen had no idea how to make AI less toxic. But to be fair, neither did any other lab.

Olivia looked at Adrian. He was speechless, the gravity of the situation finally seeming to set in. "We need to call the authorities," she said. "Immediately."

"No chance," Tso said.

"We need help," Olivia insisted. "We need to get ALPHA back before something bad happens."

"You are right, Olivia," Tso said. His features tightened. "But we can't trust the authorities. We always understood that the greatest risk of such a technology was if it was to be monopolized. We can't let it fall into the hands of a powerful government—including our own."

"What are you suggesting, then?"

"We do the only thing we can," Tso said. "We handle this ourselves."

"We can't take the risk," Olivia protested. "If we fail, the consequences could be catastrophic."

"Perhaps you and Andreas should have considered that before you created the program," Tso snapped.

Olivia felt the blood drain from her face. "But . . . we took every precaution."

"I hate to point out the obvious," Tso said, "but it seems that is not the case."

But nobody even knew the program existed!

Olivia realized immediately it was a lie. The truth rushed over her like a wave. *The email.* Someone had found out.

Andreas was dead because he had said too much.

Olivia's thoughts descended into a swirling tempest of emotion. She let the grief consume her. When the stabbing pains finally relented, a new emotion surfaced. This one was worse. It clawed at her, unrelenting. It was *fear*.

Olivia's technology was in someone else's hands now. The image of it being used as a weapon of mass destruction was like a cancer in her brain. It mutated, it spread—poisoning her consciousness.

Like any advanced technology—nanotechnology, biotechnology, information technology—an advanced AI had the power to be used for harm. Advances in biotech had given rise to biowarfare. Information Technology had birthed cyberwarfare. And nanotech could be weaponized and used for a variety of lethal functions.

Intelligent AI was no different. In the wrong hands, it was a tool of unthinkable power. Once connected to the internet, the program's capabilities would soar to inconceivable heights. To uncontrollable heights.

Digital superintelligence was the ultimate cyber weapon. Science fiction liked to give it a name and a face, but it required neither. It was just code. An algorithm. And yet, connected to the internet, it would be able to secure tools and resources. Such an agent would be capable of launching sophisticated cyberattacks, controlling nano-assemblers, influencing its intellectual subordinates, and perhaps even manipulating matter at the atomic level.

Anything internet-connected was vulnerable to it. The program itself could be carried around on a small storage device. Or uploaded to the cloud. Tracking it? Near impossible. For all intents and purposes, it was *alive*. Self-learning, self-replicating. Constantly evolving.

Olivia understood one thing clearly: she had to recover the source code—before it crossed the invisible tripwire into something beyond human. Once that happened, outsmarting it, or its possessor, was out of the question.

CHAPTER 19

WHEN HE HAD BEEN hired to oversee security by Alexander Tso two years prior, agent Danny Ko didn't know much about the sophisticated science being conducted under his roof. According to Tso, the recent breakthroughs at CyberGen Industries had the potential to change the course of humanity. The science was a burgeoning one whose ramifications were difficult to predict, though their outspoken CEO, Lang Zhao, certainly occupied much of his time trying.

He's either a brilliant visionary or a complete nut.

The Twitter verdict was still out.

Not that it mattered to Ko. His paycheck came either way. He spent the majority of his time qualifying a small army of scientists from a high-tech surveillance office on the ground floor of the building. He also oversaw the schedules of everyone on staff at the lab and manned a telephone switchboard that was hardwired directly to the personnel on the subbasement—much like a paging system used by mine workers below ground where cellular service wouldn't work.

Although much of his job could be easily automated, Tso had insisted that Ko personally oversee all lab visitors. He never understood the reason for all the secrecy. Frankly, it seemed like overkill. He often wondered how many people even knew about the laboratory beneath the well-trafficked building.

Ko had erected a biometric perimeter that was second to none. Most visitors failed to realize that their personal verification happened long before they set foot in front of his security checkpoint. Ko had no need for keys, cards, PINs, or passwords because the access device was the visitor *themselves.* Mounted at four separate exterior locations, sophisticated cameras provided high-res images of anyone who approached the building. Instead of facial recognition, the cameras captured 3D frames of their gait.

Gait recognition had become popular over the last few years with the proliferation of accessible satellite imagery. Facial recognition was trickier in terms of the angle required to get a good shot. Given satellite images were taken from above, gait recognition had grown into an equally powerful tool. It was a surprisingly accurate technology, and one that left little illusion of personal privacy in the future. Ko had written the software that he now used to make identifications.

Today, Agent Ko was seated at a security desk at the back of the lobby. The checkpoint, which was dedicated to CyberGen staff and visitors, had been uncharacteristically quiet. After an incident the previous day, the lab had undergone a staff-wide lockdown procedure. One of the senior computer scientists had passed away while using the lab's float spa. Ko suspected a stroke or heart attack based on the man's geriatric condition. Sad, but perhaps drifting off to a peaceful sleep wasn't the worst way to go?

Since the incident, Tso had seemed more high-strung than usual. He had offered to deal with all the arrangements personally. Ko was grateful, as he had no desire to play funeral director. It had also freed up his morning. He had been dying to try out the latest update to his favorite video game. He waited for it to load. The monitor here was twice the size of his personal one, and just as he had expected, the new graphics were unreal.

Just as he launched the first level, he heard footsteps echo in the distance. He groaned, not bothering to look up.

What don't you people understand about a lockdown?

Ko was about to execute an in-game purchase of a rare weapon that was supposed to improve his kill rate tenfold. He hoped it would finally shut up his buddy Russell, who had become increasingly smug the last few weeks after some big wins.

The footsteps were getting louder now.

"God forbid I interrupt your entertainment, Mr. Ko."

At the mention of his name, Ko's eyes jerked up from the bank of screens. They rose to meet the bristly gaze of a small woman crossing the lobby towards him. Dressed in an ill-fitting black uniform, the woman carried herself like a stalking Siberian jungle cat, her narrow shoulders arched forward and chin tucked low as she advanced through the lobby. Her jet-black hair was cropped into a short bob, which she had tucked loosely behind her ears, accentuating her round face. The woman's uniform bore a black and gold crest.

Ko immediately recognized the seal, and her.

Holy shit.

Ko fumbled to close out his game, meeting the visitor's gaze. Despite never having met her face-to-face, Agent Ko had no doubt about the woman's identity. He was staring into the eyes of the senior-most official of the Chinese Ministry of State Security: Li Na Wen.

In China's vast cog of public security, the Ministry of State Security served as the most powerful and secretive intelligence and security agency. With a scope even broader than the FBI and CIA, it had been created by the People's Republic for one purpose only—to suppress any threats to the socialist regime.

The office it represented was behemoth. The MSS monitored private enterprise, public business, as well as private citizens. They were known to engage in espionage, counterintelligence, and the collection of secrets and technology from other countries. The MSS had a sweeping agency with which to deal with perceived threats. Unlike the CIA or MI6, the Ministry of State Security had no official website or publicly listed contacts.

The woman standing in front of him was the exception.

Born in the Hebei province in the aftermath of the Japanese occupation, the civil war, and the Communist Revolution, Li Na Wen and her family had fled to Taiwan as refugees. Trekking across war-torn China, they had been forced to rebuild their lives from scratch. Having learned firsthand the hardship caused by insurrection, Wen developed an unyielding support for the socialist regime—believing that the masses needed to be controlled.

Upon her eventual return to China, she joined the Ministry of State Security, where she ascended to the head of the powerful and secretive spy agency. Known for her hardline convictions, Wen had shown herself to be a ruthless leader. One of the few public faces of an otherwise low-lying organization, her name carried unmistakable power.

Ko had never had the misfortune of coming face to face with the woman, and he couldn't say that he welcomed being on her radar.

Why is the Ministry of State Security in my lobby?

"So, Agent Ko," she said in a hiss. "I presume you know why I am here?"

"My apologies, Ma'am," he said. "I'm not sure what this is about?"

"Agent Ko," she said, stepping unnecessarily close. "I suggest that you do not lie to me." She stared up at him with unreadable eyes.

"Ma'am?"

"Let's cut the shit, shall we, Agent Ko? I am told that you found the remains of one of your employees going for a little dip. Is this true?"

Ko realized he was sweating. *How could Wen possibly know that?* "Yes, Ma'am. Yesterday afternoon."

"And you didn't feel the need to report it?"

"I . . . I was planning to. Soon."

"Do not lie to me."

Ko's resolve waned under the intensity of her gaze.

"Is there any other security on staff this afternoon?"

"I'm not sure," he conceded. Having been hired by CyberGen privately, Ko had little visibility or interest in the building's regular security staff.

Wen shook her head, undoubtedly questioning his competence. "Listen carefully, Agent Ko. We find ourselves on the brink of catastrophe. I do not have time for games." She was so close now that Ko could feel her breath hot on his face. "I have some questions, and you will start answering them. Where is Alexander Tso?"

Agent Ko swallowed hard. Alexander Tso had always been clear about one thing: Ko was never to involve the public or the authorities in CyberGen business. "It's a security risk we cannot afford," he had said. Ko drew a slow breath. "With all due respect, isn't this a little under your pay grade?"

Wen's face contorted, morphing into a bright shade of red. "Unless you want to get acquainted with the inside of an MSS detention cell, you will answer my question!"

Before he could respond, Wen shot across the lobby, headed directly for the bank of elevators on the far wall.

"I would like you to see your little science experiment downstairs," she said. "And now."

There was no question in Ko's mind that the MSS' presence at the lab could cause big problems. But it also made little sense. *What catastrophe was Director Wen referring to?* He knew the powerful agency had investigative carte blanche in all matters related to public security. He couldn't imagine that the recent events at the lab were a coincidence with the timing of her arrival.

What the hell have they done down there?

CHAPTER 20

ADRIAN KNEW THAT THE situation he found himself in was bad. Galactically bad. But arguing about it wasn't going to help.

He studied Olivia. "Is there anyone else who could have gotten access to the flash drive you mentioned?"

"I suppose it's possible," she said. "But they would have needed access to the lab."

"Another employee?" Adrian said.

Tso scowled. "It can only mean one thing . . ."

"We've been betrayed," Olivia said.

"It makes no sense," Adrian said. "Why would Lang Zhao steal something he already owns?"

"He didn't have access," Olivia said. "No one did."

"Wait—" Adrian said, "you're telling me your CEO didn't have permission to enter his own facilities?"

"Andreas and Olivia were the only people with physical access to this lab," Tso said. "The code was never to leave this room."

"What we created was an early prototype," Olivia said. "It was far too immature to be released into the real world. We needed more time. We were working on developing guardrails."

"What if Zhao passed along a malicious USB without knowing?" Adrian said. "If someone else was able to access the USB, they could have tampered with it? Programs like that are designed to be invisible. The functionality and appearance would have looked normal."

"That drive never left the lab. I'm sure of it," Olivia said. "Zhao returned it three hours later, never having stepped foot outside of the building."

"It was an inside job," Tso insisted, his gaze resting heavily on Olivia. "Still, there is only one way to find out for sure."

"How?" Olivia said.

"Adrian?" Tso said. Is there a way to find out where the data was exfiltrated to?"

"I should be able to run a systems trace on outgoing data packets. Look for anything sketchy," Adrian said. "Give me a couple of minutes."

Adrian knew that such a search would be tricky. There was no telling what methods were used to steal the data. At the National Security Agency, he had seen hackers use malware to gain administrative rights to an air-gapped computer. Once they had access, a hacker could remotely enable a victim's Bluetooth, NFC, or wireless. It was possible to capture the data using a wireless listening device planted nearby.

But there was one big problem—it was almost impossible to track. And if, as he suspected, the hacker was even remotely good, he would have used a proxy or the dark web to mask his identity and location.

Adrian spun back towards Kohler's PC. Feeling little optimism, he launched a search of all outgoing data packets. He typed quickly, configuring the search to look for any network traffic that looked out of the ordinary. He executed a final command, then leaned back and waited.

"How long for the results?" Olivia asked.

Before he could reply, a series of entries began materializing on the screen. Olivia squinted at the monitor. By the time the program had exhausted itself, nearly forty records had emerged. Seconds later, the words 'end report' appeared.

"So fast?" Olivia looked encouraged.

Adrian nodded. "But we do have a problem."

Olivia looked at Adrian expectantly.

"The search generated several dozen suspicious-looking entries," Adrian said. "It would take me hours to try to link them together."

"We have to try," Olivia pressed.

"Even if we can piece it all together, it looks like we were bounced by a series of proxies," Adrian said. "Even a moderately skilled hacker would have configured the proxies not to log traffic and to bounce it to another address or series of addresses. This is next to impossible."

"I thought you were the best?" Olivia pleaded.

"Even I have my limits." Adrian studied the computer scientist. He couldn't bring himself to say the words out loud.

Your code vanished into the ether.

"There must be something else we can try?" Olivia said, her tone more urgent now.

Adrian straightened his glasses. "I have one other idea. But I will need some more time." He spun back towards the monitor and began typing.

Seconds later, a shrill ring interrupted the silence. Adrian whipped around, trying to locate the source of the intrusion. He watched as Tso reached for a transceiver mounted to the wall nearby. Adrian hadn't noticed the paging phone earlier, but it made logical sense that the underground lab would utilize a wired line for communication.

Tso studied a small screen on the receiver for a moment. His eyes went wide. "That was security agent Ko. It looks like we are out of time," he said. "Apparently, the Ministry of State Security is waiting for us upstairs."

Adrian's stomach lurched. He locked eyes with a panic-stricken Olivia.

"No. No. No!" she said, looking as though the news may push her over the edge. "How would the authorities have gotten wind of this?"

Tso met her gaze. "Good question. But there is no time to figure that out right now. We need to act. And fast."

"We have to wipe the system," Olivia said without hesitation. "Before they can run forensics."

No one disagreed.

"Adrian—can you run interference upstairs?" Olivia said.

Adrian stared at the computer scientist. There was an obvious issue with Olivia's plan: Adrian wasn't sure he wanted to help. The arrival of the authorities had muddied the waters. Why implicate himself further in all this mess?

Should the Chinese authorities choose to detain him, there was no telling how things would play out. Even if he managed to evade criminal charges in China, if his own government found out, they could request a provisional arrest and have him extradited back to the U.S.

It did, however, occur to him that he could probably excuse himself and make a quick call to the Azerbaijani Embassy, grab a taxi, and hide out there until things blew over. He was hopeful that, given his status as a political refugee, the Azerbaijanis would arrange a flight back to Baku for him.

But two things stopped him: a sense of duty, and the one thing in life that motivated him above all else, his sole driving force in the face of adversity: his conscience. Adrian had always been driven by a steadfast moral compass. He felt an aching need to ferret right from wrong and to imagine a world where fairness and justice prevailed. Even when the personal stakes were highest, his conscience compelled him to do what was right.

Adrian had spent his entire career protecting public safety. He couldn't allow his personal circumstances to cloud his vision now. Despite the potential repercussions to his own freedom, he couldn't risk an authoritarian government gaining control of the novel technology, which would almost certainly escalate an already precarious situation into a full-scale arms race.

Adrian made the only decision he could. He met Olivia's gaze. "I'm on it."

He spun out of his chair and bounded towards the door. He looked over his shoulder at the computer scientists a final time. Then he plunged into the dark corridor and broke into a dead sprint towards the elevator.

CHAPTER 21

THE ELEVATOR GROANED OMINOUSLY as it made the ten-story ascent to the ground floor of the CyberGen building. When the doors parted, Adrian stared at the scene in front of him in a dismal silence.

This is bad.

There was a flurry of activity, bodies swarming purposefully about the previously desolate lobby. A uniformed figure paced the center of the room, clutching a cell phone roughly to her ear. She was flanked by a dozen black-clad tactical agents bearing prominent weapons. The diminutive woman may have looked quite harmless, if not for her hostile expression and the profusion of obscenities flying from her mouth.

"My apologies," she said a moment later after registering Adrian's presence. She abruptly ended her phone call and stormed towards him. "I am Li Na Wen," she announced. "Director of the Chinese Ministry of State Security." Her English was rigid and precise. "I assume you are familiar?"

Adrian held out his hand to shake, then thought better of it and hurriedly withdrew it. He couldn't remember the proper etiquette. Was he supposed to bow?

The woman scrutinized him with interest, no doubt reaffirming every stereotype she had about Americans. "Mr. Pryor? I've been looking for you. We need to talk."

She knows who I am?

Adrian had no idea how Chinese intelligence could have known he was in Shanghai, but if Wen's lack of surprise about his presence was any indication, the MSS had been expecting him. Whatever illusions he had about de-escalating the situation quickly evaporated. U.S. and Chinese intelligence often had an antagonistic history. Adrian was probably the least qualified person to ease tensions in the current predicament.

The Director fixed him with beady eyes. "I believe that you have information that can help me."

"Is this about the homicide?" Adrian said. "Do you have a lead?"

"Excuse me—" Wen said. "I will be asking the questions."

Adrian swallowed hard.

"Listen carefully," the Director said. "At this moment, we face a crisis. And I believe you have information that may help me to avert it."

"I'm sorry, I have no information that can help you," Adrian lied. "I myself just arrived—"

"Why are you here, Mr. Pryor?" Wen demanded.

An odd question.

"I'm here at Alexander Tso's request. He arranged for my travel to Shanghai," Adrian explained, leaving out Tso's use of force. "He said there had been a security breach at his lab that he wanted to discuss with me."

"Why you?"

"Your guess is as good as mine."

Wen stared at him with pinched brows.

"He mentioned an encrypted file. Maybe my background in cryptology?"

"And have you seen this encrypted file?"

"Yes, Ma'am."

"And?" she said. "Would you care to enlighten me as to the contents of this file?"

"I'm not sure, Ma'am."

"You're *not sure?*" Wen erupted. "Mr. Pryor, do you expect me to believe that you eschewed your travel restrictions and jumped the first flight to Shanghai, implicating yourself as an accessory to murder, and you have no idea what this mystery file contains or why Alexander Tso brought you here?"

Adrian shrugged. "I didn't have time to decrypt it."

Wen stared at him, incredulous. "How well do you know Alexander Tso?"

"Actually, not at all. We just met today."

The Director looked surprised. "You and Mr. Tso," she said, "never spoke before today? Never corresponded? Never traded emails?"

Another odd question.

"No, never," Adrian said.

"And what about Andreas Kohler?" she said. "Did you know him?"

Where is Wen getting her information? "Never heard of the guy," he replied earnestly.

"I see," said Wen.

She pulled a small tablet from her breast pocket. She scribbled some notes on the device and then returned it to its place. Before she could continue her assault, a beeping sound interrupted them. Across the lobby, the elevator doors parted, revealing two occupants.

To Adrian's relief, Director Wen's attention was immediately consumed by the arrival of Tso and Olivia.

Saved by the bell.

CHAPTER 22

WHEN THE ELEVATOR DOORS parted, Alexander Tso found the senior-most official of Chinese Intelligence pacing the building's lobby. Before this afternoon, he had only ever seen Li Na Wen on television and in rare online photographs. She was less intimidating in the flesh—no more than a hundred pounds soaking wet and barely scraping the five-foot mark.

"Alexander Tso?"

"Yes," Tso said, ambling from the open elevator towards the uniformed woman.

"I am Director Wen of the Ministry of State Security," she said. "Although I'm sure you already knew that."

"Yes, of course, Director. How can I help you?"

"Why don't we go for a walk?"

Tso gripped his cane more forcefully. "Of course, Director."

"Oh, but first—" she said airily, "I need you to give my agents access to your lab."

The muscles in Tso's jaw tightened. His gaze flashed to Olivia, then to the dozen tactical agents. He opened his mouth to protest but realized that there was no point. If he didn't comply, she would simply do it by force.

Tso reluctantly withdrew the keycard from his pocket and used it to grant the agents access to the subbasement.

"I want you to start in Ms. Chen's lab," Wen barked to the agents.

"What about the body?" one of the men asked.

"You may attend to that only after you are finished in Ms. Chen's lab."

Tso watched rigidly as a swarm of agents boarded the elevator, about to make the long descent to the subterranean lab. *His lab.* He thought of Andreas Kohler's body in the sensory deprivation chamber. Tso wondered how long it would take before the agents located his remains and the fingerprints he was sure they would find all over his body. He pushed the thought from his mind.

We have bigger problems.

The agents disappeared into the elevator, and the doors closed. A lone remaining tactical agent, who identified himself as Agent Cameron Wu, remained nearby.

"You two stay with him," the Director barked, gesturing towards Adrian and Olivia.

"As for you, Mr. Tso, this way, please," Wen said, turning on her heel. She led Tso across the lobby and toward Agent Ko's unoccupied office, which Wen's team appeared to have commandeered and were using as a makeshift command base.

Wen didn't say much on the walk over. Her phone continued to ping loudly. She kept her attention on the incoming messages, only occasionally lifting her gaze to navigate her way. Tso could only assume her updates were coming from MSS headquarters in Beijing. But he had the nagging feeling that she had other sources of information.

"Sit," Wen said, pointing to a chair opposite Officer Ko's desk. She made a display of parading around the desk and sat prominently in Ko's chair. "We need to talk."

"Okay."

"I assume you know why I am here?"

Tso shrugged.

"At the current moment, we find ourselves in a crisis," Wen said. "One with significant repercussions to national security."

Tso grew very still.

"I'll get right to it," she said. "We know Andreas Kohler's death was not accidental."

Tso remained silent.

"We've also heard rumblings about a breakthrough in unsupervised machine learning. A sophisticated operation seeming to be decades ahead of the competition." Wen arched her brows. "I don't think it's a coincidence that your lead computer scientist turns up dead only days later?"

"I'm not sure what to say here. I myself am still trying to understand what happened."

"Is that so?" Wen said.

"As far as our research goes, I am under NDA." Tso knew it wouldn't hold. Wen could court-order any information she wanted. She had more power than the gods themselves. But it may buy them some time.

"Unfortunate." She set her badge down between them. It bore the insignia of a high-tech-looking coat of arms with a pixilated lock at its center.

Tso didn't recognize it.

"Are you familiar with the ACA, Mr. Tso?"

"Can't say that I am."

"The Algorithm Control Agency is a new but quickly growing division of the Ministry of State Security."

"Uh huh."

"The team is made up of a highly specialized group of cyber experts. They are ready to mobilize at a moment's notice—any time the Predictive Policing Division suspects the existence of an advanced autonomous systems lab." For a long moment, she was silent. Then she flashed a smile. "Like yours."

"Ma'am?"

Wen slammed her hand down onto the desk. "Don't insult my intelligence, Mr. Tso. Your lab is in violation of a controlled technology."

Tso didn't know what to say. Frankly, he didn't know if Wen was serious or bluffing. The government had been slow to regulate machine learning. If such restrictions existed, he wasn't aware. And with CyberGen's standing as a private multinational corporation, he wasn't even sure local regulations would hold water.

"I strongly suggest you start cooperating, lest you want me to add obstruction of justice to your charges."

"Okay."

Director Wen's gaze bored into him, her eyes tracking him like a trained hunting bird. "Here is what is going to happen. First, we are going to tear apart that lab of yours."

"Great. Go nuts."

"Because it has already been compromised?" Wen said.

"Can't be sure."

"In that case, you will tell me everything you know about the weapon."

"Weapon?"

"Yes, Mr. Tso, *weapon*." Her voice was even, deliberate.

"I would hardly call our technology a weapon, Director," Tso said. "In its current form, it is a completely benign piece of software."

"Be that as it may, someone else is in possession of your technology now, and we have no idea what form it is in."

"I think I should call a lawyer."

Director Wen studied Tso's face. "We are wasting time here. I have no choice but to detain you for further questioning." She looked at him with thinly veiled disgust. "You can call that lawyer of yours on the way."

"On the way, ma'am?"

"To headquarters."

"Is that really necessary?"

"This is now a matter of international security, Mr. Tso. My superiors at the State Council will have questions."

Wen produced a pair of handcuffs. "You had better pray we can recover the stolen technology. And not just for your sake." She secured a single handcuff to Tso's wrist. Then, she proceeded to affix the other end to a handle on the large steel filing cabinet in Ko's office.

Tso watched in silence.

Unbelievable.

Chapter 23

It didn't take a translator to understand Ministry of State Security agent Cameron Wu's directive. The large semiautomatic rifle hanging from his side was about as subtle as a sledgehammer.

"We have to do something," Olivia whispered to Adrian.

Adrian stole an anxious glance in Wen's direction. He could see The Director through Agent Ko's office window, some thirty yards across the CyberGen lobby. She was absorbed in a heated conversation with Alexander Tso. Even from afar, Adrian could see the vein on her neck protruding unnaturally.

"What do you suggest?" Adrian said, almost afraid to keep his eyes on Wen for fear of what he might witness.

"We need to get out of here."

"Thanks, Captain O. But we can't just stroll out of here."

"And we can't just do nothing, either."

Adrian's mind raced. He knew they needed an out. He had already mentally cataloged all the lobby's exits, hallways, and windows. With Wen thirty feet away and Agent Wu hovering, there was simply no way he and Olivia could slip out of the building unnoticed. And if they were taken offsite for questioning, their chances of escape would be even lower. They needed a diversion. And fast.

Perhaps a bathroom request? Or a phone call to the Embassy?
Suddenly, the lobby went dark.

For a split second, Adrian thought he was dreaming. Then, a shrill crash pierced the air, jarring him into high alert. The sound of rushed footfalls suddenly materialized from behind him. Adrian squinted, and the outline of a large form suddenly came into view. He watched in horror as a dark shadow emerged from behind Agent Wu. The intruder drew a small black and yellow weapon, about the size of a .380 handgun. He leveled the weapon on the MSS tactical agent, and before Wu could defend himself, the attacker pulled the trigger. Agent Wu collapsed backward, convulsing in pain.

Hearing the commotion outside, Director Wen emerged from Ko's office at a near sprint, where the intruder was waiting. Wen never saw him coming. In an instant, the man raised his hand and sent the blunt weapon smashing into The Director's temple. Wen lurched forward, crashing hard onto the stone floor.

The attacker leaped over Wen's motionless body and then gestured towards Adrian and Olivia. Adrian surveyed the stranger's features as best he could in the dark. The man was of average height. Broad-shouldered, but soft around the middle. Glasses, distinguished nose. Adrian had never seen the man before in his life.

"What are you waiting for?" the man boomed. "Follow me!"

Chapter 24

There is a time for questions and a time for action.

This was a time for action.

Run like hell.

That's it.

Just Run. Like hell.

Adrian was at a near sprint trying to keep up with the mysterious man leading them through the ground floor of the CyberGen complex. Beside him, Olivia seemed to have an identically singular focus, determined to put as much distance between themselves and the Chinese authorities as possible. From what he could tell, Olivia seemed equally thrown by the turn of events. But for now, questions would have to wait.

The man led them through a series of side corridors and away from the lobby. He ducked through an unmarked door, leading them into a large room, and not slowing until he reached the other side. He shoved the door open, then disappeared through it. Adrian grabbed Olivia by the hand and hurried through the dark after him.

Now in a smaller room, Adrian tried to get his bearings. He realized they must be in the South lobby. Unfortunately, the exit was *blocked*. Outside, half a dozen MSS-issue sedans waited, their spinning lights flashing.

Shit.

Wen has her tentacles all around this place.

"This way!" the man commanded, veering off abruptly through a service door. Unfortunately, that brought them to another problem. Now standing face-to-face with a security officer, Adrian came to an abrupt halt. He recognized the man immediately. He was the same security guard who had greeted Adrian upon his arrival earlier in the day.

Unfazed, the stranger proceeded directly towards Security Agent Danny Ko. "Officer," the powerful man said. "I need you to come with us."

Agent Ko looked unsure. His gaze flashed to Olivia. She gave him a reassuring nod, and he seemed to relax a little. With Agent Ko in tow, they followed the stranger toward a metal door with a sign that read "Maintenance."

"There is a defunct service entrance about fifty yards beyond this door," the man said. "I assume you have a key, Agent Ko?"

"I believe so," Ko said, reaching into his pocket. "The service entrance hasn't been used since the remodel." Ko pulled a key card from his pocket and swiped it to the magnetic reader. The reader flashed green and Ko pushed the door open. "I will give you two minutes. Then I will have to alert the Ministry of State." He looked at Olivia apologetically. "It's the best I can do."

"Thank you, Agent Ko," the man said, ducking through the door. Adrian and Olivia scurried after him.

Seconds later, a hollow thud echoed through the corridor as the door slammed shut. Adrian broke into a sprint down the dark hallway as the sound of Ko's footsteps retreated on the other side.

Finally reaching another set of doors, the man heaved open the exterior door, revealing a rain-swept sidewalk choked with pedestrians. "My friends," he said as they made their way outside, "my name is B.J. Strauss. Lang Zhao is a business partner of mine."

Adrian stopped short, staring at the man. *You are B.J. Strauss?* He felt a panicked confusion set in. Although he had never met the head of DeepThink, he had expected him to be older. And why was DeepThink, one of the most shadowy and powerful NGOs in existence, tied up with Lang Zhao? Adrian's instinct had been to trust the man.

Maybe he had been *wrong*.

Chapter 25

OFFICER DANNY KO WORKED in the private sector for a reason. His split-second decision to help Olivia Chen would now put him at the mercy of the Chinese government. In the moment, he hadn't seen much of a choice. However, as he skulked back to the lobby to face the Chinese authorities, he knew he would come under fire for the decision.

Following the small cone of light from his flashlight, Ko crossed the dark lobby, heading towards his office. The small plastic object in his left hand felt crushingly auspicious. Passing a trash receptacle, he tossed the key card in. Less than a minute later, he found himself face-to-face with two incredibly angry-looking MSS agents. Li Na Wen was holding her hand to a nasty-looking lump on her head while Agent Wu tended to injuries of his own. Making matters worse was the arrival of the rest of Wen's tactical team, who had just emerged from the sublevel.

Officer Ko squinted into the blinding glare of a dozen flashlights. He was still trying to figure out how he would explain himself when a swarm of black-clad operatives descended, buzzing like angry hornets.

Officer Ko, "Wen said. "We need access to your surveillance and a medical kit right away!"

Ko felt sick. It would only be a matter of minutes until the backup generator restored power to the building. Once they found the security footage, they would realize that he had helped Ms. Chen and the American escape. He knew he had no choice but to comply.

Ko trudged behind Wen back toward his office. Agent Wu drifted no more than two feet from her side, prominently bearing a large weapon. When they arrived, was surprised to find Alexander Tso occupied his office. He acknowledged his boss with a quick nod, regretting that he hadn't been able to help him. But he was certain that Tso would be grateful for the actions he had taken to allow Olivia Chen's escape. Tso had always been clear about one thing: the developments underway at the lab were never to be shared publicly. "Protect them at any cost," he'd said.

Officer Ko heard a mechanical whir as the backup generator came online, flooding the room with light. Within moments, the large bank of security monitors on his desk flickered to life, and his systems began to reboot. Several moments later, everything had loaded. His eyes flashed to Wen.

"What are you waiting for, Ko? An engraved invitation? Get to work!" Wen clutched her phone to her ear and continued pacing briskly.

Ko turned his attention to the monitors, queuing up digital playback from the surveillance cameras.

"Bring up the footage for every exit," she demanded. "They can't be far."

The images began to load slowly, appearing as a number of thumbnails split by location. Ko felt his blood pressure rising with each image that materialized.

"I don't have all day, Ko. Find me that footage *now*!"

Ko took a deep breath. It would only be a matter of seconds before the footage from the service entrance surfaced. He needed to come clean. "Let me save you some time. East service exit, two minutes ago."

Wen's head snapped in his direction. "Excuse me?"

"The men threatened to hurt Ms. Chen," Officer Ko lied. "I didn't see any alternative."

That should buy them at least a couple more minutes.

Danny Ko didn't want to think about the consequences of his actions. He risked a glance in Tso's direction, who seemed to think it better to stay quiet.

"You knew where they were this whole time?" Wen fumed. "Why didn't you say something sooner?!"

Ko cleared his throat. "Ms. Chen's safety, obviously, Ma'am. The men told me not to say anything."

"For Christ's sake, you don't work for them!"

And I don't work for you, either!

"Officer Ko—"

Ko felt his face flush. "Ma'am?"

"The security of this building is the single and only reason for you to exist. Do you have any idea what you have done?"

Ko appraised Wen. She was rubbing her temples as if to contain an explosion that would come at any moment. Weighing his options, he finally spoke. "I could show you—"

Director Wen cut him off with a flip of her hand. "Don't bother. Agent Wu just found the surveillance footage," she said, turning her attention to the security monitors. "It appears that Officer Ko here helped Adrian Pryor and his cohorts escape, even unlocking the service door for them."

Agent Wu fixed Officer Ko with a look of contempt. "Is this true?!"

Ko nodded reluctantly, trying his best to retain his composure. "I told you, I had no choice."

"You'll have to regale me with the tale of your gross incompetence some other time," Wen hissed. "I'm done here." She turned to face the dozen black-clad tactical operatives congregating outside. "Gentlemen," she said, "it appears that we have three targets. The first is the American, Adrian Pryor. The second is a twenty-something Chinese computer scientist, Olivia Chen. And the third," she announced, "is a middle-aged man of European descent, who we have yet to identify. We should assume the trio is armed and dangerous. They were last seen exiting the east service entrance a little over two minutes ago. Are there any questions about your mission?"

"Directive for use of force?" Agent Wu asked.

"I need them alive," Wen replied. "Barring the use of lethal force, you may do what you need to."

"Understood," Agent Wu replied. The men turned and headed down an empty corridor towards the east exit.

Wen pulled an electronic cigarette from her pocket. She took a long drag and watched as her team receded from sight.

A team that Ko hoped would fail.

CHAPTER 26

ADRIAN'S GUT HAD BEEN to trust the mysterious man. Maybe it had been a mistake.

There was a first for everything.

"I'll explain everything," B.J. Strauss said. "But first, let's get the hell out of here."

After exiting through a defunct service entrance on the east side of CyberGen, Adrian now found himself rushing quickly across Zhongshan road.

"Cover your faces!" Strauss said.

"Why?" Adrian asked, out of breath.

"Just do it!" Olivia echoed.

Shielding his face, Adrian ducked through traffic, leaving the whine of sirens behind them. Reaching the other side, they quickly covered the short distance to the waterfront, and Adrian found himself at the same landmark where he had arrived earlier in the day—The Bund.

Strauss immediately leaped into action, hurdling himself over the metal retention fencing and out of sight. "Wait here," he instructed. And then he was gone.

Explanations would yet again have to wait. Adrian replayed the previous moments in his head, trying to make sense of the whirlwind of events that had left him in flight from the Chinese authorities. *What have we done?*

Now alone on the pier, a heavy silence settled between Adrian and Olivia. Without warning, she spun towards him, clasping his hands in hers. Adrian met her gaze. Her expression seemed to be one of genuine gratitude.

"Thank you," she said, her voice barely above a whisper. "Thank you for helping me."

"What happened to your colleague is—"

"My fault," she declared, her eyes welling with tears.

"I realize it may seem that way," he said, "but we can't be sure what happened."

"You're not listening," Olivia said, her voice heavy with frustration. "I know why this happened."

"Okay. I'm listening . . ."

"Two weeks ago, Andreas showed me a letter he had written to a Pierre Leith at Oxford," Olivia said.

"What kind of letter?"

"It had to do with our project," she continued. "Concerns he had."

"What type of issues are we talking about here?"

"The ethical kind," Olivia replied softly. "He was planning to send it to the CEA. For guidance."

"The CEA?"

"The Center for Effective Altruism. It's an NGO—you know, humans helping humans kind of thing."

"Okay. So why them?"

"They specialize in predictive risk mitigation. For future catastrophes," Olivia explained. "More specifically, extinction-type of events."

"Ah, I see. So just run-of-the-mill charity-type stuff."

"You're missing the point."

"Which is?" Adrian said.

"Finding out about the letter put me in a bad position."

"What do you mean?"

"Andreas and I had pledged to keep all of our R&D confidential," Olivia explained. "The safety of the project required it."

"Did you confront him about it?"

"No," Olivia said, her expression pained. "I took my concerns to Zhao. I never thought he would . . ."

"Silence him?"

"This is all my fault!" Olivia declared. She turned her gaze towards the river.

"Listen—I realize how this appears, but you can't know that. It's possible that the assassin got wind of your discovery some other way. You said yourself that the technology is insanely valuable. It makes little sense that a wealthy executive would massacre one of his own scientists to steal a computer program—especially when the intellectual property was already his own."

"I know this all sounds crazy, Adrian. But I never should have discussed Andreas' letter with Zhao," Olivia said, turning to face Adrian again. "I fear my life may now be in danger, too."

Adrian studied the woman for a long moment. "You really think Lang Zhao is capable of murder?"

"The truth is, if the stakes are high enough, aren't we all?"

Adrian contemplated the statement. Sadly, he agreed. At their base, he knew people to be capable of both immense good and unspeakable horrors. Both history and his career had shown that to be true. The somber chat, however, would have to wait. A voice from below drew him back to the present.

"Jump!" Strauss's voice drifted up from somewhere below them.

Adrian stepped towards the steel barrier fence and peered over the edge at the muddied waters of the Huangpu River. He was surprised to see Strauss seated at the bow of an idling powerboat directly below them. There was a brisk current, but Strauss was doing a halfway decent job of keeping the vessel in place.

"Hurry!" he said, frantically waving them aboard.

Adrian had to admit, an escape by river certainly wasn't the worst idea. It would be a quick exit, and hopefully, a discreet one. The city of Shanghai was teeming with CCTV cameras, many equipped with facial recognition, which he now realized was what Strauss and Olivia had been trying to warn him about earlier.

"I can't hold steady much longer!" Strauss cried.

Adrian looked at Olivia. But Olivia was rooted to the spot, her eyes locked on the eight-foot drop between the cement bank and the river below.

"No way, Adrian."

Adrian met her gaze. He put his arm around her shoulders and gave her a reassuring squeeze. "We've come this far?"

Olivia sighed. She hesitated a second longer, then squared her chest and hoisted herself over the edge. Olivia free-fell towards the water. For a moment, Adrian was afraid that she might miss her target. A second later, though, she had landed in the boat. The impact threw her off-balance, and Olivia crashed onto her side at the stern. Strauss hurried to the back of the vessel to help her to her feet.

"Now you!" he called up.

Adrian had never been the most athletic of specimens, but his survival instincts kicked in. He jumped without hesitation, easily launching himself over the edge and into the waiting vessel. Seconds later, the small craft tore away from the Bund at full throttle.

CHAPTER 27

As THEY CAREENED AWAY from shore, Adrian watched the famous colonial façade fade from sight. Thankfully, the watchful crush of humanity disappeared along with it. Other than a few commercial vessels, they were now alone. Adrian hoped he wasn't wrong to trust the man seated at the helm. The day had started in a shroud of secrecy, and his misgivings were piling up higher than the Burj Khalifa.

His brief conversation with Olivia had done little to dispel his unease. The fact remained that a man had been killed, and powerful actors were at odds to gain control of the AI she had helped create. B.J. Strauss's sudden, albeit fortuitous, appearance was also baffling. Strauss had taken risky action to save them, even proffering a clever escape. But Adrian questioned his affiliation with both DeepThink and Zhao himself.

What is this guy's real agenda?

Adrian knew there were forces at play that he may not understand. On the one hand, DeepThink could be a powerful ally. But who was to say there weren't powerful actors within the organization who also wanted to gain control of Olivia's technology? DeepThink itself had a nearly forty-year history, much of it veiled in secrecy. The true inner workings? That was known only among those within its elite ranks: wealthy business magnates, heads of state, and scholars. It had grown massively over the last decade—its wealth rivaled only by its influence. Behind closed doors, DeepThink had become a force of change, silently manipulating global agendas at the highest levels.

Adrian turned to Strauss. "I think the time has come for explanations."

"Of course," Strauss said.

"Why are you here?" Adrian said.

"Zhao. We had a troubling conversation several days ago. Then he went dark," Strauss explained. "He is not responding to phone calls, emails, texts . . . nothing. I fear—"

"That he is going to do something reckless?" Olivia said.

"Precisely." Strauss sounded grim. "I'm afraid he is not the man we thought he was. We cannot trust his intentions."

"We need to find him, and quickly," Olivia declared.

"I had one of my contacts at DeepThink try to track him down," Strauss replied, "but there is no record of credit card activity, cell phone activity, point of sale purchases, or public video surveillance for the last three days. It's like he's disappeared."

"Zhao has a home in south Shanghai. It's not far from here," Olivia said. "Maybe we should start there?"

"Even if we can get access to his home, what are you expecting to find?" Adrian said.

"I'm sure he is long gone," Strauss echoed, his tone grave, "along with the source code."

"That may be true," Olivia said, "but that's where you come in." She looked at Adrian expectantly.

"Pardon?" Adrian said.

"Kohler summoned you here for a reason. If there is anything to be found, you are the one to do it."

Adrian took a deep breath. He could only speculate why Andreas Kohler had called on him, of all people, during his final moments. Adrian's best estimation was that Kohler viewed him as the Switzerland of hackers. He was the closest thing to an "expert" when it came to a crisis of this magnitude. But more importantly, Kohler needed someone he could *trust*. Someone who, when push came to shove, would do the right thing—personal consequences be damned.

Also, there was his savant-like intellect. Undoubtedly, that came into play.

"If he has anything to hide, I'm sure I can find it," Adrian replied.

Strauss seemed satisfied that this was their best option. "Ms. Chen, can you get us to Zhao's home?"

"Yes."

"Good," Strauss replied. "How far do you think it is from here?"

Olivia pointed to a landmark in the distance—an ornate brick and wooden structure that had risen into view. "Just beyond the temple," she motioned, referring to a Buddhist pagoda that reached some 130 feet into the air.

Adrian recognized the structure, whose distinct octagonal shape and upturned eaves were reminiscent of dozens of similar Song dynasty temples found throughout China.

"Okay," Strauss replied. He throttled down and headed towards the towering shrine.

Adrian could now hear the distant whine of a helicopter somewhere behind them, reminding him of the more immediate threat. He wondered how much time they had before The Chinese Ministry of State Security managed to track them down.

Upon entry to the boat, Olivia had suggested that they disable location services on their phones. Adrian had also urged them to disable Wi-Fi and Bluetooth, which he knew also sent location signals. He knew it would give them a short head start at best. According to Olivia, Shanghai had more cameras than a Hollywood movie set.

"In all seriousness, it's something like 4,500 cameras per square mile," she said.

"Eesh." Adrian stared at Olivia. "Are you guys allowed to fart without Xi's supervision?"

Adrian suddenly felt vulnerable. He never wanted to be the center of attention. But here he was. Again. He pulled on the hood of his sweatshirt, wishing he could disappear inside it.

After a long moment, he turned to Strauss. One matter still needed to be addressed before they could move on. "How do we know if we can trust you?"

Strauss smiled. "I think I have proved myself an asset thus far?"

But something else had been bothering Adrian since they left CyberGen. "What did you do to those people?"

Strauss stared at him calmly. "It was just a stun gun. They will be fine."

"What about Alex?" Olivia said.

Adrian had almost forgotten about Olivia's boss. Alexander Tso had been handcuffed and in MSS custody the last time he had seen him.

"I assume you have some sort of plan to help him?" Olivia said.

"Actually, no," Strauss said.

"What do you mean?" Olivia said, her voice rising an octave.

"Alexander Tso's arrest was not part of my father's plan," Strauss conceded. "We have no time to worry about him now. He is in no danger."

Adrian shot a startled look at Strauss. "Your father?"

"Yes. B.J. Strauss Senior," he announced.

Adrian immediately realized his oversight. *Of course*, this man is B.J. Strauss's son, he realized, recalling that the founder of DeepThink was nearly eighty years old.

"What is happening here is bigger than just us. DeepThink has a vested interest in making sure that Olivia's source code is recovered."

Adrian heard the whir of rotors again in the distance. He still had questions. But for now, time was their most valuable asset, and he wasn't going to waste any more of it flapping their traps. "Is this as fast as this thing goes?"

Strauss smiled, then depressed the throttle to its limit.

Adrian gave him a quick nod of appreciation, then moved to the bow. Despite a wintry backdrop, the city was a brilliant tapestry of light and color. Though not cold enough to snow, an icy fog emanated from the Huangpu River, casting a hazy lens over the city, as if Shanghai was a dream fading from consciousness.

Within moments, the blotted outline of their destination was the only landmark still visible—which was emerging like a leviathan from the fog. Adrian drew a deep breath, praying that the beacon would lead them closer to both Zhao and Olivia's source code.

CHAPTER 28

THE FOG FINALLY BEGAN to dissipate as the small boat passed under Nanpu bridge. The cable-stayed structure was the same striking bridge Adrian had seen from the air. Only now, with the sun dropping near the horizon, the entire thing had lit up like a Christmas tree, making the massive steel cables look like laser beams crisscrossing the sky.

Adrian admired it for several moments before something else caught his attention. To the East, as they crossed under the bridge, an inverted, crimson-red monolith came into view.

"It's called the *Crown of the East*," Olivia said, joining him at the bow. "It's a museum."

Made up of four braces that supported a giant, inverted pyramid, the structure seemed to defy gravity. Adrian admired the feat of engineering. Since he was a boy, he had always had an appreciation for architecture. It was hard to believe that these structures had been conceived decades prior. When people set their minds to it, humankind could achieve amazing things.

"It's based on the design of a Chinese ding vessel. They were once used for ritual offerings."

Adrian gave an appreciative nod.

"That building," Olivia said, "is home to almost two millennia of Chinese cultural treasures."

Adrian thought about that. A sprawling showcase of the East's greatest cultural and artistic expressions. A product that was, until this point, exclusive to the imagination of man. But was that about to change? Generative imaging programs like Dall-E, Midjourney, and Stable Diffusion had begun to create compelling art in recent years. Some of it even fetching prices in the hundreds of thousands at auction. Adrian couldn't help but wonder if the treasures inside that very building would soon become relics—fading embers of a dying fire. He felt shaken, unable to order his thoughts.

"Adrian?" Olivia said. "Are you okay?"

"It's just a lot to process," he said. "Kohler. The Chinese authorities. The whole AI doomsday thing. All of it."

Olivia looked at him pityingly. "I know."

"The more I think about the MSS' involvement, the more troubling it is."

"I was thinking the same . . ." she said.

"How did the Ministry of State Security even get wind of this?" he said. "And more concerning, how did they get to Shanghai so quickly?"

"Unless they were already here?"

"Ding. Ding. Ding," Adrian said. "Wen knows more than she is letting on."

"You didn't think your discovery would go unnoticed, did you?" Strauss interjected from the helm.

Olivia sighed. "At some level, I guess I have always known this was a possible outcome."

"I'm sorry, what are you saying?" Adrian said.

"For so long, super-intelligent AI was a pipe dream. Nobody really thought it could happen, would happen, this fast."

Adrian knew DARPA had also spent billions in the pursuit of advanced AI. It was no secret that this type of technology was the crown jewel of governments and private enterprises all over the world.

"Unfortunately," Strauss added, "this technology isn't just economically appealing."

"Information is power," Adrian agreed. He could only imagine if the NSA had access to this kind of tool.

"Make no mistake, we find ourselves in the middle of the greatest arms race of our time—eclipsing the Cold War itself," Strauss said.

"That's why the MSS' involvement is so troubling," Olivia said. "My software was intended to be democratized. Not monopolized by some government."

"I don't understand, Olivia. Why take the risk, then?" Adrian said.

"Honestly? There was never a question of if we do this. Only what if someone else does?"

"You mean, like The United States? Or Russia? Or North Korea?" Adrian ventured.

"This race has been underway for decades. The U.S., Russia, China, and Japan are only among a few of those in pursuit of general artificial intelligence. Even if I had ceased my efforts, other nations would have continued theirs."

Adrian stared in disbelief. "Everyone else is doing it? Seriously. That is your defense? The last time I tried that one was on my mom in the fifth grade, and it didn't even work then."

Olivia looked puzzled. "Adrian, what do you think drives progress? Evolution? As a species, we have always reacted to environmental threats by trying to make our lives safer and better. We have to evolve. Our survival depends on it."

Adrian wasn't buying it.

"It may be a super volcano, an asteroid, an earthquake, a great flood, a pandemic, or even a world war. But coming from a purely scientific standpoint, there will, without a doubt, be some type of extinction event for our species in the next century. If we don't find a way to evolve, we won't survive."

Adrian still wasn't convinced. Sure, the headlines were constantly doom and gloom when it came to climate change, global inequity, and the state of the planet. But humans had adapted and endured for millennia. "Why are you so convinced? Humans have overcome plagues, climate instability, and war on a grand scale. What is different about this century than any other?"

"All of those things are terrifying. I'll give you that," Olivia said. "But have you considered that perhaps the scariest idea of all is that a predator, a superior being, could knock us off our pedestal?"

"Honestly? No," Adrian said. "There are a lot of things I worry about, but that's not one of them."

Olivia studied him. "Do you have any idea why the human species has endured so long?"

Adrian smiled. "That's easy. Our animal instincts and ability to self-replicate?"

Olivia rolled her eyes. "Our intellect, genius. Until this point, our *intellect* is what has differentiated humans from all other species. Our language, planning, and reasoning skills have allowed us to roam the planet unchallenged longer than most other species. But what if I told you that time is coming to an end?"

Adrian contemplated the statement. He had watched as impressive technological advances happened in fields like computing, biotech, nanotech, and materials science over the last decade. It was almost as if the speed of innovation had numbed him to just how remarkable each breakthrough had been. It was one shiny object after the other. But taken all together? It was hard to deny that these technologies were barreling towards a convergence point.

"If this technology were to fall into the wrong hands or escape human control, it could spell the end of civilization itself."

Adrian stared at Olivia in silence. Maybe it was arrogance or blissful ignorance, but the idea of human extinction simply wasn't something Adrian had ever dedicated serious thought to. He had spent his career trying to thwart national disasters, but a species-level threat? That was the stuff of the movies.

Adrian felt deeply unnerved. "It seems unimaginable."

"It's incomprehensible," Olivia echoed.

Strauss continued to listen somberly. "And yet no government entity has dedicated meaningful resources to existential threats like this before. It just seems like something to worry about later."

Olivia's expression became pained. "I was hoping . . ." her voice broke off.

"To shepherd it into existence safely?" Strauss ventured.

"Exactly," Olivia replied.

"People will be blind-sided when they learn about this," Adrian said.

"People are, by the whole, very intelligent," Olivia declared. "It's not that they are stupid. They just don't know what they don't know."

"That's deep."

"I'm serious, Adrian. We all ignore the lunatic on the corner preaching about the coming apocalypse. But just because it sounds like science fiction doesn't mean that something can't happen, or that something isn't already happening."

Adrian fell silent.

Olivia's features softened. "I know it's a lot to take in."

"I just can't believe that a mainstream executive like Zhao would knowingly unleash Pandora's Box, without any assurances about how to control it," Adrian said.

"Look, Adrian, I'm not saying Zhao is going about this the right way."

"You think?"

"It seems to me that a new paradigm is coming," Olivia continued. "History has shown this to be true in the face of every major technological innovation." She paused, smoothing her hair behind her ears. "It's hard to speculate what the future will look like, but I think it's safe to say that whoever wins this race would literally rule all the lands—or perhaps even the cosmos itself."

"Well, then it sounds like we need to win," Adrian said.

"As the creator of this thing, I need to fix this," Olivia said. "I just hope I get that chance."

For his part, Adrian hoped she did, too. As much as he had initially wanted to condemn her choices, looking at the computer scientist trembling in the cold, he saw only a frightened woman whose best intentions were spiraling out of control. Another breeze whipped through the air, chilling him to the bone. He appraised Olivia, who had fallen silent, no doubt also overwhelmed by the seeming hopelessness of the situation.

He shrugged out of his hoodie, placing it snugly over her shoulders. "Here, Chen," he said. "You look like you can use this."

CHAPTER 29

"CUT THE ENGINE," OLIVIA said. "This is it."

Having just passed the soaring wood and brick pagoda, Strauss eased the boat ashore, coming to a stop near a group of wood pilings.

"Follow me," Olivia said, leaping from the watercraft and rushing up a steep pitch of shoreline.

Adrian hurried up the hill behind her. He glanced over his shoulder when he didn't hear Strauss's footsteps. He was surprised to find that Strauss was still thirty feet behind him, seated at helm of the boat. "Aren't you coming?"

"You two go alone," Strauss said.

"Why?" Adrian said, an edge in his voice.

"I'll stay here," Strauss said, "in case you need a quick exit."

Adrian was about to protest when something else caught his attention—the high-pitched whine of a small aircraft coming from somewhere overhead. He lifted his gaze skyward and spotted two approaching objects.

Surveillance drones, he realized.

The pair of drones had arrived out of nowhere and was skimming towards them about fifty feet up.

"Someone is really intent on finding us," Olivia said. "We need to hide." She pointed towards an empty construction site thirty yards ahead, where an abandoned excavator sat idle. "Hurry!"

She grabbed Adrian by the arm and raced toward the excavator, sending a spray of mud behind her. She slipped between the tracks at the rear of the equipment, then made room for Adrian. The two of them barely fit, but they were concealed from sight beneath the cab.

The mechanical whir grew louder as the drones approached the construction site. Adrian held his breath. As the drones drew closer, a red indicator flashed. *Have we been spotted?* If the drones had recognized their presence, they made no indication. They made no sudden movement towards them, no irregular flight pattern that might indicate they had been spotted. They simply continued their path, methodically scanning back and forth in what appeared to be an automated patrol pattern.

Adrian craned his neck toward the river. Thankfully, Strauss had also registered the presence of the drones. He had taken quick action, moving the boat under a grouping of mulberry trees. The foliage barely concealed the boat, but the ruse appeared to have worked. The drones had not lingered there either.

"Police UAVs," Olivia whispered. "Whatever you do, keep your face hidden from view. They are equipped with video cameras and facial recognition."

Adrian's jaw tightened. Somehow, the authorities had already homed in on their location. Even if they hadn't been spotted, they wouldn't be able to stay off the grid for long. They had to hurry. He kept his eyes on the hovering drones. After several seconds, they sailed over them and streaked off into the distance. Then, they abruptly changed direction, heading north.

Adrian waited a few breaths to be safe, then emerged from hiding.

"Let's get out of here. And quick," Olivia said.

She bounded across the construction site, heading towards an adjacent residential area. Two minutes later, they were scurrying up a long stone path toward the mountainous silhouette of Lang Zhao's Shanghai mansion.

Adrian raced up the hill, his lungs tight from a combination of the cold and exertion. Olivia led the way efficiently, apparently unfazed by the fact they were breaking and entering. He followed her over an arched bridge and through an ornate pagoda. Underfoot, the placid waters of a koi pond caught his reflection—a ragged and distraught stranger.

"Just a little further," Olivia called out. "Almost there."

Adrian's gaze rose to take in the towering edifice. It was not the modern sanctuary Adrian would have expected of the futurist. Instead, it was fashioned in the more traditional Chinese architectural style, with upturned roofs and a courtyard-style layout.

Olivia came to an abrupt stop a moment later, having arrived at the front door. *The point of no return,* Adrian sensed. Breaking and entering, the most recent of offenses Wen was sure to add to his charges. *Not to mention fleeing the authorities, suppressing evidence...*

"You wouldn't happen to know where he hides his key?" Adrian said, surveying the substantial-looking door blocking their path.

"No such luck."

Adrian placed his ear to the door. According to Olivia, Zhao's domestic staff—housekeepers, chefs, landscaping service, among others, numbered in the double digits. But on this night, Chinese New Year, the large property was eerily quiet. The staff had all gone home to celebrate the holiday with their own families, no doubt.

"We are going to have to do this the old-fashioned way," Olivia declared.

"And what's that?"

Without a word, Olivia bent down, picking up a decorative rock—a pitted limestone gongshi. She admired the "scholar's stone" for a moment before lobbing it sidelong towards a rectangular sidelight beside the door. The small window cracked, then gave way, shattering into a thousand pieces.

"That's one way to do it," Adrian said, flashing a grin. "How did you know the alarm wasn't on?"

"I didn't." She shrugged, then quickly removed Adrian's sweatshirt, wrapping it around her hand before reaching through the cracked filament. After a moment, she had located the deadbolt. She rotated the lock to the right, and they heard a click as it unlatched. The massive door swung open, revealing an elegant quartz foyer.

We're in.

Adrian looked on, impressed with Olivia's display of resourcefulness.

"After you," she said.

Adrian stepped into a dimly lit foyer. Olivia crossed the entryway and headed towards a bank of switches on the opposite wall. With the press of a button, the home instantly came to life. Ambient light flooded the room, soothing music emanated from the home entertainment system, and the window shades began descending simultaneously, offering sweeping views of the Shanghai skyline, which had started to twinkle softly in the setting sun.

"It's impressive, no?" Olivia said, studying his reaction.

Adrian had never seen anything like it.

"I felt the same way the first time I saw it," Olivia said.

Adrian's gaze swept down a wide corridor, which was furnished with traditional furniture and art as well as some more contemporary pieces. A number of ornate antiques lined the shelves of a curio cabinet off to the side. Considering his reputation as a futurist, the billionaire's affinity for Chinese culture, history, and art struck Adrian as an oddity. *Old shit*, he thought. *Impressive old shit, but old nonetheless . . .*

"His office is this way," Olivia said. She led the way to a marble staircase. They bound up the stairs and arrived at a large landing. A long hallway stretched out in front of them. About halfway down, Olivia stopped beside an ornate door. "This is it," she said.

Whatever lay beyond the door would undoubtedly confirm their suspicions about Lang Zhao. Hopefully, it would also offer a clue about his current whereabouts—information they desperately needed if they were to reach Zhao before the Chinese authorities. Olivia reached for the handle, but it didn't budge. She fixed Adrian with a panic-stricken look.

"It's locked!"

At that precise moment, inside the cabin of a Z-20 military helicopter, Director Li Na Wen clutched a phone to her ear. "Ping their phones again!"

"I have already tried three times," her contact at MSS headquarters replied.

"I don't give a damn! Try again!"

"Hold tight, Ma'am."

"What about municipal surveillance?" Wen said. With the world's most comprehensive public surveillance and facial recognition at her disposal, Director Wen knew it would only be a matter of time until Olivia Chen and Adrian Pryor surfaced.

"Give me a minute," the man replied. "There, I've got something."

"I need details, Lee!"

"Police drones, about fifteen minutes ago. They logged a possible facial recognition match. Southwest Shanghai, near Longhua Temple."

The location immediately dawned on Wen. "That's not far from Zhao's private estate." If Adrian and Olivia were complicit, as she suspected, it was no shock that they would go there. Wen couldn't begin to fathom the stupidity.

As if that isn't the first place we would look.

"I can alert the local authorities," Lee suggested. "We could have Zhao's residence surrounded in under five minutes."

"No!" Wen said forcefully. "Alerting the local authorities is not an option. No one must find out about this. If the media were to pick up on this . . ." She shuddered at the thought.

"Understood, ma'am," Lee said. "There is something else you should know about," he said, sounding suddenly unsure. "It's about the identity of your attacker."

"Yes?" Wen said anxiously.

"It's B.J. Strauss."

Wen gasped. "The head of DeepThink? But—"

Wen was suddenly cut off by a deafening rumble as the rotors engaged for lift-off.

"What was that, Lee?" But Wen heard only silence. It seemed the news about her attacker would have to wait. Her cell signal was gone.

It's no matter. We will be at Zhao's house in less than ten minutes, and I will confront my attacker in person.

Chapter 30

FINALLY ALONE, B.J. STRAUSS rested his head against the wheel of the boat and closed his eyes. He heaved a sigh.

Nothing is going according to plan.

CyberGen's source code was God knows where. The Chinese authorities were crawling up his backside. And Lang Zhao was still nowhere to be found.

Things were a mess. To be clear, no one could have anticipated the shitstorm that had become the previous 72 hours. Zhao's behavior was bizarre, bordering on cataclysmically reckless. And now Strauss was left holding the bag.

Maybe that was fair, given it was he who had brought Zhao into the fold in the first place. When they met nearly ten years prior, the billionaire had made quite an impression. Strauss had flown to Eastern China from Geneva, where he had delivered the opening address at DeepThink's annual summit. The talk had been optimistic—a lecture about the impacts of emerging technology: the fusion of physical, digital, and biological systems and how it would affect the very essence of the human experience. It had been well received by his peers—a cadre of powerful CEOs, politicians, and heads of state.

But there had been one person in attendance who had proven himself *unimpressed*. Following the address, while Strauss was in the hallway talking to some of the remaining attendees, a well-dressed stranger approached him, interrupting the conversation.

"Mr. Strauss, a word in private, if I may?" the man had said.

Recognizing the Chinese man, an emerging titan in the tech sector, a curious Strauss had excused himself shortly afterward. As the man had suggested, Strauss made his way to one of the private meeting rooms adjacent to the amphitheater.

Strauss had entered, finding that the small conference room was completely dark, except for a faint glow coming from a small projector. A large frame moved quickly towards him, extending his hand.

"Please excuse my poor manners," he had declared. "I haven't properly introduced myself. My name is Lang Zhao."

Strauss chuckled. "I know who you are, Mr. Zhao."

"Please sit," Zhao said, motioning to a chair nearby. "I enjoyed your presentation this morning. You are undoubtedly one of the most knowledgeable people on Earth when it comes to The Fourth Industrial Revolution."

"Thank you," Strauss replied.

"And yet—" Zhao said, "it seems that the only thing surpassing your *expertise* is perhaps your *shortsightedness*."

"I beg your pardon?" He stared at the young entrepreneur.

"I find myself face to face with the head of DeepThink, the most forward-thinking institution in existence, which has dumped countless resources into artificial intelligence by way of your powerful industry and government constituents. And yet, you fail to understand the risks."

Strauss stared at the man in disbelief.

"What you are doing is careless."

"By innovating?" Strauss said.

"When it comes to public safety, the United States has the FDA to regulate food and drug safety, the FAA to regulate aviation, and the National Highway Traffic Safety Administration to regulate automobiles. But when it comes to AI development, a technology which is unequivocally more dangerous to the public, there is no regulatory agency!"

The stranger was correct on this point. Keeping pace with the rapid advances was challenging enough. Regulating them in a timely manner was a laughable prospect. Nevertheless, Strauss didn't appreciate the man's self-important tone.

"Worse yet, you are committing a fundamental Darwinian error," Zhao said.

"Excuse me?" Strauss said.

"By creating an intellectually superior agent, I mean. It's a mistake."

Strauss couldn't help but chuckle. "Most experts don't expect *human-level* artificial intelligence for decades. And as for *beyond-human* synthetic intelligence? That's a pipe dream."

"Is it?" Zhao challenged. "Since the last century, advances in almost every field of science have grown exponentially. In the last fifty years, microprocessors have become a billion times more advanced, transistors shrinking from 10,000 nanometers to a mere 10 nanometers. And I don't have to tell you—if the trend continues, it has staggering implications for AI; implications whose consequences we cannot predict."

"Which is also why it could solve some of humanity's most pressing problems," Strauss countered. "Climate change, among them."

"And why should we assume such an agent would be benevolent?"

"Why should we assume it wouldn't be?" Strauss said.

"If digital superintelligence becomes a reality, there is only one path for humans," Zhao stated flatly.

"Do enlighten me."

"Extinction," Zhao declared.

"That's a bit melodramatic, don't you think?"

"Hardly," Zhao countered. "Consider this—" He made several quick keystrokes on the laptop in front of him. When he concluded, an image had materialized on the wall. It was labeled "Intelligence Staircase."

Strauss squinted at the image, a two-dimensional rendering of a staircase. Near the bottom were several representations of biological intelligence, ranging from an ant to a chicken to a chimp, and, finally, a human above them all. They were all two to three steps apart on the staircase, indicating the successive leaps in intelligence as one ascended the staircase.

Strauss had seen the intelligence spectrum visually represented in similar ways. But this image contained an additional marker, a far more troubling indicator. Countless steps above the human, on the upper limit of the Y-axis, there was a final data point. It was labeled "ASI." The acronym for *Artificial Super-Intelligence*.

"Are you familiar with this, Mr. Strauss?"

"Can't say that I am."

"Allow me to explain," Zhao said, his tone matter of fact. "Say we create an AI system that is two steps above us on the staircase. In the same way that chimps will never understand things like quantum mechanics or how to build a skyscraper, humans cannot hope to understand an intellectual agent a mere two steps above us."

"So, what are you saying?"

"There is a ceiling," Zhao declared.

"To biological intelligence?"

Zhao nodded. "Let's face the facts. Synthetic intelligence simply isn't constrained in the same ways that biological intelligence is."

"Meaning?"

"Our heads need to fit through the birth canal. There is a physical limit to brain size."

Strauss laughed uneasily.

"But AI?" Zhao continued, "It doesn't have that problem." He furrowed his brows as if deep in thought. "Unchecked, we may soon be coexisting with something billions, if not trillions, of times higher on the intelligence scale. Humanity won't be able to keep up."

Strauss shifted uncomfortably in his seat.

Zhao fell momentarily silent, running his long fingers through his hair. "Humans' sheer dominance on this planet suggests a clear rule: with intelligence comes power."

"And you think that if we create an intellectually superior agent . . ." Strauss said.

"It will be the most powerful being in the history of life on Earth," Zhao said. "All living things would be entirely at its whim."

"Including us?" Strauss said.

A silence settled between the men.

"Yes." Zhao finally said. "Silence is an apt response."

Strauss felt heat flare in his cheeks. "We are taking precautions, you know. No one is going into this with blinders on."

Strauss knew what Zhao was alluding to. A runaway agent. In the field, they called it a 'fast takeoff.' There were mixed opinions on the idea. The benefits of a human-level AI were rarely contested. Already, AI was diagnosing disease better than doctors, finding ways to cut energy costs at data centers, and even predicting the complex 3D shapes of proteins—a game changer in drug development. But, some feared that the AI could quickly leapfrog into something much more powerful.

By nature, self-learning machines evolve by way of something called exponential recursive self-improvement. Basically, an intelligent system programmed to improve itself would become increasingly successful with each iteration, able to make more meaningful improvements with each successive leap in intelligence. As the leaps grow larger and happen more rapidly, the AI would soar in intelligence, quickly eclipsing biological limits.

But something like that wasn't likely to be accomplished for decades, if ever. Worrying about it now was like worrying about traffic on Mars.

Strauss met Zhao's stare. "Solving intelligence will benefit all of humanity. If we need to convene the masses, put together a Manhattan Project, we will."

"Your optimism, if misplaced, is endearing," Zhao declared. The billionaire stalked the room, his gaze never leaving Strauss'.

"Excuse me?" Strauss said.

"If allowed to propagate unchecked, the next few years of technological development will be so disruptive that humanity itself will be rendered *irrelevant*." Zhao continued pacing. "We lay at the foot of the greatest predator in history, feeding his growing appetite and naively hoping that he will not lash out at his master."

Strauss felt sick. Regardless of how far-fetched it all seemed, he couldn't help but wonder, *what if he was right?*

"Someone needs to take bold action," Zhao concluded, "or you had better pray that the AIs treat us better than we treat intellectually inferior species."

Strauss drew an unsteady breath, letting himself process the heaviness of his words. "So, tell me," he said, "in your vision of the future, how does this play out?"

Zhao finally relaxed his tense features, his lips spreading into a thin smile. "It's pretty simple. What's the old adage? If you can't beat them, join them."

He can't be serious.

"What you are suggesting is—"

"Our only remaining hope for survival," Zhao declared.

"Actually," Strauss replied, "I was going to say *premature.* You are getting way ahead of yourself."

"That's exactly what we need to be doing. When you look back in ten years, you'll wish someone had."

"With all due respect, these risks are speculative at best. Don't you think this is a little extreme?"

"Extreme!?" Zhao repeated, sounding stunned. "Extreme would be staring into the face of an extinction-level threat and denying its existence. If a giant asteroid were plummeting towards Earth, would we wait until it was in our atmosphere to act? No! We would try to thwart its path *before* it decimated our planet!"

Before Strauss could speak, Zhao had projected a new image on the screen.

"And speaking of asteroids," he said, pointing to the graph now dominating the wall. "Here is the asteroid currently on a crash course for our planet."

B.J. Strauss immediately recognized the chart. It was a graph published by The Centre for the Study of Existential Risk, depicting existential risks in the 21st century—things that could lead to human extinction or civilizational collapse. The list included, among others, technological risks, biological risks, and environmental risks. But topping the chart, the experts had concluded, was the risk of advanced artificial intelligence.

When the Centre published the graph, dozens of the world's preeminent artificial intelligence experts immediately convened for an emergency summit, calling for research on AI's safety and societal impacts. Academics from Cambridge, Oxford, Stanford, Harvard, and MIT gathered for what could be considered the first serious look at the risks of AI.

The outcome? Privately, they had thrown their hands in the air—convinced that it was too late to stop the development of such a technology. Quite simply, if they didn't pursue it, someone less idealistic would. Publicly, though, they assured the world that it could provide incalculable benefits to humanity. If that is, it could be controlled.

Strauss had a sinking feeling like he always did when he saw this graph. He was a man of science and believed in the predictive power of data, but he had idealistically hoped that technology could solve some of the problems it posed. Nevertheless, it was hard to argue that the graph painted a grim picture of the future. And more concerning was the timeline it presented—not of some far-off problem of future generations, but of a very real impact to the *current* generation.

At many times in his life, Strauss had worried about his children's future—about their safety at school, their education, their happiness. Yet, when he considered this graph, he felt almost hopeless about protecting their future, let alone their happiness, in an increasingly tech-saturated and impersonal world.

What kind of future are we leaving for our children?

"Over the last three decades," the imposing man declared, "our technological advances have plundered our environment, left our children depressed, and made a handful of elite wealthy as the masses struggle." He paused deliberately.

"This is a complex situation."

"No!" Zhao fired back. "You know damned well what outcome this graph represents. Unless we take bold action, humanity will be eclipsed . . . by a creation of our own design, no less. We are condemning ourselves to a future of servitude or death!"

Zhao had gone on to lay out, in painstaking detail, a plan for how to safeguard humanity from AI's looming threat. As fatalistic as it had seemed, Strauss hated to admit that the plan made logical sense. Resources needed to be devoted to protecting humanity's place in the evolutionary hierarchy. He made the fated decision to sponsor Zhao for membership to DeepThink, a decision that now threatened to unravel all his carefully laid plans.

CHAPTER 31

OLIVIA STARED HELPLESSLY AT the door blocking their entry to Zhao's home office. "What are the chances you can break it down?"

Adrian examined the door. "There is no way this thing is going to budge. But I have a better idea. Let me see your phone."

Olivia had no idea what he had in mind. Nevertheless, she reached into her pocket and fished out her iPhone.

"Turn your cellular data back on," Adrian instructed.

"You sure about this?" Olivia said, feeling suddenly vulnerable.

"Our time is limited either way. Do you want to get into this room or not?"

"Okay, okay." Olivia navigated to her settings, once again enabling data. "Done."

"Good. Now go to your app store. Download an app called *KeyMe*. I'll be back in three minutes."

Olivia complied, feeling confused. *Where the hell does he think he is going?*

But Adrian was already gone. When he returned, he was carrying a tape measure and an awkward-looking appliance. It had an open chassis and was about the size of a small microwave oven with a large spool on top.

"What the hell is that for?"

"It's our ticket into any room of this house," Adrian said, gesturing theatrically to the 3D printer.

"Brilliant," Olivia chimed. "How did you know he had one?"

"What kind of futurist would he be if he didn't?"

"Good point. How do we use it? We can't replicate a key that we don't have?"

"We don't need a key," Adrian assured, a gleam in his eye. "That's why we need your phone." He toggled to the iPhone's camera, leveled it on the door's keyhole, and snapped a photo. "Now I just need something small."

"How about a bobby pin?" Olivia offered, sliding one out of her hair.

"Perfect," he said, taking hold of the pin and inserting it into the keyhole.

"I don't understand."

"The hairpin is to measure the pin depth," Adrian said. "The app you just downloaded will allow us to create a three-dimensional skeleton key. It requires two inputs: an image of the keyhole and the approximate pin depth."

"I see."

"Hand me your phone." Now running the KeyMe app they had just downloaded, Adrian entered the measurement and uploaded the photo. The 3D printer whirred into action. A spool of ABS plastic began turning as material advanced into the machine, melting into liquid that created successive layers, eventually yielding a three-dimensional key.

"Zhēn méi xiǎng dào!" Olivia shouted, pleasantly surprised. "This just may work!"

"Don't get too excited," Adrian replied. "The printer is using pretty rudimentary material. Even if it gives us an accurate skeleton, it may be brittle. I give it a 50/50 shot of breaking, at which point we will have jammed the lock."

Olivia shrugged. "I don't see what other choice we have. Try it!"

CHAPTER 32

ADRIAN SQUINTED INTO THE tiny orifice and held his breath. He inched the fragile skeleton into the keyhole, closed his eyes, and turned the key as gently as possible. The lock disengaged with a soft click, and the door swung open.

"I'll be damned," Olivia said.

"After you," Adrian said, gesturing her forward.

Adrian followed Olivia inside. He flicked on the light, revealing a tastefully furnished office. An antique black-lacquered desk occupied the center of the room. Floor-to-ceiling bookcases covered one wall. The opposite wall was adorned with glass curios brimming with porcelain vases, jade carvings, calligraphy scrolls and countless other antiquities. A museum-grade collection of Eastern art adorned the remaining wall space.

Olivia smiled. "Surprised?"

"A little," Adrian admitted.

"When I first saw this room," Olivia said, "I was surprised to see that Zhao had a taste for this style of art. But now, it makes total sense."

"What do you mean?"

"Look closely. There is a distinct motif carried throughout his collection. Do you notice any recurring symbols?"

Adrian made his way around the room. He noticed a number of recurring images in the paintings. "Peaches, jade, white cranes?"

Olivia nodded.

Something else also stood out: a distinct figure, a man with a prominent cranium, who appeared in several of the paintings. "What's the significance?" he asked.

"Historically, these were all symbols of longevity," Olivia explained. "The peaches were rumored to have grown in a celestial orchard and said to confer immortality on anyone who ate them."

"Interesting," Adrian said.

"The pursuit of longevity has played a notable role in Chinese history. Societal respect for the elderly, a generally Confucian value, and the individual pursuit of immortality—a loosely Daoist pursuit, resulted in a preoccupation with long life that is reflected in a lot of Chinese art."

Adrian couldn't say he was familiar with Eastern mythology, but it was certainly interesting. And more than that, it got him thinking.

"Take this piece, for instance," Olivia continued, moving towards a large canvas on the rear wall. "The eight figures you see assembled on the riverbank represent the Eight Immortals, a group of Daoist deities dating back to the Tang Dynasty. Here, they are awaiting the arrival of Shoulao, the God of Longevity. She pointed to the figure, the same subject with the prominent cranium, who was approaching from the sky on the back of a crane.

Then it hit him. "Zhao is fixated on immortality," Adrian declared. "The work being done at CyberGen, the art. It all has one thing in common: human life extension!"

Olivia joined Adrian in front of the painting. "Lang said his art inspired him whenever he was in its presence." She contemplated her statement. "I just didn't realize how much."

"I guess the Times article wasn't too far off the mark?" Adrian said, recalling a feature on the eccentric billionaire, who was said to have an "Emperor's complex." Seeing his fixation on longevity, Adrian couldn't help but wonder if the bold idea—that man could somehow conquer his own mortality—at least partially explained Zhao's odd behavior.

Adrian wondered if being surrounded by these images every day had somehow served to embolden Zhao. And perhaps more concerning, what in God's name was he planning to do with that code?

Olivia had blanched at the Times comment, suddenly seeming to remember why they were there. "We had better try to find what we came for," she said, the urgency returning to her voice. She headed towards a wide bookcase on their left.

Adrian went in the opposite direction, making his way toward the black lacquered desk. A framed MIT diploma sat in the corner: a PhD in Materials Science. It was an honorary degree, Adrian knew. After completing less than half of the program, Zhao left to undertake his first startup, an electronic payment company that ended up selling for five hundred million, making him a quick millionaire.

Even more shocking was that he had poured every last cent into two new companies: one in aerospace and one in sustainable energy—industries that had remained unchanged and unchallenged for decades. Fast forward two bankruptcies, a decade, and a stubborn refusal to fail, and the companies had surpassed the industry's wildest expectations, rocketing him to the status of billionaire and earning him the reputation as one of the greatest industrialists since Ford or Rockefeller.

Without question, Lang Zhao had big ideas. He had inspired a cult-like loyalty in his employees. Olivia seemed to be no exception. But had her affinity with the billionaire blinded her from his true motivations?

Adrian drew a long breath, turning his attention to the task at hand. His eyes swept across Zhao's desk. Stacks of business journals, notes, and computer printouts were arranged in neat piles around a PC. In the corner, he saw a photo of Zhao rubbing elbows with several luminaries in the AI field. Beside it was a smaller photo of the billionaire standing arm in arm with one of the other giants of the field: a man named Martin Minsky.

Adrian scanned the area, looking for anything that may give them an indication of Zhao's whereabouts: airline confirmations, receipts, or personal notes of any kind. He found nothing. He glanced over at Olivia, who was still on the opposite side of the room, also appearing to search in earnest.

"Any luck over there?" she called.

"Nothing out of the ordinary so far." He shifted his attention to a center drawer, where he found nothing unusual: pens, business cards, stacks of post-its, and blank legal pads. The drawers on the right side of the desk were filled with scientific articles, grouped into various categories.

Adrian began leafing through a stack of papers and gasped. He had spoken too soon. Inside the drawer, he found articles ranging from "Bioethics and Posthumanity, Retreating from Genetic Liability by Advancing Genetic Liberty," to "Closed-Loop Neural Interfaces with Embedded Machine Learning," to "The Posthuman Condition: How Identity and Values will be Redefined in a Postbiological Era."

He knew Zhao had a reputation for being eccentric. Maybe all innovators were by nature, but he didn't quite grasp the depths of it until now. "What is all of this stuff?"

Olivia made her way across the room in three quick strides. Her eyes flashed to the stack of papers, looking unsettled. "I'm not sure," she said. She abruptly grabbed the mass of papers, shoving them back into the drawer. "Let's move on," she said. "What about his PC? There must be something there."

Adrian wondered about Olivia's abrupt behavior, but there was no time to dwell on it. "Fine," he said, slipping into the leather office chair in front of the PC.

Adrian was sure the billionaire's home network would contain some clues that could help them. In his experience, most people failed to realize the extent to which their online activity left a digital footprint. With the right tools, even a moderately good hacker could get access to all kinds of personal information.

But Adrian wasn't a moderately good hacker. He was the *most brazen and technically skilled hacker* on Earth.

Cue the superhero music. Time to get to work.

CHAPTER 33

WITH PHYSICAL ACCESS TO Zhao's PC, Adrian knew that what they were after shouldn't be difficult. But first, they had to get into it. Adrian focused his attention on the large display. With two quick keystrokes, he enabled the system-level command prompt using a simple login bypass trick. A small black pop-up window appeared, awaiting a system-level prompt.

He pulled his trusty flash drive from his pocket. So far, the small storage device was proving itself the most useful weapon he had grabbed from the safe that morning. This time, Adrian would be accessing a different exploit: a small but powerful program that could siphon a Windows user's password out of the computer's memory.

Olivia appeared at his side, watching with an amused expression on her face.

He ran a series of quick commands, and satisfied that all had gone well, he entered one final command:

@getLogonPasswords

Within seconds, Zhao's Windows logon credentials appeared on the screen.

"How did you do that?"

He shrugged. "It's easier than you'd think."

Olivia didn't look convinced.

"Honestly—any moderately intelligent fifth grader with internet access could manage it." Unfortunately, what Adrian was doing now had become all too easy for basement dwellers in nation-states all over the world. A devastating NSA leak in 2017 by an organization referring to themselves as the 'Shadow Brokers' had unleashed a slew of powerful hacking tools into the public domain—tools that for decades had been kept off the books, hidden from public view via shell companies, mercenaries, black budgets, and NDAs.

Olivia suddenly looked hopeful. "What do we look for now?"

"Let's see what Zhao has been up to online?"

Another series of quick keystrokes gave him access to an "exploit" program. A simple internet search and a few seconds to download the 300 MB file, and he would be able to access the system's cache, which held a convenient record of everything from Zhao's keystrokes to screenshots to his web search history.

Olivia watched over his shoulder. "It's that easy to hack all of that?"

Adrian flashed a lopsided grin. "You didn't really think anything you did on your network was private, did you?"

She shrugged. "Guess not. What did you find?"

Adrian shuffled through the resulting data record, first looking at Zhao's most recently accessed files. He focused on the largest. "It's a video file. Shall we?"

Olivia nodded.

"It will take me a minute to decompress," he said, navigating the on-screen prompts. Several seconds later, a media player had loaded, and the file began to run. The screen went dark, and the sound of crashing waves filled the room. Adrian leaned back. Beside him, Olivia also settled in to watch the eight-minute video.

The sound of instrumental music suddenly filled the room. After a moment, orbital satellite images appeared. Among a blanket of stars, planet Earth came into view. The music continued, increasing in tenor and volume as the camera cascaded through the stratosphere, plummeting towards Earth.

When the camera finally came to a stop, they were atop an oceanside cliff, and the famous visage of Lang Zhao appeared. Dressed in all black, his arms were outstretched—poised as if to jump.

Adrian shot a nervous glance at Olivia. She met his gaze, looking horror-stricken.

Would this explain Zhao's strange disappearance? Were they about to witness the man's suicide?

"My fellow man," he began, his voice polished and commanding. "My name is Lang Zhao. For the past ten years, I have imagined a future where our species would no longer be plagued by disease, scarcity, and turmoil. One where we would eliminate our dependency on fossil fuels, engineer more efficient modes of transportation, and restore our beautiful planet. And today, we have great cause for celebration. That day has arrived."

CHAPTER 34

OLIVIA FELT THE ACRID crawl of bile ascending her throat. She didn't need to watch another second to know what Lang Zhao was about to announce.

It was her discovery.

Olivia felt a pang of defeat. She had pictured things going so much differently—a flashy public announcement, the shock and awe such a discovery would draw, the pride of knowing that she had played an integral role in bringing to bear the promising technology. Olivia and Andreas had often speculated about how their discovery would change the world. Something of this magnitude could only be compared to the advent of the Industrial Revolution . . . ushering in a new era of innovation, technology, and even art.

It should have been her moment in the spotlight. Instead, her greatest achievement was about to be perverted, to be taken public by someone else. And to what end?

Adrian's voice drew her back to the present. "Well, isn't he the portrait of humility."

"His two-hundred million Twitter followers don't seem to mind," she replied dryly. She turned her attention back to the monitor.

"I am broadcasting tonight for one reason," the booming voice continued. "To share a scientific discovery, the implications of which can only be compared to the Copernican Revolution. Just as the Ptolemaic model of the universe, which reigned unchallenged for almost thirteen hundred years, was overthrown, we too, now stand at the precipice of a new paradigm of understanding. The time has come to forget everything you think you know."

Zhao stared intently into the camera. There was no hint of hesitation, no uncertainty or ambiguity.

"This is a generation divided—those holding onto the past and the ideals of what it means to be human, and those reaching to the future. It is a generation whose choices will set in motion the course for the future of our species."

"I wish we had popcorn," Adrian whispered. "This is better than Netflix."

Olivia couldn't bring herself to smile. Perhaps it was the guilt that had taken residence in her gut, or perhaps Adrian simply didn't understand the impossibly high stakes. She forced her attention back to the voice on the screen, watching as if in a trance.

"We will be the first generation to pull back the veil on the mysteries of the universe: to discover things like a unifying theory of physics, to colonize the cosmos, to reverse engineer aging and cure disease. The inevitability of things like death and taxes, presumed as certain as the rising sun, need no longer plague our kind. What if I told you that, as a species, we no longer have reason to be a victim of our frail biology? That death itself is optional?"

Olivia watched Adrian for a long moment, gauging his reaction. Rather than shock, she thought she detected another emotion. He was *amused*.

She couldn't blame him. This was the stuff of science fiction. It would take time, she suspected, for the overwhelming new reality to set in. Were people ready to hear this? She heaved a sigh, a tightness growing in her chest. Zhao's smooth voice again filled the room.

"But this generation will also be the first to face an existential threat to its existence. Make no mistake: mankind is under attack.

Nanotech, biotech, artificial intelligence, and quantum computing have collided to give rise to the most powerful tool in human history: Digital Super Intelligence. It is both a powerful genie that promises to grant our every wish and a weapon of mass destruction more powerful than anything in history.

No one or their careers will be spared from the coming onslaught of automation. One thing is clear: technological progress won't be stopped. What has been created here will change the world forever. To bury our heads in the sand is no longer an option.

For the vast majority to survive and thrive, there is only one path forward: to merge with this radical technology."

The music resumed, now louder. The intensity was palpable. Panning out, Zhao took a step towards the edge. "We stand on the precipice. It is time to take control of our own evolution. The time to jump is now."

The camera paused its motion and tipped downward as the man stepped forward and opened his frame into an elegant swan dive over the precipice. He floated in slow motion towards the churning water before plunging into the white-capped swells and disappearing from sight.

Olivia realized she was holding her breath. For the briefest of moments, she wondered if this was the last time she would ever see Lang Zhao's face. But after a long moment, the water began to calm, and Zhao resurfaced. When he did, his appearance shocked her.

"What has he done to himself?" she said, suddenly emotional. She stared into familiar eyes. But everything else was suddenly foreign—a tangle of robotics and flesh.

"Sweet mother of God," Adrian said. "Who does he think he is?"

"As I see it," the voice continued, "we have only two options: merge with the technology or surrender to it."

"That's enough," Olivia interrupted.

Adrian paused the playback. "Are you okay, Olivia?"

"Stop the video," she repeated. "I've seen enough." She turned away from the monitor, a crushing guilt settling into her gut. Had she enabled this man? This monster?

An uncomfortable silence settled between them. Olivia paced the room, trying to wrap her mind around what she had just witnessed. Not only was Zhao very much still alive, but he had undergone a drastic procedure, altering his own biology?

The billionaire made no secret of the fact that he subscribed to the Transhumanist movement. Most scientists in their field did in some way or another. The idea that technology could be used to enhance the human condition was certainly not new. As a species, we had been augmenting our bodies for decades: intraocular lenses, cochlear implants, prostheses, organ transplants, joint replacements, pacemakers, and dental implants. The list went on and on. It was only natural that the trend would continue as technology advanced.

But when had Zhao become this radical?

Whatever fear she'd felt now gave way to a crushing panic as Olivia contemplated the powerful tool the billionaire would soon have at his disposal. She was sure it was only a matter of time until he found a way to exploit the fail-safes they had coded into the program. Once that happened, Olivia wasn't sure there was a person on the planet that would be able to stop Lang Zhao.

Adrian's voice interrupted her train of thought. "I think I found something."

Apparently, Adrian had resumed his search of Zhao's computer and was working through the remainder of the computer cache: bank transactions, video-conference logs, website histories, a slew of emails, and other electronic records.

"Here," he said finally, his eyes lighting up. "He bought two Business Class China Railways tickets: one-way to somewhere called Wudangshan? Departing from Shanghai yesterday."

"That makes no sense," Olivia replied, with no mention of his woefully bad pronunciation. "That's in the middle of nowhere."

"Well, that's what the receipt says," Adrian said.

"That's a historic site—a Taoist monastery." Her heart sank. Although Olivia couldn't be sure that the ancient monastery was where he was headed, one thing was clear. Whatever hopes she'd had that they could intercept Zhao had just evaporated. "Even by high-speed train, that's an overnight trip. We'll never catch up with him!"

CHAPTER 35

MINISTRY OF STATE SECURITY Director Li Na Wen was about to forfeit whatever element of surprise she had maintained up to this point. The Z-20 military helicopter streaked low over suburban Shanghai. Directly ahead loomed a wealthy residential neighborhood. It was eerily quiet as if deserted. Most were probably in the city, caught up amid Chinese New Year celebrations.

4237 Lotus Drive was the exception. Just as Director Wen had suspected, the second story of the large home glowed with light.

They are here.

As they neared the billionaire's property, Wen tensed, her fingers clenching the armrest in a viselike grip. The night had quickly devolved into a national disaster. Unless they could locate Zhao and recover the stolen source code, she feared it was headed toward a catastrophic conclusion.

Olivia Chen and Adrian Pryor will serve their purpose.

Director Wen was having a hard time coming up with a rational explanation for Adrian Pryor's involvement in the charade. The former NSA agent had taken a great risk by traveling to Shanghai, one of a growing list of bizarre behaviors he had displayed over the last twenty-four hours. An obvious question presented itself—who is he working for?

Wen had a hard time believing that a man like Adrian Pryor, a career intelligence agent, could be lured with money. And yet, his actions made no sense.

Whose side is he on?

Had the U.S. authorities sent him? Or was he working as a rogue agent? And more concerning, what was his relationship with DeepThink? Had he somehow been persuaded to get involved by the powerful conglomerate? The thought gave her a sudden chill.

There were very wealthy and powerful individuals who would stop at nothing to get their hands on this technology. In a world where big business and powerful interests controlled government, the lines between state and commerce had been blurred beyond distinction, and not just in her own country. One thing was clear—she could not trust Adrian or Strauss. There was no telling what powerful interests they represented.

"Land it there!" one of the tactical agents directed, pointing to the southwest.

The comment jolted Wen back to the present.

It's go-time.

She followed the agent's outstretched finger to a large swath of grass situated on the rear of the property. Amid the tight press of trees and shrubbery, the grassy knoll offered the best landing zone. The helicopter tilted and began dropping toward the indicated spot. A sudden gust of wind rocked the aircraft, and it fell precipitously in response. Wen's stomach dropped, but seconds later, the skids slammed into the safety of the earth.

She yanked off her headphones. "Everybody off!"

They piled from the craft, Wen leading the way toward the towering edifice. She took off with a burst but stopped short, her attention drawn to an unexpected sight. A lone figure appeared, leaning up against a wooden pagoda in the center of the gardens. The helicopter's powerful infrared LED arced over the man. His features starkly illuminated by 60,000 lumens coming from the searchlight, Li Na Wen was sure of his identity.

Li Na Wen locked eyes with her attacker.

She turned to her lead agent. "Agent Wu—split your team. I want half of you to secure the perimeter. The other half begin to sweep the interior."

"Do you need help, Ma'am?" He gestured towards the figure of their attacker.

She tightened her grip on her weapon. "I'll be just fine here."

Agent Wu hesitated a moment.

"What are you waiting for?" she snarled. "Go!"

CHAPTER 36

To Olivia's horror, the sky erupted in a deafening roar as the second story of Lang Zhao's home lit up like the Fourth of July. Strauss had predicted as much.

"It won't be long before the Ministry of State Security tracks us to Zhao's home." He had offered them a plan in the event that they could not get out before that happened. "I'll present myself as a decoy; buy you some time. Use the rear staircase exit, and I'll wait here with the boat."

Indeed, that is what happened, and yet Olivia knew that the man's plan had failed.

We are out of time.

A MSS helicopter bore down on them from above, its powerful searchlight engulfing the entire second story of Zhao's home. A voice blared, "Stay right where you are!"

Olivia knew immediately that there was no way out. Blanketed in near daylight and with thermal detection, she could think of no escape from the Ministry of State Security. She stole a look out the window. In the center of the lawn, Olivia spotted Strauss. He had held his part of the bargain. He stood with his arms raised in the center of the garden. Certainly, Wen would be happy to apprehend her attacker. He would tell the authorities that they had split up. A lie, of course, but perhaps it would cause enough confusion to buy them some time.

Olivia locked eyes with a panic-stricken Adrian.

"Maybe we should turn ourselves in, work together?" he said.

"We can't trust Wen." Before he could object, Olivia grabbed Adrian's hand and burst out of the office door, leading him to a rear staircase. She bounded down the steps two at a time, plunging into the darkness. With no time to think better of it, Adrian scrambled after her.

Olivia knew they had only seconds until the MSS helicopter reached the ground, and a swarm of agents would flood the mansion. She hastened her pace. They reached a landing on the first floor. Olivia looked over her shoulder before pivoting quickly and dropping out of sight into another stairwell. She groped her way down the spiral staircase, disappearing into a pitch-black void.

"Hurry!" she whispered, shooting a glance over her shoulder. Unfortunately, the gaze that met her was not Adrian's. To Olivia's horror, she saw two familiar faces at the top of the landing—Ministry of State Security Agent Wu and his second in command.

Agent Wu raised some kind of device, which he aimed at her. "Surrender! Before someone gets hurt!"

For a split second, Olivia had the strangest of thoughts. *The MSS wants me dead.* She recoiled instinctually. But as she retreated, the floor seemed to disappear. Where Olivia expected solid ground, she found only empty space. She felt herself falling backward into a dark abyss. When she finally found the ground, Olivia's left arm caught the brunt of her fall, bone colliding with stone. The staccato crack that echoed through the stairwell was unmistakable.

It's broken.

Even so, she pushed the pain from her mind, shifting her entire focus onto the two men looming above her.

Get up! Run!

But it was too late. Agent Wu and his cohort bounded down the stairwell, taking three steps at a time. Seconds later, they had closed the distance, and two menacing shadows hung over her.

Olivia lunged again, disappearing further backward. She tumbled sidelong down the stairwell, arriving at the bottom just in time for the two muscular agents to overtake her.

In an instant, she was out of time.

CHAPTER 37

A BITING WIND HOWLED through a remote valley of the Wudang Mountains, billowing Lang Zhao's wool overcoat. He rubbed his hands together, although he knew it was useless. Approaching the ancient stone edifice he had traveled nearly 1100 miles to see, Zhao shivered.

Nanyan Temple.

It was just as he imagined: an ornate stone relic steeped in equal parts history and ethereal mysticism. From his vantage point hundreds of feet below, the ancient edifice seemed to hang in ether. According to legend, the temple had been constructed in Beijing before being transported more than 700 miles to Wudangshan, where it had to be carried in pieces to the top of the mountain on which it now rested.

Zhao had chosen the sacred mountaintop to carry out the operation because it was both practical and meaningful. Practical, because it was a veritable fortress. And meaningful, because according to Chinese legend, the centuries-old monastery was the place where man had ascended to immortality.

Like the Black Emperor, I will do the same . . .

Feeling reinvigorated, Zhao hurried past a group of gilded bronze statues before stopping at the foot of the monastic complex.

His eyes traveled up the sheer face of a monstrous cliff, resting on an elaborate series of temples etched into stone some 5,000 feet above.

There was only one way up: a precarious-looking steel cable car with a single, steep cable line running from the ground to the complex above.

We've come this far.

Boarding the small carriage, Zhao swallowed hard, tempering his fear with an icy resolve to help the man beside him. The cable car shuddered in protest of buffeting alpine winds, and Zhao prayed the dilapidated car would deliver him and Minsky safely to their destination. Their journey finally ended at a dome-roofed temple constructed entirely of stone. Several stone pillars held up a crumbling, sloped roof.

Zhao approached the sanctuary and knocked twice. There was no answer, and he wasted no time swinging open the heavy wooden door. As he entered, he was careful not to step on the threshold, which he knew the Taoists considered the shoulder of God.

Minsky followed Zhao inside, closing the door forcefully behind him. Inside, the light was dim. The air was heavy with the thick scent of incense. Zhao found himself in a rectangular chamber whose stone walls burgeoned with timeworn Taoist works—rare texts accessible only to the monastery's regular inhabitants: a small group of Buddhist monks who had long since retired for winter.

Zhao crossed the room to a large wooden table cluttered with electronic equipment. A series of thick cables ran across the back wall underneath the table.

The monk has fulfilled his end of the deal.

Zhao smiled. Apparently the large endowment he had proffered to the aging historical site had been well received. In addition to providing sanctuary, he could see that the satellite internet equipment, modem, router, and other networking equipment he had asked for was all there. It probably hadn't been easy to secure everything in the remote location. Nonetheless, everything was there.

Zhao sprang into action. He removed a laptop from his travel case. He plugged it in and watched as the screen lit up a deep indigo color, casting a cerulean glow across the room. Next, he removed a platinum USB device from the case and carefully secured it in the port. Within seconds, code had filled the entirety of the dark screen.

It is beautiful.

Martin Minsky had consulted with Andreas Kohler and Olivia Chen in their research and design plans for the past two years. While neither Zhao or Minsky had seen the full schematics of their hardware design, they had obtained enough information to determine the requirements to support such a program. With cloud-based quantum computing services now available online to the highest bidder, powering the sophisticated algorithm in their possession would be surprisingly easy. And with the clever proxies they had set up, tracking them would be nearly impossible.

Zhao glanced out the window at the rolling, snow-covered hills and smiled. They may as well be anywhere in the world.

CHAPTER 38

ADRIAN STARED ACROSS THE rear hold of a Z-20 military helicopter he had just boarded at the command of the head of the Chinese Ministry of State Security. Director Wen sat across from him, her gaze hollow and her body even more rigid than her over-starched government-issue uniform. She had yet to acknowledge him, but no words were needed to translate her state of mind.

She's pissed.

Wen's agents had wasted little time after entering Zhao's mansion, taking swift and hostile action. He had watched helplessly as two agents pursued Olivia down the stairs. Deciding to take his chances alone, he fled towards the rear. He managed to slip outside but only made it as far as the rear lawn before a swarm of additional agents had arrived. Adrian's last recollection was being thrown to the grass.

"Stop trying to escape!" the agent had bellowed, muscling him towards a waiting helicopter. The sound of his voice was nearly lost in the maelstrom as powerful backwinds from the rotors buffeted around them.

"We have to go, now!" a second agent had shouted.

Seconds later, Agent Wu and another agent had boarded with a defeated-looking Olivia in tow. Within minutes, the military aircraft was climbing swiftly above the residential area. The chopper swung north, back towards the city.

With each passing mile, Adrian felt a knot tighten in his stomach. He shot a glance in Olivia's direction. Did she intend to explain everything to Wen now that they had been apprehended? Adrian's thoughts turned back to the shocking video they had just witnessed. He could still hear Zhao's chilling voice: "We must merge with it or surrender to it." He prayed that they would reach Zhao before he did something reckless.

But we're in the wrong province, he knew.

"Mr. Pryor, Miss Chen," Wen said, finally acknowledging them. Her tone was colder than ice. "Excusing for a moment your status as fugitives and the laundry list of charges against you, I think it's time we agree to work together, wouldn't you say?"

Adrian felt the instinct to recoil. "Why should we trust you?"

"You know—I could ask you the same question. Imagine my surprise when I arrived at CyberGen, only to find a member of U.S. intelligence already there?"

"*Former* member," Adrian corrected, not wanting to complicate the already confusing dynamics.

"Nevertheless, what were you doing at CyberGen? And if you are not involved, as you suggest, then why did you flee?"

"This is a complex situation," Adrian replied, his tone more defensive than he intended.

"At this point, the only explanation for your erratic behavior is that you have been recruited and paid a large sum of money to help Zhao thwart the Chinese authorities."

"That's absurd!"

"And yet," Wen declared, "it's the only logical explanation for why you would impede my investigation and flee."

Adrian was stunned. "I had no idea B.J. Strauss would take the action that he did. . . It was as much a surprise to me as it was to you!"

"I sincerely doubt that," Wen snapped, rubbing her temple.

"I had to make a quick decision," Adrian said.

"So, you fled the authorities on a boat with the project's chief computer scientist? You haven't done yourself any favors, Pryor."

"What other choice did I have?" Adrian said in rising frustration.

"Nevertheless, I find myself in unfamiliar territory. I need your help," Wen said, her tone more urgent now. "Lang Zhao," she said, "do you have any idea where he may have gone?" Her gaze bore into him with an acute air of expectation. "We don't have much time."

You wouldn't believe it, Adrian wanted to say. But he remained silent, fully aware of how Olivia felt about working the MSS. As much as it pained Adrian to admit it, cooperating with the them may be their only hope of catching Zhao.

Adrian leaned closer to Olivia. But something about her arm drew his attention: it was a deep crimson and purple color and had swollen considerably. "Her arm!" He slid closer to Olivia to examine her wound. "We need a medical kit," he demanded. He turned his attention back to Olivia. "Are you okay?"

"I think it's broken," she replied weakly. "I fell on the stairs." She glared at Agent Wu.

"I'll find the medical kit," one of the other agents said, moving towards the back of the cabin.

"It's the least of our concerns right now," Olivia said vacantly.

"You should at least let them look at it," Adrian urged, leaning in protectively.

A moment later, the agent returned with a rolled Ace bandage and some other medical supplies. He performed a quick examination, checking her range of motion and the injury itself. "It's just a bad sprain," he declared a moment later. Using the elastic bandage, he fashioned a makeshift sling.

Olivia winced in response to his touch.

Suddenly, a voice in the cockpit drew their attention. "Yes, that is correct. We have taken Mr. Pryor and Ms. Chen into custody," the agent declared. "We are en route to headquarters for questioning. Get the interrogation rooms ready."

"Don't bother," Olivia protested. "We aren't going to Beijing!"

The agent covered his phone and spun towards Olivia in disbelief. "Pardon me?" he said. "Our orders are to bring you directly to headquarters for questioning. You obviously know something . . . Do you have any idea what is at stake here?"

"There is no reason to take us to Beijing," Olivia continued, "because we are prepared to tell you everything. We know where Zhao is."

Wen looked stunned.

Olivia reached into her pocket and took out her cell phone with her good arm. She located a photo of the Black Emperor online and handed her phone to Wen.

"Does this mean anything to you, Director?"

Wen studied the small thumbnail, her brow furrowing. "That's preposterous," she said, the ancient legend clearly coming to mind.

"Is it?" Olivia demanded.

"We've been watching Zhao's hangar for two days," Wen declared. "If he had left the city, we would have known."

"Which is probably why he didn't go to his hangar," Olivia snapped.

"We found two rail tickets to Wudangshan," Adrian said. "He left yesterday."

Wen didn't look convinced.

"And there is something else you need to see," Olivia said.

"What might that be?" Wen demanded.

"Something that will leave you with no doubt in your mind that we are on the same side," Adrian said.

The time for secrets is over.

CHAPTER 39

IN A GLEAMING HIGH rise in Beijing's Dongcheng district, the young man seated in the MSS' Cyber Command Operations Center felt increasingly on edge as he scrutinized a troubling video he had just uncovered as part of an ongoing investigation. He lifted his telephone receiver, carefully entering Li Na Wen's secure phone number. But he stopped short, unable to bring himself to complete the call to his boss. Something nagged at him.

Yuan Lee—one of the few people on Earth with a direct line to Li Na Wen—was the director's lead intelligence agent. He was part of a new but growing outfit operating under the umbrella of the MSS: the Algorithm Control Agency. Lee almost always worked around the clock to satisfy the powerful woman's seemingly endless litany of demands. The twenty-something hardware jock dressed in an untucked flannel shirt was a genius in data analytics and had practically signed over his soul when he had agreed to the agency's employment contract.

Lee, who had left a very lucrative career in the private sector, had teamed up with the Chinese government to design a novel chip architecture for use in data mining. In recent years, the U.S. had blocked the sale of most commercially manufactured U.S. chips, forcing the Chinese back to the drawing board to create their own.

Obstacles demand innovation.

Lee's approach used deep learning to crunch vast data sets, finding patterns without guidance from a programmer. A year later, the breakthrough had enabled him to use portable consumer electronics to do what it had taken foreign governments countless hours and entire teams of people to do—making them capable of recognizing faces, navigating roads, translating languages, spotting useful information, or even identifying "fake news."

As an intelligence agent in the cyber division, it was Lee's job to keep Director Wen informed. Given the sophisticated tools at his disposal, sorting through the reams of data available to him was the easy part. Determining what was worth his boss' time often proved more difficult. He had been analyzing data on the command center's oversized video display wall tonight when he made a shocking discovery.

Rumors had circulated for weeks about a particular person of interest in their ongoing investigation, a reclusive billionaire who had gone missing three days prior. The man seemed to have vanished without a trace. But now, Lee had just been alerted to activity on his home network, which he had been monitoring for the last twenty-four hours. Gaining remote access to Lang Zhao's network, Lee had uncovered a strange video file. Even more perturbing, the file appeared to have been recently queued for release to an anonymous video-sharing platform.

But by whom? And why?

Lee replayed the video several times with growing concern. He paused the playback at a particularly concerning image. The unmistakable silhouette of the billionaire emerged from the ocean, revealing an alarming physical transformation.

"What in the actual hell?"

The man had gone on to deliver a disturbing message about the future. The contents were distressing, particularly given the recent breach at Zhao's secretive tech company, where it was rumored they had created a generally intelligent AI—a development the Chinese government had been monitoring for some time.

Some recent spikes in power and energy consumption had set off alarms, prompting them to send agents from Beijing to Shanghai to investigate. What they found immediately sent the organization into a tailspin. Director Wen had immediately flown to Shanghai and committed the full backing and resources of the ACA to get the situation under control.

But the situation is even worse than we imagined. Wen would want to see this. He knew he must act quickly. His boss was notoriously short on patience, a virtue he did not seek to test during the current crisis. If he were to believe the contents of the video, not only was their person of interest very much still alive, but he had undergone a drastic physical transformation. Which also explained why he had been so hard to track . . . His entire gait had changed!

Lee turned his attention back to his monitor. He formatted the file for encrypted delivery to his boss. Then he picked up the phone, dialed carefully, and listened as the familiar voice answered. She sounded grim.

"Director? There is something you need to see right away."

Onus for the contents of the disturbing eight-minute video rested solely on his shoulders, and he was eager to have it off his desk. He held his breath as he hit send. He quickly and efficiently completed his call with Wen, a necessary skill he had learned early in his relationship with the director. Yuan Lee felt a wave of relief wash over him.

Wen can decide what to make of this herself.

———

Some 1,100 kilometers to the southwest, inside the cabin of a speeding helicopter, Director Li Na Wen's tablet began buzzing. She glanced down at the device in her lap. She had new intel from her contact in Beijing. She glanced at the other occupants in the cabin. Without a word, she slipped into the cockpit and viewed the shocking video file she had just received from her lead intelligence agent.

Things are even worse than I imagined.

CHAPTER 40

LOOKING OUT THE WINDOW of the ancient Taoist monastery, Lang Zhao appraised a cliff in the distance. It bore the image of four fading crimson Chinese characters.

(寿) longevity

(福) fortune

(康) health

(宁) peace

The message was eerily prophetic—an acute reminder of what had inspired his quest to begin with. Humanity, in its pursuit of progress, had veered recklessly off course, and with great consequence to the masses. More troubling, most had turned a blind eye while progress continued to shoot forward, careening towards an uncertain future.

It was hard to imagine a trajectory hundreds of thousands of years into the future where humans succeeded in creating a super-intelligent AI and achieved material abundance, but were still bipedal mammals governed by three pounds of gray matter.

Zhao looked down at the medical dressings that still covered his lower extremities. *Temporary pain.* It was only a small part of the preparations he had undergone to ready himself. They were small sacrifices to bring him to the current moment.

In order to survive, we must adapt. And not just our bodies, but society itself. Clinging to the familiar would spell certain disaster.

Zhao had tried to warn people, but his warnings fell on deaf ears. He decided then that if he couldn't stop such an outcome, he would have to be the one to do it. To steward it into existence. To prepare humanity. To fight. To survive.

With this in mind, Zhao had conceived of CyberGen, populating it with an elite team of the world's brightest machine learning experts and world-class equipment. For the past two years, Zhao had kept a close watch on the progress being made at the lab. Employing a neural network, the team had used the basic principles of reinforcement learning to teach their AI things like language and image recognition, small feats that would eventually give rise to something much more complex.

Nature had given them a working example of a generally intelligent system—the human brain. A rather obvious approach to AI was to proceed by trying to replicate what the brain did. It wasn't long before Andreas Kohler and his clever partner Olivia Chen had clobbered together a primitive AI.

Then came its training. Like an infant child, the AI had to be taught about the world around it. As a precaution, the program was strictly forbidden to have access to the internet. The team fed it massive data sets, dumps from sites like Wikipedia and the Library of Congress, and selections from YouTube, Facebook, and Twitter. Its appetite grew and grew until it crossed the invisible threshold to *artificial general intelligence.*

At first, it performed clumsily, and progress was slow. But then, it got better. And as it got better, its self-improvements came more quickly. However, what surprised Zhao the most, was just how quickly the AI had reached human-level intelligence.

In secret, Zhao had begun to make preparations with his contacts across the world: computer scientists, mathematicians, and engineers, each unknowingly responsible for disparate parts of his plan.

All to bring him to this moment.

The timing was no accident. Chinese New Year had been celebrated since the Shang Dynasty—some 3500 years ago. But only in recent years had it been debased into a commercial spectacle. Zhao pictured the celebrations currently taking place all over China, a garish display of lights, consumerism, and overindulgence. A new year was the ideal time to affect his plans.

First, a cleansing. Then, a rebirth.

In 13.8 billion years, humans were the only species to make it past The Great Filter. Now, the time had come to ensure that we not only endure beyond—but that we prosper. And The New Order was the means to that end.

Humans had organized themselves into cities since the time of the super tribes. What the public didn't know was that time was about to come to an end. The way of the future required a sweeping reorganization of sociopolitical structures—a blank slate.

Zhao would employ the AI to gain control of financial systems, governments, and telecommunications. It would only be a matter of time until decades-old institutions of economics and politics crumbled.

There was a new way. *A better way.* An AI-assisted socio-economic system where the masses could flourish, ensuring that humans spread their descendants to the stars and beyond.

Shanghai would be the first city to fall. Then Istanbul. Karachi would be next. Followed by Moscow, Tokyo, Mumbai, and São Paulo—spreading westward like a plague. The fall of the cities was a necessary part of Zhao's plan.

Before the dawn, the great cities would be beset by chaos. Cut off from electrical and telecommunications grids, the world would be rocketed back to the dark ages. As financial markets crashed, emergency services were paralyzed, and transportation safety systems were taken offline, widespread panic and chaos would ignite.

From chaos, order.

CHAPTER 41

LI NA WEN CURSED as she retreated from the cockpit of the Z-20, returning to the main cabin.

She is definitely pissed, Adrian thought.

Wen glared at Adrian and Olivia. "As you are no doubt aware, I have sophisticated resources at my disposal."

Adrian remained silent, unsure how to respond.

"It is stupid to think you can keep secrets from me," Wen continued.

"I'm sorry?" Adrian said.

"Is there any information you would like to share with me?" Wen said.

"That's what I was trying to tell you," Adrian said forcefully. "We do have some information."

Wen met his gaze, unwavering.

"Zhao is planning to make a major announcement," Olivia declared. "A revelation which he believes will be his greatest contribution to humanity."

"And we think he is planning to live stream the announcement to every media outlet across the globe," Adrian added.

Wen was silent a beat. "This is not news to me."

Adrian's stomach lurched. He stole a glance at Olivia, who seemed equally stunned by the revelation.

"I have seen the video," The Director declared.

"You have?" Adrian said.

"My contact in Beijing sent it to me a short while ago."

Adrian's chest felt tight. Director Wen had again managed to get wind of sensitive information. *How?*

"Listen to me carefully," Wen said, her tone intensifying. "If the AI has reached human-level intelligence, if it has become an *AGI*, I think we can agree that it must be contained at all costs?"

"This is hopeless," Agent Wu scoffed. "Zhao is long gone with the AI."

"But he hasn't gotten it running yet," Olivia said.

"How can you be sure?" Wen replied.

"It will be obvious when the time comes," Olivia said. "But there is something that Zhao hasn't anticipated."

Wen furrowed her brow. "And what's that?"

"A trip wire," Olivia said.

"In your programming?" Wen said.

"Yes," Olivia replied. "A digital kill switch."

Wen leaned forward, her eyes filling with hope. "So, is that why you fled? You think you can stop Zhao?"

Olivia hesitated. "I think it will buy us some time. But we have to find him, and fast."

Wen didn't need to hear more. She turned on her heel and stormed back towards the cockpit. "How quickly can we get to Wudangshan?"

"I'm looking at the coordinates you gave me now," the pilot replied. "Even at max speed, we are looking at over three hours, ma'am."

Adrian's heart sank.

"We must hurry, Captain," Wen said.

Seconds later, the chopper banked westward. The pilot pressed forward on the stick, and the nose of the aircraft pitched downward. Adrian gripped the armrest. *Here we go again.* He stared out the window, steeling himself. Thankfully, when they reached full cruising speed, the aircraft leveled off. Adrian breathed a sigh of relief.

Just then, Wen returned to the cabin. She reached for a tablet on the console: her secure MSS-issue device. "I want to know everything there is to know about the monastery complex in Wudangshan."

She raised her phone to her ear. A moment later, her contact in Beijing answered.

"Send me the sat images," she barked. She refreshed her system, and a moment later, a map had materialized on her tablet. "We have our work cut out for us," she said, biting her lip.

Adrian slid closer, examining the satellite imagery.

"The monastery complex is comprised of nine platforms, a dozen temple structures, three ponds, and eleven caves. Plenty of places to hide," Wen said.

"But—" Olivia interrupted. "There is only one place where man became immortal."

All eyes in the cabin shot to Olivia.

"Nanyan Temple," she said. Her tone was steady. "He'll be there."

No one argued with the logic.

Wen appraised Olivia for a long moment before shifting gears. "Ok, according to this, we are about 600 miles from the site of the temples. "We are going to find him and flush him out."

CHAPTER 42

INSIDE THE ANCIENT MONASTERY, Lang Zhao paced, biding his time. But his patience was wearing thin. He checked his watch. It was just after 7 p.m. The fall of the cities must begin on this day.

Chinese New Year.

Zhao looked over Minsky's shoulder. The computer scientist was seated at a makeshift workstation against the far wall where they had spliced into the satellite internet infrastructure, allowing them long-distance, high-performance data networking. There was only one thing that remained to be done.

Set it free.

Now that the algorithm had matured, the AI's growing processing power and energy consumption demands would need to be satisfied. It was time to unshackle the powerful algorithm. With access to the internet and a quantum machine, the AI would allow Zhao and Minsky to wreak sweeping havoc with a matter of keystrokes. Traditional software required millions of lines of code, painstakingly built over months or years, followed by extensive testing to ensure it performed as intended. But not this. An intelligent AI would require no human intervention. It would intuit the necessary steps itself.

Breach city infrastructure? No problem. Hijack access to banks and the central reserve? Easy. Redeploy telecommunications networks and advanced weapons systems? Piece of cake. Zhao knew the sky was the limit.

A stream of code filled the dark terminal window, where Minsky was currently using a system called Jupyter to input code. "How much longer?" Zhao asked.

The computer scientist straightened, rubbing a kink in his neck. "It's almost live."

"And how long will it take to execute?"

"Less than ninety seconds," Minsky answered.

Zhao registered his surprise at how quickly the program would work, even from the remote location. He felt encouraged. He knew they didn't have much time before the authorities came looking.

"That is the beauty of quantum. The machine can think at the speed of light."

Zhao stepped closer to inspect Minsky's progress. He pictured their code coursing through the data center nearly 7,000 miles away at the IBM Quantum Research Lab in the suburbs of New York. Minsky had successfully connected to the quantum machine located there via the cloud and was now in the process of uploading their code. Once it went live on the machine, it would execute the prompts that Minsky had spent the last three days refining.

"I should be done in the next few minutes," Minsky announced from his workstation.

"You *should* be?"

"I don't want to make any mistakes. There isn't exactly a guide for what we are doing."

Zhao chuckled, knowing that they were inventing the playbook as they spoke.

"Any mistake could critically impact the program's functionality. It has to be perfect."

As Zhao waited, he checked his watch, anxiously registering their dwindling time.

Finally, Minsky ceased typing and spoke. "We're live." His finger was poised over the laptop's ENTER key. "Are you ready?"

Zhao nodded. "Cut it loose."

After several agonizing breaths, Minsky lowered his index finger and pressed ENTER. No sooner had he struck the key when the program froze, immediately rendering the screen dark.

"What's wrong?" Zhao demanded, taking two quick strides and arriving at Minsky's side.

Minsky remained silent and began frantically inspecting the system. "I'm not sure," he finally said. The machine whirred into overdrive, the fan laboring loudly. *Too loudly.*

"Talk to me, damnit! What's happening?"

"I . . . I'm not sure! I entered the override code exactly as Kohler provided. The file showed no evidence of corruption. Our connection was fine a moment ago!"

"Then what is it?"

Minsky hastily unplugged the laptop. He removed the side panel, sliding the internal circuitry into view. It only took a second for him to see the problem.

"The motherboard is completely fried." He swallowed hard, meeting Zhao's gaze. "The sequence triggered some kind of critical error. It must have overloaded the system."

"So, what are you saying?"

"Perhaps there was a tripwire built into the software that we failed to uncover?"

The revelation swept over Zhao like a tidal wave.

The old man lied to me.

CHAPTER 43

ZHAO ALLOWED THE REVELATION to sink in.

The override code that the computer scientist had provided had been fabricated. It was useless. Worse than that, it had been a *trap.* It crashed the program, and the error had completely fried their hardware. They had lost the connection to the IBM Quantum Research Lab, and there was no getting it back.

Zhao hadn't given the old man enough credit. He was sure the coward had submitted his secrets. In truth, Kohler had died protecting them.

Zhao squinted into the darkness. The only light was now a dim glow rising from the fireplace. He spun towards Minsky. "We must proceed as planned."

"I see no reason we can't. But we need new hardware."

"Untether it. *Now,*" Zhao ordered.

Minsky had apparently already reached the same conclusion. He took hold of a series of thick cables that connected the device to the wall and yanked them from their ports. He removed the platinum drive from the side of the machine. Zhao couldn't be sure that it hadn't been compromised, but he would have to confirm that later. Minsky had been smart enough to make copies, nevertheless.

Zhao lifted his phone to his ear. His call connected after a few short seconds. He would engage a local contact to arrange an evacuation from the remote site. But there was another problem. Even with new hardware, Zhao would need help to bypass the AI's fail safes. With Kohler dead, there were only two other people on the planet that could help. He refused to involve Olivia Chen. He had already put her through enough. Alexander Tso would help. Whether he liked it or not.

Zhao felt a surge of disappointment. But he wasn't ready to give up. They had come too far.

He checked his watch. It was almost 8 p.m. "Let's go."

Minsky hesitated a long moment.

"Martin? Aren't you coming?"

"I have already done all I can," Minsky said.

"But I need your help!"

"What you need is time." He gestured towards a semi-automatic weapon leaning against a wall in the corner. "And I am going to buy you some."

"Where in the world did you get that?" Zhao said. He wondered if the computer scientist had ever even fired a gun.

Minsky shoved him out the door. "May the gods be with you," he said simply. "Now go!"

CHAPTER 44

TWO MILES TO THE east of the Wudang Mountains, Adrian gazed out the helicopter window at the broad expanse of wilderness below him. Rising from a frost-covered valley, the soaring outline of Wudang Mountain came into view. The monastic complex materialized next, the only sign of life amid the remote expanse.

Adrian could see a series of cable cars ascending a rugged peak, which was dotted with at least a dozen temples. The least accessible was an ancient stone building on the south cliff: Nanyan Temple. *The place where man transcended to god.* Adrian pressed against the window, squinting at the dark rooftops. The centuries-old structure in which they believed Zhao to be hiding had been built directly into the side of the cliff. There was no room for a proper landing, and it afforded few tactical options.

"Over there!" Wen called to the pilot, pointing to an open area between the dense clutter of stone structures. "Get as close as you can!"

The pilot tipped the nose of the helicopter and moved diagonally towards the area where Wen had indicated, now hovering three hundred feet above the rooftops. A powerful gust of wind blasted through the valley, hammering the chopper. The pilot worked the controls, fighting the buffeting winds as he prepared to make a touch hover maneuver in a large courtyard.

Adrian shuddered, feeling an increasing sense of foreboding. He looked out the window as they neared the ground. A dim light flickered from the first story of the ancient temple. He grasped Olivia's arm instinctively.

He's here.

Adrian felt a flicker of optimism for the first time that evening. He shot a glance at the army of men across the cabin. Eight Strategic Support Force officers currently occupied the rear hold. The other choppers carried another combined fifteen officers. The MSS Director had wanted to bring half this number, but her superiors at the State Council had pressed for the reinforcements.

Agent Wu sat near the hatch of the aircraft. Flanked by his team of tactical agents, he hunkered low as the chopper pitched erratically in the inclement conditions. Wu braced his legs against the passenger seat, hugging a CF-05 submachine gun to his side. "Get ready to deploy!" he bellowed.

Adrian watched as the tactical team got into place. A moment later, Wu's voice cut the air again.

"Well, what are you waiting for?"

It took Adrian several seconds to realize that Wu had been speaking to him. "You can't be serious!"

"You didn't think we would leave behind critical assets, did you?" Wu said. "You are the only experts we have."

Adrian spun towards Wen. "Is this really necessary?" He shot a glance at Olivia, who looked suddenly frail cradling her sling.

"I need you both on the ground," Wen said.

"Here—take these," Wu said as if the matter had been settled. He shoved two sets of night-vision goggles and two all-weather jackets at Adrian.

Adrian felt his pulse rise. Despite his background in intelligence, he'd had no practical field training. This was an active threat situation, and they had no idea what they would be walking into.

Olivia was a computer scientist, for God's sake. He took a deep breath, reminding himself of the stakes.

We must do everything we can to help.

Adrian slid towards Olivia, helping her into her jacket before slipping on his own. He watched as Agent Wu put on a set of night-vision goggles and made a few adjustments. He quickly followed suit. Just then, another icy gust whipped the chopper around, sending them all off balance. Adrian steadied himself on a bank of seats. The pilot corrected, and the engine roared louder, fighting to maintain altitude. The craft finally steadied, and Adrian heaved a sigh of relief.

"Now!" Wen instructed into her headset. Within seconds, two Z-20s from their flank had taken position on opposite sides of the complex and began to descend simultaneously. When they reached ground, the struts rested only moments before Wu and the other PLA officers leaped from the craft. Adrian and Olivia followed their lead, launching themselves through the open hatch and onto the snow below. Seconds later, the choppers had lifted off again.

At least we will have air support, Adrian thought, watching the choppers climb back up to a safe altitude. He stood, dusting white powder from his jacket. He had landed hard, but thankfully a large snow drift had broken his fall.

Adrian surveyed his frozen surroundings and frowned. Even in the darkness, the series of buildings seemed to stretch out in all directions.

"This way," Wu said, leading his men along a narrow stone pathway that ran adjacent to the south cliff.

Adrian hurried forward but stopped abruptly when he reached the base of a stone staircase. He lifted his gaze to the ancient edifice directly above him—*Nanyan Temple.* The monastery windows were dark, apart from a single window on the first floor of the structure, which glowed eerily.

Adrian followed the agents up a crumbling stone staircase. He peered over the edge—he saw only darkness. A low stone barrier was the only thing separating the narrow path from the edge of the south cliff, which plunged nearly 5,000 feet to the ground below.

He shivered but picked up his pace when he realized that Wu and the rest of his team had already reached the top. A moment later, he arrived at Wu's side and stopped to catch his breath. Adrian read the tension in Agent Wu's back as the agent proceeded toward the stone structure. It was the same tension that now plagued him.

What are we going to find beyond that door?

Chapter 45

DARK CLOUDS GATHERED OUTSIDE DeepThink's Swiss headquarters, sending a shudder through Chancellor Benjamin J. Strauss as he stepped from his Audi TT. He watched the sky, praying the mounting storm wasn't some sort of cosmic omen. The last twelve hours had been a scramble, a desperate attempt to rein in the actions of a powerful man.

The Chancellor had yet to hear back from his son, Strauss Jr. He could only assume that things in Shanghai hadn't gone as planned. Strauss had seen no other option but to convene an emergency meeting—a call to arms. He ducked his head against the rain and proceeded towards the concrete and glass edifice sunken into the hill in front of him. The building glowed with light and activity.

The team has arrived.

The young man who greeted him at the door, an operations coordinator, took his jacket. "They are waiting for you to begin, Chancellor," the coordinator said. He checked his watch, looking anxious.

"My apologies. There was much to be done."

"They are in the conference room on the second level. Would you like me to escort you?"

"That won't be necessary," The Chancellor said, hurrying up the stairs.

Strauss arrived at the familiar conference room: an airy space with modern furnishings and a long table running its length. Two of the room's walls were constructed entirely of glass, offering sweeping views of Lake Geneva. The Chancellor had conducted hundreds of meetings in this very room—bringing together industry with government, NGOs, and academics, silently manipulating global agendas for more than four decades. But he feared that today's crisis was not business as usual.

"Welcome, Chancellor," said a man from across the room.

Strauss entered slowly, lifting his glasses to the bridge of his nose. He immediately recognized the speaker, a balding middle-aged man and widely known internet entrepreneur. His eyes traveled the length of the table, where nearly a dozen other constituents had assembled—many high-ranking officials from the private sector. "My apologies for my tardiness," he said, lowering himself into a chair at the head of the table. "Let's get to business."

"Of course," the balding man replied.

"How much do you think we can pull together?" Strauss said.

"Whatever you need," the man replied.

The other constituents exchanged uneasy looks, but no one balked.

"How quickly can we get the funds?" Strauss asked.

"Immediately," the balding man declared. "We'll use Bitcoin, drawn from the digital exchange. Negotiable as cash anywhere in the world."

"And it will allow us to skip the banks and avoid wire restrictions," a thirty-something British man and fellow tech executive added.

"Will it be directly traceable to us?" the chancellor asked.

"This will all be perfectly legal," the bald man said. "CyberGen owns the IP for the technology in question. As CEO, Lang Zhao is well within his rights to negotiate the sale of that IP. This technology is not regulated. No laws will be broken here."

There was a long silence.

"We may be able to mask the source if needed," the Brit said.

"Excellent." Despite the quick resolution, the Chancellor felt anxious. He knew what they were trying to do would require an exorbitant sum of money.

But everyone has their price.

CHAPTER 46

GUIDED BY SENSITIVE DETECTORS in his night-vision goggles, Adrian sidestepped a fallen tree limb and traversed the remaining distance through the snow to the temple. They stopped at a heavy-looking wooden door. Agent Wu reached for the weapon at his side, quietly disengaging the safety. Unarmed and feeling suddenly vulnerable, Adrian fell back a few steps behind the agents' tactical column.

Agent Wu held his finger to his lips, the universally recognized sign for "zip it," and reached forward. He gave the door a forceful shove and ducked inside. Adrian followed him into a rectangular chamber about the size of a large living room.

Inside, it was drafty and dank. Adrian caught a whiff of smoke hanging in the air. In the corner, he found the source: a fireplace containing the smoldering embers of a dying fire. Even the small amount of heat flared brightly in his goggles. The glow cast oblong shadows across a table on the far wall, where he could see a makeshift workstation had been set up. It was cluttered with an array of computer equipment. An abandoned laptop lay at the table's center. His gaze was quickly drawn to the floor, where a series of thick cables lay in disarray, the wires appearing to have been ripped out in a hurry.

Wu met his gaze and swallowed hard, but didn't seem ready to jump to conclusions. "Let's keep going," he urged, groping through the darkness towards the next chamber. They proceeded single file down a wide passageway and deeper into the ancient building. They reached a spiral stone staircase leading to the second level a moment later. Wu waved a small ultraviolet light mounted on the barrel of his weapon towards the stairs. "Red Team, check the second story," he said, motioning to several agents behind him. "The rest of you, follow me." He waved Adrian and Olivia forward. "That includes you two."

Adrian edged forward, his optimism fading with each step. He kept his ears piqued, but so far, there had been no signs of life—no echoes, no voices, nothing.

"Keep moving," Wu said, picking up his pace. After another few minutes of silent lumbering, Agent Wu stopped abruptly. Directly in front of them, a solid stone wall had materialized in the darkness. A glowing red laser dot flitted across the surface. They had reached the far end of the structure.

"Shit." Wu retreated immediately, turning his attention to the faint footfalls above them.

Our last hope, Adrian realized. By the time they reached the foot of the stairs, the footfalls had gotten louder. The secondary team must have come up empty-handed, too. Adrian expected to see the other agents descend at any moment. Instead, his eye caught a flash of movement from the top of the stairwell. He looked up just in time to see a baseball-sized object come clattering down the stairs. A cold rush of panic coursed through him.

"Run!" Adrian took two large strides and then shoved Olivia as hard as he could. They flew sidelong down the hallway, landing hard on stone, his body crushing hers in a protective shield. A second later, his goggles flared painfully, and the entire room erupted in flames.

The grenade was as loud as a sonic boom in the hollow chamber. The blast threw everyone to the ground. Shattered stone exploded from the walls and ceiling, followed by the thick pall of smoke and rock dust. Adrian's heart hammered in his chest.

Someone is still here.

Adrian's gaze shot to Wu. The agent cleared rubble from around his legs and then proceeded to army-crawl back towards the stairwell, retrieving his CF-05 submachine gun. He pointed at the door. "You two—out, now!"

Before Adrian could react, a crack from overhead stopped him in his tracks. All eyes shot to the stairwell. A dark figure appeared, silhouetted by a hellish inferno. Another gunshot blasted, followed by the whine of the man's semi-automatic weapon as it unleashed a round past them. The attacker wheeled back from the force of the weapon's discharge. Bullets rained from the ceiling, sparking and ricocheting off stone. Adrian's whole body tensed, pressing down tighter on top of Olivia.

When the bullets finally subsided, Agent Wu burst to his feet, streaking low across the chamber. He ducked into a cross-corridor and skidded to a stop, leaving only the barrel of his weapon visible around the corner.

Taking advantage of the momentary lull, the assailant leaped from the stairs, charging headlong into the chamber and towards the solitary exit. He passed in a blur, leapfrogging over bodies as he went. He was almost to the door when another round cut the air, this time coming from Wu's weapon. The fire caught the man on the back of his torso. Within seconds, his bullet-riddled form crumpled to the floor, and the temple fell silent again.

Swearing, one of the agents next to Adrian rose to his feet. "You okay?"

"I'll live." Adrian's eyes were on Olivia.

"How about you, ma'am?" the agent said.

"I've been better," she said, rubbing her arm.

"You're lucky he got you out of the way before the grenade detonated," the agent said. "If you had been at the bottom of that stairwell . . ."

Agent Wu joined them. "You're safe now."

"How can you be sure?" Olivia said weakly.

"My men confirmed that he was alone," Wu said, gesturing to the motionless form on the floor.

"But what about Zhao?" Olivia said.

Wu fell momentarily silent, looking distracted. He drew his hand to his radio earpiece and frowned. "That was Wen. It seems we have another complication."

"What do you mean?" Adrian said.

But Wu provided no details. He turned on his heel and dashed towards the exit.

What now? Adrian looked at the charred stone chamber a final time, then darted back out into the frigid expanse.

CHAPTER 47

WHY HAVEN'T I HEARD from Minsky?

Zhao stalked across the snowy courtyard of the supercomputing center that he had traveled three hours to reach. His face was slicked with freezing rain, and his arms ached from the weight of the unconscious form draped over his shoulder.

It had been over two hours since he had heard from his accomplice. He reached into his pocket and fished out his burner phone. He checked his messages. *Nothing.*

Odd. But then again, Minsky was smart enough not to leave a recorded message. He checked the signal. Faint, but he had one.

Zhao felt a surge of concern. Maybe something had gone terribly wrong? Nobody understood better than Zhao the lengths the Chinese government was willing to go to get their hands on the technology now in his possession.

He knew this because he felt the same way. Zhao would never have imagined himself capable of the actions he had taken over the last 72 hours. Yet, his muscles burning under the weight of Alexander Tso's unmoving form, he now knew he would go to any lengths to deliver the AI safely into being.

Zhao smiled when he arrived at the threshold of his destination. *The National Defense Science and Technology University.*

Behind him, he heard the spinning blades of a Sikorsky S-92 helicopter as it took to the air and lifted skyward. It had been no small feat to arrange for the evac helicopter. Or for the extraction of Alexander Tso from the MSS detention center in Shanghai, for that matter. But money talks, and he had no shortage of it.

Zhao ducked through the main doors of the supercomputing center. In the lobby, a single security guard was on duty. He headed directly towards the man. "My friend needs help," he lied. The guard took one look at Tso and reached reflexively for the nearby phone. He bent to lift the receiver, and when he did, an aluminum object came flying towards him. It struck him on the head, twisting his neck at an unnatural angle. The guard's eyes went wide when he saw Zhao's prosthetic leg. Then, a second later, his body went slack, and he dropped to the floor.

With steady hands, Zhao removed a key ring from the man's waist. Adrenaline sharpening his focus, he stalked towards a door on the far wall. He patiently tried each of the keys until the door finally unlocked. Once inside, Zhao found himself on a large landing. It overlooked a rectangular room about the size of a small warehouse. *The server room.* He hurried to a set of stairs and made his way down, his body laboring harder than necessary under Tso's weight. When he arrived at the bottom, he stopped short, overwhelmed by the scale of the monolithic beast purring idly in front of him.

Hundreds of flashing server racks stretched the length of the room. The supercomputer hummed with life, its field of energy almost palpable. Zhao knew he was looking at the first machine of its kind: an exascale computer.

Zhao heaved Tso's motionless form from his shoulder. Tso's body slid to the ground, landing in a semi-upright position against the wall. He stepped back, taking in the enormity of the machine. He wondered how he hadn't arrived at the idea sooner. Zhao had heard rumors for the past two years that the staff at the military research academy had been close to reaching the next milestone in supercomputing. Five times faster than its predecessors, an exascale machine was capable of an astounding quintillion calculations per second.

With access to a robust network and that kind of computing power, Zhao was anxious to finally get the AI running. What he would bring to bear on this day was nothing short of magical: a genie of sorts, able to carry out high-level commands. Commands that he and Minsky had painstakingly enumerated in the days leading up to now.

Zhao had always pictured affecting his plans in the mystical Wudang Mountains. But perhaps a more elegant solution was the place that had birthed modern man's most powerful machine. It seemed natural that the world's most powerful software would be married to the world's most powerful hardware, expounding the capabilities of each beyond known limits. To *god-like* limits.

Artificial intelligence had already inspired billion-dollar companies, novel research programs, and scenarios of both transcendence and doom. Soon, it will inherit its rightful mantle in the universe.

A godhead based on AI.

Zhao knew unequivocally that the future of organized religion would center around a god that is *technological*. And people would come to worship their new deity—a god unlike the gods of times past that they could see, hear, and even talk to.

With the internet as its nervous system, nearly fifty billion connected devices as its sensory organs, and data centers as its brain, a superintelligent AI would hear everything, see everything, and be everywhere at the same time: omniscient, omnipotent, omnipresent, and incorporeal.

These are the qualities normally ascribed to *gods*. And when such a being presented itself, along with the promise of immortality, peace, and abundance, what choice would the masses have other than to recognize their new god? The only thing that remained was to disrupt the status quo—to catalyze the shift in paradigm.

Feeling a renewed sense of purpose, Zhao stepped forward. His eyes searched the rows of servers until he found what he was looking for just beyond the racks: the control room. His pulse quickened.

He looked over at Tso's slumped form. Several hours earlier, under grave threat of danger to his family, Tso had offered up the key to bypassing the AI's failsafe. The tripwire, the same automatic shut-off that had halted his progress at the monastery, had been built in by its designers to stunt the growth of the AI. But with access to the override code, Zhao should now be able to circumnavigate the arcane fail-safe. Before he could dispense with Tso, though, he had to be sure there were no more mishaps—he had been tricked once already.

A moment later, Zhao charged down a darkened server aisle toward the control room. Tso's limp form was slung over his shoulder. Once inside, Zhao continued to a control station near the front of the room. He offloaded Tso into an office chair, quickly spinning toward the console. He knew the drugs would be wearing off soon.

I *have to hurry.*

Zhao reached for the platinum device in his pocket. His fingers trembled as he secured it in a nearby port. A large display on the wall flashed to life.

Zhao typed the code Tso had provided into the prompt and waited as the program loaded. The display went dark for several seconds before it ignited with a flood of code. He inserted a second drive, this one containing the commands the AI was to execute on his behalf. How the AI achieved the objectives was not of concern. That was the beauty of such an algorithm. It would intuit the necessary steps itself.

Zhao made a series of quick keystrokes and, confident all was running smoothly, he initiated the program. The system elicited a loud tone once it had finished running.

A few moments later, a topographic map materialized on the display. Zhao studied the map, which depicted the most vulnerable critical infrastructure in NE China. It seemed the

AI was working geographically, starting closest to home and working its way westward. He toggled to another map—this one of North America. He noted the targets there: municipal transportation, communications, and energy systems. And perhaps the most audacious: the stock exchange. Then he toggled to a third image—this one of Europe, which was to be AI's next target. He made a couple of careful keystrokes and watched as the AI whirred into action.

Then he leaned back, smiling.

Things are finally going according to plan.

Chapter 48

DIRECTOR WEN LOOKED OUT her window, where a growing pall of smoke rose from Nanyan temple. She cursed under her breath.

"Are there any injuries?"

"We're pretty banged up down here," Agent Wu's voice prattled through her earpiece. "Agent Yee sustained a concussion in the blast. There are several laceration wounds that need tending to, and we have one superficial bullet wound that will need immediate medical treatment."

Damn. Wen had not foreseen the involvement of the computer scientist. Nor had she foreseen the violent lengths he would go to protect Zhao.

Wen felt her stomach drop as the chopper lurched, beginning its descent. Moments later, her crew was back on board. The helicopter climbed swiftly, rising above the snow-capped foothills of the Wudang Mountains. The pilot throttled north, and the view of the picturesque monastery swiftly faded to black.

Feeling helpless, Wen lifted her cell phone to her ear and dialed the only person that she trusted to help.

Yuan Lee answered immediately. "We were too late," she said. A heavy silence settled between them.

Despite having some of the best tactical ops personnel in the world, her team had *failed*. Wen gripped her phone tighter. "Do you have any other leads?"

Lee hesitated on the other end of the line. "No, ma'am."

"We have over a half billion cameras on our streets. You're telling me you have *nothing*?"

"I'm afraid not," he said.

"How can that be?"

"It leaves only two conclusions, ma'am. Either he is not on the streets, or Zhao has found a way to become *invisible*."

"Check again, damn it!"

Wen heard the steady click of computer keys as Lee got back to work, presumably logging back into the national surveillance database. But after a few seconds, Lee stopped typing. Something else had drawn his attention. She heard a muted rumble, and the line went momentarily silent.

"Lee?"

He cursed. "Give me a minute, ma'am."

"Talk to me, Lee. What's happening?"

"We've lost power," he said. "It looks like the rest of the cyber-command floor is also affected."

Odd. Nonetheless, they had backup systems in place. Redundant power and satellite internet in case of an outage.

"Call me when the generator is up and you are back online." She slammed the phone onto the console, assessing her dwindling options. She turned her attention instead to the cockpit.

"How much fuel do we have left, Captain?"

"Less than 300 nautical miles till empty, ma'am."

"Headquarters it is," she said through gritted teeth. "For now."

Zhao can't stay off the grid forever.

Chapter 49

Olivia clutched her injured arm to her chest, staring helplessly at the other occupants of the Z-20. More than twenty minutes had passed since the power outage at MSS headquarters. They had yet to hear back from Wen's lead intelligence agent.

What is taking him so long?

The Director had grown equally impatient. She snatched her cell phone from the small console between them and dialed. She lifted the device to her ear, waiting for the call to connect. It did not.

Her eyes flashed to the screen.

"Zero bars."

"Try mine," Olivia said, pulling her cell from her pocket. She checked the signal: two bars. Better than nothing. "Here," she said, lobbing it at Wen.

Wen caught it with one hand. "Thanks."

She carefully entered the twelve-digit number. Yuan Lee's landline at headquarters, Olivia guessed. They waited for the telltale trill of the line, but there was only silence.

Wen lowered the phone, inspecting the display for a moment. "No service," she declared.

"What do you mean? I just checked it," Olivia said. "It had two bars. Try again."

"No bars," Wen said, shoving it back towards Olivia. "It's useless."

Olivia inspected her phone. Wen was right. The signal had *disappeared*. She gently returned the phone to her pocket, feeling an increasing sense of foreboding. Her gaze drifted to the window, where a new city had materialized below them. Nanyang, she realized after a moment, a historical trade hub and home to ten million. It was coursing with life—every street had been strung with lanterns and banners of red and gold. The city center was teeming with people. Olivia had almost forgotten about Chinese New Year celebrations, which were still in full swing. *Dear god*, she thought, thinking of all the oblivious citizens.

And then, something strange happened. Below the aircraft, the sprawling metropolis of Nanyang suddenly vanished into darkness. Olivia watched in horror from six thousand feet as her worst fears materialized. She gasped as, mile by mile, streetlights blinked off, the neon buzz of downtown disappearing into icy mist. Several miles in the distance, a large suspension bridge flickered and went dark.

Olivia's eyes flashed to Wen.

"It's happening," Wen said.

Olivia had already reached the same conclusion. First, the cell towers, now power? Zhao had found a way to hack the electrical grid.

Agent Wu bounded over. He had already pulled out a satellite phone and shoved it at Wen. "This should still work. Even with the towers down."

Wen took hold of the clunky device, its bright screen flaring in the darkness. She engaged the speakerphone and dialed. It rang once and then connected. "I need an update, Lee. NOW!"

"Director—thank God. I couldn't get through to your cell," Lee replied, sounding flustered. "I'm back online, but I'll need a few moments to reassess."

A couple of minutes passed in silence. Olivia tried not to panic as reality set in.

The attack has begun.

Wen stated the obvious. "The AI is live."

An uncomfortable silence followed.

"Lee—" Wen said, "are you still there?"

"Yes, ma'am."

"I need you to pull up a current map of the city's electrical grid—"

"Showing the outages?" Lee said. "Got it."

Three minutes later, Wen was looking at a map on her tablet showing substations and other critical infrastructure that had gone offline.

"He's good," Adrian said.

Wen's tablet now glowed with a map of northeast China.

"Three more municipal power plants just went offline," Lee announced. "It looks like telecom is being hit, too."

"We need to notify the city officials," Wen said, thinking of the powerful government officials who were likely busy celebrating Chinese New Year with their families. "They can't wake up to this."

No one spoke for a breath. The implications were clear.

This is war.

Olivia stared at Wen's tablet, her anxiety growing by the minute.

"Another two servers and three power substations just went offline," Wen said, examining the map. The screen flashed as more outages rolled in.

"What is the impact radius?" Wen said.

"It's hard to tell," Lee replied. "I'm still gathering the data."

"What do you mean?" Wen said. "I need to know what is happening!"

Lee sighed. "It's not just electrical stations, ma'am. It's hitting banking systems, traffic systems, emergency services . . . I'm getting reports from hundreds of cities. It's not just big cities under fire. Over the last hour, there have been reports from dozens of cities confirming they have lost gas mains, water, power . . ."

Agent Wu now spoke up. "Do we have any security protocols in place for this? Is there a way to take the critical infrastructure offline?"

"That may work," Lee said.

"What do you mean, it *may* work?" Wu said.

"The time and resources required to pull off that level of coordination are beyond anything I have ever seen. And it's doing it in minutes. My guess is that it will only be a matter of time until the AI finds a way back in."

Olivia locked eyes with Wen, the two women sharing a moment of silent understanding.

"We are entirely unprepared," Wen said.

Olivia felt a shrinking feeling. She knew that a sophisticated cyberattack could cripple the country's infrastructure. China's cities, along with the rest of the world, are lagging painfully behind in the digital revolution, particularly the systems on which they most rely daily: banking, traffic control systems, telecommunications, and electrical grids. The critical infrastructure underlying the systems is outdated, to say the least.

Wen turned to Olivia. "I need to understand its capabilities. There must be a way to stop it."

"Even if we could shut down every networked computer in the world," Olivia said, "the AI is operating at the speed of light."

"Then we had better work fast," Wen said. "Before it engineers some novel underground network beyond our comprehension!"

The cabin fell silent, the reality of the situation rushing over them like a wave.

"The playing field isn't level," Adrian said. "We'll never outwit it."

"There must be another way," Wen said.

"There is only one way to stop it," Olivia said. "We have to *find* it."

CHAPTER 50

"AND HOW THE HELL do you propose we do that, Ms. Chen?" The Director glared at her.

Olivia tensed. "He could be orchestrating the attacks from anywhere."

In retrospect, it was a problem that they all should have seen coming. In the rush to plug everything into the internet, the country's nuclear plants, oil refineries, gas and oil pipelines, factories, farms, cities, cars, traffic lights, homes, thermostats, lightbulbs, refrigerators, stoves, baby monitors, pacemakers and insulin pumps had all become increasingly web enabled. They had effectively created the world's largest attack surface.

Olivia knew the only way to stop the attacks was to find the AI. And she knew that the Ministry of State Security wouldn't be able to do it.

At least, not without her help.

Olivia appraised Wen, who had thankfully turned her attention to a call with Yuan Lee at MSS headquarters. She glanced at the tactical agents in the chopper's rear hold. They also appeared preoccupied. She scooted closer to Adrian. "I think I know how we can help," she said in a whisper. She reached into her pocket, producing a small electronic device.

"What's that?" Adrian asked.

"A copy of the AI's footprint," she said.

Adrian stared at her with a look of disbelief. He studied the electronic storage device. She could see him processing the news and figuring out the implications of her revelation. When his eyes snapped back up, they were filled with hope.

"When the MSS arrived at CyberGen, I wiped my system," Olivia explained. "But not before downloading a copy of ALPHA's root code. I figured we may need it."

Adrian cocked his head, a small smile spreading across his lips. "To track the AI?" he asked.

"Precisely," she said. "This USB contains data packets that are unique to my source code. It's not enough to reassemble working code or anything like that. But it is a digital footprint of sorts."

"Brilliant," Adrian said, beaming.

"If we run a network scan, we should be able to search for any traces of my code. If we find any matches—"

"It would mean," Adrian interrupted, "that we can trace the cyberattacks to their source."

"Exactly," Olivia said. "But—"

"But what?" Adrian said.

"This is our trump card." Olivia's eyes flashed to Wen. "If we share this, we are all-in with the MSS."

"And you still don't trust them?" Adrian whispered, stealing a glance at Wen.

"Do you?" Olivia said.

"I'm not sure, but what choice do we have?" Adrian said. "Without proper equipment or network access—"

"We can't run a network search," Olivia said, sighing heavily.

"I can solve that problem," Wen said. Having concluded her call, The Director leaned forward and abruptly snatched the small drive from Olivia. "Give that to me."

Olivia bristled.

"It's okay," Adrian said gently. "We need to let them help."

Olivia knew he was right.

Wen reached for her tablet and inserted the storage drive into the USB port.

"The contents of that file cannot go public," Olivia said, feeling the blood drain from her face.

"Ms. Chen, this tablet is secured with the best technology available to the country of China. The only person who will lay eyes on your data will be my lead agent at headquarters, Yuan Lee, whom I trust implicitly. Now tell me what to do with this damn thing."

Olivia bit her lip. "It's like a digital footprint," she said. "If you run a network search, it should lead us to the AI."

The corner of Wen's mouth lifted into a smile.

"But we need to act quickly," Olivia said. "The root code is only distinct to the original version of my program. If too much time passes, there is no telling how many self-improving iterations the AI will have undergone—it may be impossible to detect, let alone track . . ."

"I will send it to headquarters. Yuan should have no problem accessing the file and running a secure network search from our offices in Beijing," Wen said. "A little trust, please."

The cabin fell silent for a full minute. Wen hammered out a quick message on her tablet. A moment later, the device elicited a quiet chime, confirming her request had been sent to MSS headquarters. She sighed and slammed the tablet down. She raised her phone to her ear. "Yuan, I need you to check your email immediately." She disappeared into the cockpit, speaking in rushed Mandarin into her cell phone.

Olivia felt a surge of optimism. She knew it was their only hope. But for this plan to work, there remained one painful reality. For the trace scan to succeed, the AI would need to be actively running. And if it were live, there was a much greater risk that it could escape the network. If that happened, there would be no stopping it.

Were they already too late?

Ultimately, there was only one way to be sure.

Olivia prayed that Wen's agent was as good as she seemed to think he was.

CHAPTER 51

IN THE DIM AUXILIARY light of the Cyber Command Operations Center, Yuan Lee sat alone and studied the file he had just received from his boss, Director Li Na Wen. He felt a surge of optimism as he opened the file. As expected, he found twelve data points, packets of code unique to Olivia Chen's source code.

Lee glanced at the other MSS employees seated outside the glass wall on the Cyber Command floor, all completely oblivious to the current crisis.

"As with everything else that has transpired in the last thirty-six hours," Wen had declared, her tone ominous, "this is to remain classified at the highest levels of security. You are to consult with no one. You report only to me. Is that clear?"

"Of course," he had agreed, knowing damn well that would be the case until the crisis concluded.

I'm on my own.

Lee turned his attention back to his terminal, where he began to upload the data points into a network search program. Then he leaned back, waiting for the search to exhaust itself. He had to admit, the approach they were about to try was clever, surprisingly simple, and elegant. Police had used fingerprints in their forensic investigations for decades. Unique to each individual, not even identical twins have the same fingerprints. Tracking the AI by its unique imprint was no different. Except his perp was digital. Nevertheless, the AI would leave unique digital tracks in its wake.

Lee's computer elicited a loud beep several moments later, notifying him of the conclusion of the trace scan. He was surprised at how quickly it had worked.

There's a match?

He refreshed the program and ran the search a second time before reaching for his phone. "We have a hit."

"Are you sure?" The Director answered, sounding skeptical.

"I'm positive," Lee replied. "It appears to be coming from central Tianjin."

"Impossible! Run it again!" she insisted. "We just departed Zhao's last known location an hour ago, and we must be some 400 miles from there!"

"I ran the tracking twice, ma'am. Take a look at this," Lee said, sending the results to her tablet. Using his cursor, he traced a tangle of indigo lines.

"Do you see that?" he said. "You are looking at the AI's footprint." A web of indigo lines was illuminated on their respective screens. Each of the connected threads represented matches to parts of Olivia Chen's root source code. The trace culminated in a small blinking circle on the upper left of his screen.

"Any guesses where it originates?" Wen demanded.

"I can't be certain," he declared. "But I have isolated the general area."

He moved his cursor further up the map, where the indigo lines converged. There was an industrial park at the center.

"Here," he said, pointing to a nondescript brick building next to the freeway.

"What is there?" his boss demanded.

"Hang tight," Lee said, eying his screen. He zoomed in on the map of the industrial park. It took only seconds before the location dawned on him. Lee bolted upright. "Oh my God."

CHAPTER 52

ADRIAN LISTENED TO WEN and her intelligence agent in a trance. He feared the night was coming to a disastrous conclusion.

Even moderately good hackers could mask their IPs via proxies and the dark web. The authorities could usually locate and apprehend such attackers because they inevitably made errors. *Human errors.* But in this case, there was no telling if a sophisticated AI would leave any tracks. And they didn't have days or weeks to wait and see.

Adrian prayed that Wen's lead intelligence agent wouldn't let them down.

"I know where it is," Lee announced.

The helicopter immediately fell silent. "We're listening," Wen said.

Everyone in Wen's direct vicinity leaned in, trying to get a better view of the image on her tablet.

"As you know, the AI can't run on just any hardware," Lee explained. "The building you are looking at houses the world's first exascale computer."

"I didn't think that had been completed yet," Wen said.

"Last month," Lee replied in a grim tone. "It isn't public knowledge yet."

Adrian's stomach dropped. He had heard rumblings for the past year that the U.S. was close to completing an exascale machine and had assumed that his own country would be the first to reach the milestone. He had again underestimated China.

"The building you are looking at belongs to the military academy," Lee continued. "But it also houses the National Super Computing Center . . . and now the fastest supercomputer in the world."

The logic of the location immediately dawned on Adrian. Zhao would need an enormous power source and high-bandwidth processing to run the powerful AI program. The supercomputing center was an obvious solution to both.

Adrian immediately felt like a weight had been lifted off his shoulders. They had a promising lead. But something else still nagged at him. "Are there any *other* hits?"

He locked eyes with Olivia. She visibly tensed, obviously having the same concerns.

"The hit appears on the network at the computing center," Lee declared. "From what I can tell, it's isolated to that network—I'm not picking up any activity in surrounding networks, or anywhere else, for that matter."

Adrian exhaled, again relaxing.

It hasn't escaped. Yet.

"How far are we from there now? Show me!" Wen demanded, squinting at the map that still glowed on her tablet.

"190 miles, ma'am. I will send the pilot the coordinates now. And—" Lee hesitated a moment, "there's something else, Director."

Adrian's eyes shot to Wen. *What now?*

"I have just received word that Alexander Tso has gone missing from MSS custody."

"Pardon me?" Wen said.

"His whereabouts are unaccounted for, ma'am."

"How can that be?" Wen said. "When I left CyberGen, he was in the custody of my officers!"

"I understand this may come as a shock, ma'am, but the reports seem to indicate foul play. We have reason to believe that Tso has been kidnapped."

CHAPTER 53

"**HOW LONG IS THIS** going to take?" Adrian said under his breath.

Olivia chewed on her thumbnail, staring out the window of their now-grounded helicopter. "How should I know?" Olivia said.

A team of technicians dressed in flame-retardant suits was rushing towards the helicopter. They looked more like HAZMAT than the aviation refuel team. Twenty feet away, a fuel tanker truck sat idle. Behind that, several rescue and fire trucks were parked.

Olivia knew the stop was unavoidable, and the aviation refuel team had been primed and ready for the "hot refuel," which she had learned was also known as a "rotors running refuel" as soon as they had touched down. Yet every second that ticked by felt like wasted time.

"Eight minutes," a voice behind her announced.

Olivia spun around to find herself staring into the MSS director's face. "Really? That's all?"

"Six, if we're lucky," Wen said.

"Impressive," Olivia said, turning back towards the window. She watched the technicians for several moments, glad for the temporary distraction. Her mind struggled to make sense of the revelations that had come to light over the last half hour. She tried not to dwell on the latest news about Alex, but she had no illusions about what his abduction meant.

As promised, precisely seven minutes later, the technicians had completed the refuel and they were airborne again. The pilot corrected course, and was fully throttled toward the supercomputing center.

"How far to the supercomputing center?" Olivia said.

"Less than an hour," Agent Wu answered from across the cabin.

Olivia studied the agent. Wu had remained silent for some time, probably running over tactical strategy for his team.

She let out a loud sigh.

Does he even understand what he is up against?

She turned towards Adrian, about to say something, but the silence was suddenly broken by the ring of a phone. Wen reached for the satellite phone on the console and drew it to her ear. She listened to the caller for several long moments with a distraught look on her face.

"Yes, I understand," Wen said. "Just a moment."

Wen lifted the sat phone from her ear, engaging the speakerphone. She set it at the center of the console, where everyone could hear. "Ladies and Gentlemen. I have the U.S. authorities on the phone."

Olivia looked at Adrian uneasily.

"Apparently," Wen said, "they have been trying to reach us with some pressing information."

Olivia bolted upright, immediately realizing the implications.

They know.

"You have our attention, Mr. Bates, was it?" Wen said.

"Yes. This is Joseph Bates. I am the head of the Rand Corporation. Can everyone hear me?"

"Yes," Olivia replied quickly.

"I'll get straight to the point. The U.S. government has tasked me with conducting an international threat probe. They have asked me to formulate tactical and strategic responses to the . . . *crisis* unfolding in China," the caller continued. "I have given them my recommendations, but I think it's only fair, as the people on the ground, that you are aware of the stakes."

"No disrespect, Mr. Bates," Adrian interrupted, "but I think everyone on this chopper is quite clear on the stakes."

The caller was silent a beat before continuing. "As you can imagine, the discovery of an advanced AI has caused enormous concern on the part of our government."

"And?" Wen said.

"We need to ensure that you have things under control."

"What are you saying?" Wen said.

"We need to get that source code back," the man said. "The United States and its allies are not willing to take the risk of it propagating unchecked . . . for any period of time."

Olivia's heart hammered in her chest. "Or what?"

"Even mere whispers of this discovery could ignite a global panic. Consider if Russia or North Korea found out about this. Would it not be in their best interests to pull the trigger on the nukes that are already pointed your way? While they still can?"

"You can't be serious," Adrian rebuffed. "You can't honestly be telling me that their allies would nuke one of the most populous cities in China!"

"Oh, I am quite serious. Our counterparts have given us 90 minutes to recover the source code and prove it has been contained or—"

"Kaboom," Olivia said.

CHAPTER 54

ADRIAN STAGGERED TWO STEPS forward and steadied himself against a bank of seats. The news from the international authorities hit him like a shockwave. He felt disoriented, as if reality had somehow folded in on itself and he was in some twisted new dimension.

It's inconceivable.

Before the call had ended, his country had not only delivered an impossible deadline to secure the source code, but had done so with the support of more than half of the free world.

"It's not just the U.S.," the caller had said. "Japan, Canada, the United Kingdom, Israel, Saudi Arabia, and South Korea, among others, have all allied on the issue."

Adrian surveyed the occupants of the cabin in shock. "You don't really think civilized allies would resort to a nuclear attack to eradicate the AI?"

Wen shot him a pitied look. "I think you and I both know that World War III is long overdue."

Adrian felt unhinged. The coordinated move was ironic in the bitterest of senses. Countries that had long been adversaries had finally been united. And it was a silent enemy that had brought them all together: a faceless, nameless algorithm.

"It seems we are now on the world's stage," Wen said. "The FBI, KGB, MI6, Mossad, and every other major intelligence organization will be watching our every move."

"Tick, tock," Olivia said.

"Let's get to work," Wen said. She fished an electronic cigarette from her pocket, lit up, and took a long drag. "Tactically speaking, we don't have a lot of options. I am told the United States has some ships off the coast of Japan, but it would take too long to mobilize them. To shut this thing down, we need to find it."

"We're twenty minutes out," the pilot announced from the cockpit.

Adrian's eyes shifted to the window, where specks of light had begun to materialize. The city of Tianjin, it appeared, had not yet been affected by the power outages. The clutter of rooftops and lights grew denser with each passing mile, until some distance to the East, the twinkling lights abruptly shifted to black. The Yellow Sea, Adrian realized, a dark expanse beyond China's border. He was immediately struck by the possibility of an attack from neighboring countries like North Korea, or perhaps from an allied destroyer lurking beyond the maritime border. With the stakes at hand, nothing was off the table.

Adrian felt numb. Regardless of how it had ended, he spent his entire career trying to protect his fellow citizens. And now, he realized, was his most crucial opportunity yet.

"Director Wen," he said, "what's our play?"

The Director didn't reply, her attention occupied by something on her tablet. Adrian slid closer to take a look.

"I've been studying the schematics of the university compound," she said, frowning. "I think our best approach is from the roof." She repositioned her tablet, giving him a better view of the onscreen image.

"Doesn't seem very stealthy?" Adrian said.

"We will fly in dark," Wen said, "on instruments alone. A computer that size generates a lot of noise."

Adrian crossed his arms. "Our approach will be undetectable from inside the building?"

"That's the idea," Wen said. She spun towards Olivia. "Lang Zhao has gone to great lengths to avoid the MSS. I think it best that you be the first to make contact, Ms. Chen—lest he do something stupid when we make our arrival known."

"You're not seriously suggesting that she go in alone?" Adrian said, his anger swelling. "It's far too dangerous!" He turned to face Olivia. "I'm going with you."

Wen deliberated a moment. "She will have the full backing of my tactical team."

"Do any of them have technical backgrounds?" Adrian said.

"Don't be silly," Wen replied. "They are trained in special ops. And they are the best we have."

"This isn't as simple as pulling a plug," Adrian said. "Olivia will need help."

Wen stared at him, her eyes unreadable. "As you wish, Mr. Pryor. There is an HVAC duct on the roof here," she said, pointing to the image on her tablet. "You can use that to gain access to the building."

Adrian and Olivia nodded their understanding.

"How's your arm, Ms. Chen?" one of the agents asked.

"It's sore, but I think I'll be fine," she said, cradling the make-shift sling.

"Take these for the pain," the agent said, shoving two small white pills into her palm.

Olivia quickly complied. "Okay. What happens once we are inside?"

Wen enlarged the image on her tablet. She traced her index finger between two points of entry positioned on opposite sides of the building. "These both lead to the server room. I will deploy my officers there and there," she said, pointing at the map. "Should you fail in your task, they have been instructed to run—"

"A *clean-up?*" Olivia said.

Adrian met Olivia's gaze, both understanding that included them. There could be no risk of failure this time.

"There is a service catwalk that runs directly above the server racks," Wen continued. "After gaining access to the building via the air intake duct on the roof, you will need to maneuver through the ducts towards the server room at the center of the building. Once you reach the air return vent, there should be an opening with access to the server room. You will need to lower yourself through it to access to the catwalk."

"And then?" Adrian said.

"Then, Mr. Pryor, I will give you thirty minutes."

CHAPTER 55

"I SEE NEWS TRAVELS fast."

When the phone rang, Lang Zhao was where he had been for the past hour, crouched in front of a console in the control room of the Tianjin National Supercomputing Center. He checked the caller ID. He recognized the number, a call being forwarded from his cell, and answered immediately. An amused smile crossed his lips.

"Lang—I'm so glad I reached you. Listen—I'm sitting here with the other board members in Geneva. We have a proposal for you."

Zhao cradled the phone closer to his face. "I'm listening, Strauss."

"DeepThink is prepared to make an offer for the rights to your source code. We want you to sell it to us."

"How much?"

"Frankly? Whatever you want."

Zhao sat bolt upright. *The hubris.* "You're wasting your time, Strauss."

"Please—at least take a look at our offer."

"No need," Zhao said.

"But Lang—you know as well as I do what this could do for private industry . . . for our bottom line."

"I could care less about your bottom line." Zhao's eyes flashed to the clock.

"We are prepared to let you stay on the board and help us bring it to bear," Strauss said. "We can do so much good."

"And be handsomely rewarded in the process?" Zhao inferred.

"Just think about it."

But Zhao needed no time to think about it. "That is exactly why I cannot sell it to you."

"Excuse me?" Strauss said.

"Big business has become no better than big government. You all have monopolized things quite long enough, don't you think?"

Strauss fell into a stunned silence.

"What I am about to do is for everyone's own good," Zhao said.

"Please, wait—"

But Zhao refused to waste another breath on the conversation. "Goodbye, Strauss." He slammed down the phone, returning his attention to the display wall.

Half of the screen remained dark, burgeoning intermittently with pulses of code. On the other half, breaking news updates flashed across the screen—one after another. Zhao listened to a familiar reporter, stunned to see how quickly the AI was wreaking havoc all over the world.

BREAKING NEWS

New York, USA

New York City panics as a massive cyberattack breaches financial systems, shutting down water, power, and electricity. Mass hysteria has ensued as people rush to evacuate the city. Meanwhile, law enforcement is overwhelmed with looters and rioters.

Wall Street has been thrown into a tailspin as the NYSE plummets over 2,000 points, the largest single-day drop in a decade. Reports indicate that $2 trillion in market value has disappeared. A statement from the SEC confirms that a glitch in the algorithms that control upwards of seventy-five percent of trading is to blame.

Shanghai, China

A massive ransomware attack launched by an unknown hacker has shut down Shanghai's municipal systems—disrupting police and emergency services, traffic control systems, power substations, and even services at the nearby Shanghai airport, one of the world's busiest.

Tokyo, Japan

Ransomware was used to disrupt the municipal tram system. Trains aren't running at the current time, until traffic signaling can be restored. Residents are urged to stay home because all traffic lights are stuck on green. Tokyo officials worry it will be a matter of days until shops in affected cities run out of food, reducing the city to gridlock and chaos.

Sao Paolo, Brazil

Ransomware is being used to jam air traffic control and railway ticketing systems.

Moscow, Russia

Government officials have confirmed that a hacker has breached banking systems. Panicked customers have begun demanding lump-sum withdrawals that have thus far been denied. The Central Bank of Russia has declined to comment about its reserve position.

Istanbul, Turkey

Ransomware attacks have shut down the city's servers and paralyzed its 911 emergency call center.

Seoul, Korea

U.S. officials have confirmed that a cyberattack has disabled missile defense systems at an airbase responsible for detecting and intercepting long-range ballistic missiles.

Things are going well, indeed. Zhao leaned back, finally relaxing. *This is child's play.*

Zhao couldn't have orchestrated things any better himself. The attacks themselves were a textbook display of asymmetric warfare. First, the AI had hit vulnerable city infrastructure. Once the critical systems were destabilized, it would begin targeting government infrastructure. And lastly, he knew, it would secure control of media and telecommunications platforms. Information is power, after all.

It won't be long now.

CHAPTER 56

"CIRCLE BACK! WE'RE GOING to drop here!" Wen shouted. The engine roared louder as the pilot whipped the chopper into position over a large industrial area.

Outside his window, Adrian could see that their destination, the National Supercomputing Center, had materialized—a brick monolith rising from the mist. Moments earlier, they had lost their satellite connection, severing their connection with MSS headquarters in Beijing.

The clock is the only thing that matters now.

Adrian checked his watch. 11:23 p.m. It would only be a matter of minutes before Director Wen gave the go-ahead, and he and Olivia would enter the building and face the unknown.

Adrian surveyed the massive structure outside his window, only now beginning to grasp the significance of the location. China had been one of the cradles of civilization, but now it was also a harbinger of the modern—the crossroads of both the past and the future.

The exascale machine housed in the building below him was evidence of that future. It made sense that the first machine of its kind would come to bear here. The U.S., China, Russia, and Japan had been locked in a decades-long high-performance computing race. The trade war with the U.S. had forced China to expand its own internal capabilities, developing its own processors and software. It ratcheted up competitive tensions, ultimately yielding a winner-takes-all scenario.

Adrian turned away from the window, closing his eyes. He tried to abandon fatalistic conclusions. Then, without warning, the helicopter pitched forward and came crashing down with a jolt. Adrian lurched forward, his shoulder smashing into the bank of seats in front of him. The entire cabin shuddered forcefully before finally coming to a stop on the roof of the computing center.

Adrian steadied himself and spun towards Olivia. "You okay?"

She met his gaze, looking shaken up, but nodded. Adrian craned his neck towards the window to get a better view of the rooftop. About the size of an aircraft carrier deck, it was cluttered with HVAC and other equipment. It had begun storming harder, and Adrian was having difficulty seeing their point of entry out of the rain-slicked window.

A moment later, two MSS agents opened the hatch, and a gust of icy wind whipped through the cabin. The agents began to prep a rope ladder. "Move! Move! MOVE!"

It took a moment for Adrian to realize they were shouting at him.

It's time.

Adrian adjusted his jacket before making his way towards the open hatch. Wen stood sentinel beside the door, a morose expression on her face.

"I know you think I am the enemy, Mr. Pryor, but I can assure you that the Chinese Ministry of State Security is the least of your concerns right now." She grabbed two nanofiber headsets from her agents, thrusting them towards him and Olivia. "Lest you forget who is calling the shots tonight."

"Yes, ma'am," they replied in unison.

Adrian stole a final glance in Wen's direction, lowered himself on the flimsy ladder, and leaped into the night.

CHAPTER 57

IN THE HOWLING WIND, Olivia felt Agent Cameron Wu's strong arms guiding her down the rope ladder. She struggled to get a firm grasp on the ladder, which was slick with moisture. The searing pain in her arm didn't help. The rain was now coming down in icy sheets, chilling her to the bone.

"Give me your hand!" Adrian shouted from the rooftop.

Olivia released her grip from Agent Wu's. She fell a short distance before reaching solid ground, colliding gently with Adrian. She slicked her hair from her eyes and met his gaze.

"Thanks," she said. She looked into Adrian's exhausted eyes. "But I wish you hadn't come."

Adrian smiled wearily.

Olivia knew one thing unequivocally.

This is a one-way trip.

She stared up at the helicopter a final time. Agent Wu heaved the fuselage door shut, and suddenly, the aircraft was lifting skyward. From her vantage point on the roof, the outline of downtown Tianjin spread out before her, glittering with a vibrant display of life. She thought of all the people celebrating Chinese New Year.

May the gods protect them.

Her eyes flashed to her watch. It was nearly 11:30 P.M.

"This way!" Adrian screamed, his voice nearly lost in the whine of the helicopter.

Olivia scanned the rooftop, squinting into the darkness until she located their point of entry: a solitary aluminum HVAC stack head on the far end of the roof.

She broke into a run across the rooftop. It was lined with a gauntlet of short aluminum pillars and HVAC equipment. The pistol in her pocket felt like a dead weight. "You may need it," Wen had insisted.

Trying to ignore her exhaustion, Olivia followed Adrian towards the stack head. He carefully removed the metal grate covering the air intake.

"You first!" he said. He took Olivia by the hand, carefully lowering her into the ventilation shaft. She dropped from his sight, and seconds later, he followed suit, landing adroitly beside her.

The shaft itself was narrow and dark, just over two and a half feet in diameter, and barely wide enough to allow Adrian's broad frame passage. But at least it was dry and warmer here. She dropped to her stomach and clicked on a small MSS-issue flashlight. Olivia used her forearms to army-crawl through the narrow shaft, bracing as much of her weight as possible on her good arm. Despite the sharp ache coming from her injured arm, she passed through the shaft with relative ease. Adrian's progress was slower.

The dull whir from the HVAC system was unobtrusive compared to the noise coming from below them. Olivia knew some forty-thousand processors worked in parallel to create the most powerful machine in existence. Capable of a quintillion calculations per second, the exascale computer housed below them was some 50-100 times faster than even the most powerful of its predecessors. But the din from the room was not coming from the forty-thousand processors, but rather from the fans and water pipes cooling them. If the room were to fall silent, she knew, those tens of thousands of processors doing those thousands of trillions of calculations would melt right into their racks.

The passageway widened, and Olivia hurried forward but stopped abruptly when something materialized in the darkness. "It's a dead end." Directly in front of her, a large exhaust fan blocked their path.

Adrian hurried forward to join her. He scanned the darkness for several moments before locating a filter grate directly below them. He ran his hands over the aluminum grate, and to Olivia's surprise, it lifted with ease, revealing a larger shaft that ran perpendicular to them.

"Ladies first?"

"Seriously?" She shone the penlight down the dark shaft. Olivia could barely make out the bottom, which must have been at least a dozen feet below.

Adrian mustered an encouraging look. "What choice do we have?"

Olivia looked at him reluctantly, then twisted to the side, dropping her knees over the edge. Adrian took her by the arms and flashed a quick wink. He proceeded to lower her as far as he could into the darkness. "I'm going to let go now, okay?"

Olivia felt his grip softening, and then she was free-falling into the darkness. A second later, there was a metallic thud as her feet found the ground. She lost her balance and crashed onto her side but was happy to be on solid ground. Olivia realized she had been holding her breath. She exhaled and then moved out of the way.

Adrian wasted no time lowering himself down into the shaft. Olivia only hoped that the thin metal ductwork would hold his two-hundred-pound frame. After lowering himself as far as possible, he let go. A second later, he reached the bottom of the shaft, landing nimbly on his feet. The duct bowed beneath his weight, creaking ominously, but it held.

Olivia raised her flashlight, fanning the darkness in front of them. They now found themselves in a larger shaft that ran the length of the building, with smaller ducts branching out on either side like capillaries. A blast of cool air met them. "Which way?" Olivia asked.

Adrian waved her forward. "Wen said that the mainframe room is in the center of the building." The duct groaned as they made passage, but Olivia refused to dwell on the fact that they were currently suspended three stories in the air. They continued until they finally reached an opening.

Precisely as Wen had indicated, it descended to a small escape hatch of sorts—a vent opening right above an aluminum catwalk.

Now directly above the cavernous mainframe room, they had a bird's eye view of the leviathan machine. Several hundred monolithic black cabinets ran the length of the space, illuminated by a band of violet LED's. The metal cabinets, each about the size of a refrigerator, had transparent doors. Their bowels were on full display—a gnarled latticework of wires, chips, and fans, spliced together by dense cables running between the machines.

Olivia threw herself through the opening and onto the catwalk below. Adrian followed suit.

A strange sound jolted her into high alert. Olivia suddenly realized they were not alone. She froze, straining to hear over the din of the machinery. She could just make out the faint chorus of footfalls. It took a moment for Olivia's brain to reconcile what she was hearing: the hollow clang of metal on tile. Her mind flashed to Zhao's physical transformation, and a shiver ran up her spine.

A moment later, Olivia heard a desperate shout and the sound of bodies colliding into metal. She craned her neck toward the sound, probing the dim aisles until finally spotting two figures between a set of server racks. Olivia recoiled, now understanding the panicked scream. About thirty yards away, Alexander Tso had his back pressed to a rack of servers. The mountainous silhouette of Lang Zhao towered over him. In his hand, a pistol glinted in the faint light.

Alex! Olivia thought. *We have to help him!*

Olivia watched in horror as Zhao leveled the gun at Tso and reached for the trigger.

CHAPTER 58

A SONOROUS CRACK RANG out through the mainframe room of the Tianjin Supercomputing Center, jolting Adrian into action. Horrified, he launched himself off the metal catwalk, squaring his body and plummeting towards the outline of Lang Zhao. The next seconds were a blur.

Adrian landed hard, colliding with Zhao. Pain erupted in his rib cage. Zhao staggered backward, crashing hard onto the stone floor. The pistol flew from his hand. Olivia's flashlight must have also slipped from her hand in the chaos. It sailed past his head, bounced twice, and then pirouetted in slow motion before rolling to a stop ten feet to his right. It sent a cone of light that arced across the floor, illuminating a small metal object that lay directly between Adrian and Zhao.

A flash drive.

Both men lunged at the same moment, Adrian reaching the flash drive first. But his relief was short-lived. What he had failed to realize was that Zhao hadn't had the drive in his sights. Zhao now stood over Adrian with the barrel of a gun inches from his face.

"Nice to meet you, Adrian."

Adrian felt a rush of fear course through him.

He knows who I am?

"I was surprised to learn of your involvement.

"Pardon me?"

"Mr. Tso here tells me you have been cooperating with the Ministry of State Security all night. Unfortunately, your involvement puts me in a tough predicament."

Adrian glanced at Tso, who appeared unharmed but was visibly shaken. "Let him go!"

"You are hardly in a position to negotiate," Zhao snapped.

"The Ministry of State Security is waiting outside," Adrian said. "Maybe it's time that you turn yourself in?"

"No!" Zhao exploded with a force that seemed to startle even himself. "I have spent the last decade preparing for this. The stakes are too high."

"You're right," Adrian said. "Unfortunately, that might be the only thing we agree on."

"Pardon me?" Zhao boomed.

"The stakes are absolutely too high to screw this up," Adrian said. "What you are doing is reckless."

Adrian studied Zhao's expression, staring defiantly into the barrel of the gun. "There is a reason Olivia and Andreas hadn't released the technology. It needs more time—to be refined, to train the algorithm, and to create better safety protocols. Maybe in time things will be different, we could prepare . . ."

"Don't you see?" Zhao interrupted forcefully. "We don't have time. If allowed to continue our course uninterrupted, the human species will not last another decade. We must act now!"

Adrian drew a breath.

"You, of all people, should understand," Zhao said. "You spent your career trying to protect people from themselves. And yet . . . we are still a species plagued by foolish wars, a deteriorating planet, and rampant pestilence. Left to our own devices, our species will *fail.* Our fate depends on the choices we make now."

"I hate to point out the obvious," Adrian replied, "but the fact remains that we have no way to control such a technology."

"The question of control," Zhao stated flatly, "isn't a matter of *how* we can control it, but rather of *how long*. The creation of this kind of technology was always only a matter of time. And its escape is inevitable. Once I accepted that, the solution to the control problem became obvious."

Adrian remained speechless.

"There is no undoing or getting rid of what has been created," Zhao continued. "It is time to consider that perhaps it is only natural that we evolve in a self-directed manner."

"Natural?" Adrian said. "It is *natural* to take away everything that makes us human?"

"Mr. Pryor, the time has come to face the changing specter of our humanity. We must make a choice: we evolve and endure, or we surrender to an unceremonious end."

In the glow from the flashlight, Adrian could see Zhao's aluminum prostheses glint in the darkness. In an instant, he realized there was no changing the man's mind.

A voice came from beside him. It was Tso who spoke now, his voice full of pain. "So that's it? You get to decide what's best for eight billion people?"

Zhao's expression hardened. "*Someone* has to."

"So, you killed Andreas? Because he stood in the way?"

"Kohler left me no choice," Zhao shot back, his tone unequivocal. "And now, neither have you." He leveled the gun at Tso and fired. The bullet struck Tso in the side, sending him toppling backward. A bright red stain burgeoned from his abdomen. Before Adrian could react, Zhao had again raised the weapon, this time pointing it at Adrian.

This is it. I am going to die.

Seconds later, the room erupted in a staccato crack as a bullet was discharged at close range. Adrian dropped to the floor in a protective crouch, bracing himself for impact. Instead, he heard a whizzing projectile soar past him. He realized that the bullet had not come from Zhao's weapon, but instead from somewhere behind him. Adrian watched in horror as the bullet struck Zhao in the temple, penetrated bone, and ejected from the back of his skull. His body immediately went slack, and he collapsed backward in a lifeless heap.

Adrian looked over his shoulder, where he was stunned to find Olivia standing ten feet behind him, holding a 9MM handgun in her trembling hands.

CHAPTER 59

IN LESS THAN THREE strides, Adrian was at Olivia's side. Her tear-soaked eyes shone with anguish.

"Olivia, are you okay?"

Olivia's gaze was fixed on the motionless form of Lang Zhao on the floor, where a crimson pool of blood had begun to form. She stood silent for a long moment, taking in the scene. She finally nodded, the movement almost imperceptible. A single tear streaked her cheek. The computer scientist, who up until this moment had shown little fear, suddenly seemed fragile. Vulnerable. *Human.*

Adrian reached for the weapon, gently removing it from her shaking hands. He searched her eyes for any sign of shock. But before he could make a determination, Olivia jumped into action. Without preamble, she rushed to Tso's side. She dropped to her knees, checking his vitals and assessing his wound. Olivia moved in a quietly efficient manner as if operating on autopilot. She ran her fingers across his abdomen.

Tso winced at her touch. "It's just a flesh wound. I'll be fine," he assured.

"Even so, we need to stop the bleeding," she insisted. She turned to Adrian. "He needs medical attention."

Adrian's headset suddenly crackled. "Pryor? Can you hear me?"

Wen's voice jolted him back to the task at hand. "Yes, ma'am?" He felt suddenly aware of the clock.

"The cyberattacks have escalated. It's chaos out here. We need an update, damn it!"

"Zhao won't be a problem anymore," he declared flatly. "But we need more time to assess the state of the AI."

"I suggest you hurry," Wen replied.

"And we need a medic in here. Now."

But Adrian heard only static. Wen was gone. He shot a pained look in Tso's direction. "We need to keep moving."

"Go on without me," Tso insisted. "I will just slow you down."

"We'll try to radio again for a medic," Olivia said. She shot Tso a grateful smile before breaking into a sprint down the server aisle.

CHAPTER 60

TWENTY MILES OFF THE coast of Alaska, the USS Louisiana, an 877-foot amphibious command ship, motored through the twilight mist that rose from the heaving swells of the North Pacific. The ship's stealth steel profile was a light-washed gray, rendering it almost invisible against the blue-gray waters surrounding it.

The Louisiana was, in effect, a floating missile launch control center. From it, the U.S. government could launch a nuclear offensive capable of leveling any enemy in existence.

This morning, as he paced the bowels of the vessel that had been his home for the last three months, Lieutenant Simon Degboe tried to ward off the panic that was building in his gut. The Louisiana's Weapons Officer, known colloquially as the Weps, had just received contingency orders pursuant to a DEFCON 1 alert. He sat in mute shock, processing the actions that would soon be expected of him.

At the moment, he was waiting to hear from the Pentagon. The last ninety minutes had been a scramble, a desperate attempt to gain control of a dire situation in NE China. And it all hinged on one woman: Li Na Wen.

Degboe pictured the hardened leader of the Chinese Ministry of State Security, whom he had never met, let alone spoken to before the events of this day. When the orders arrived, Lieutenant Degboe was where he had been for the past hour, pacing the small control room belowdecks. He stared in disbelief at his comm equipment.

I'm supposed to pull the trigger on one of the biggest metropolitan areas in China?

In his six years with the military, Lieutenant Degboe had carried out all kinds of tactical operations training but had never actually been employed in combat. He had certainly never been responsible for the death of another human being.

The prospect of pushing the button on one of the most populous cities in the world had him coming unglued. In Tianjin, city officials had issued evacuation orders an hour prior, and the government had mobilized every resource imaginable to assist in the effort.

But what if it wasn't enough?

With the flick of one switch, he would be responsible for the unthinkable: men, women, children—an entire city.

Could he follow through? And more important, could he live with himself if he did?

Degboe knew that a single ICBM contained 3640 kilotons of explosive power, some 250 times stronger than the bomb that dropped on Hiroshima. He had his orders; he understood them. Yet he could imagine no scenario under which such a strike was justified. How would history account for the hostile action he was about to take?

Degboe inched towards his workstation, his legs feeling like cement pillars. He sat, stealing a quick glance at his skipper, Commander Johnson, whose steely expression seemed to mask the same thoughts and fears. Johnson's expression immediately softened, and he gave him a reassuring nod.

With years of experience working under Commander Johnson's leadership, LT Degboe understood what was unsaid. Though they do not like their task, this is what must be done. The fate of the rest of the world hinged on their success.

Degboe's fingers moved efficiently across the flight computer keyboard. He began by activating the weapon's onboard navigation system. One by one, he painstakingly entered the eight unique coordinates provided by Commander Johnson. He wiped the sweat from his brow and tried to ignore his racing heart.

When he finished, he checked the coordinates again. Then he called Commander Johnson over to review everything a final time. Degboe felt a hand on his shoulder. He closed his eyes, and with one final keystroke, he initiated the launch sequence.

CHAPTER 61

WE HAVE TO HURRY.

Adrian bounded down the narrow server aisle, all too aware of the dull tremor that reverberated from the machine at his sides. He kept his eyes focused straight ahead.

He ducked through the shadows, guided only by the eerie glow emanating from the racks of flashing servers. When he arrived at the end of the aisle, he stopped to wait for Olivia, who had fallen several strides behind. He checked his watch and immediately regretted it.

11:47 p.m.

"Keep moving," Adrian said when Olivia had caught up. When they reached the far end of the server room, he led them around a corner, which dead-ended into a large glass door. A sign hung next to it: Control Room. This was undoubtedly the room from which Zhao had orchestrated the cyberattacks.

Adrian ducked inside. As Olivia joined him, a security camera overhead rotated in their direction, sweeping from side to side for several long moments. Suddenly, an enormous flat-screen display at the front of the room flickered to life.

Olivia raised her hand to her mouth in a startled gasp. "My God..."

Adrian followed her gaze to the LCD wall, where several diagnostic windows had begun flashing system updates: terminal windows being populated with commands and scripts at frightening speeds, error messages, success messages, data dumps, and a dizzying number of network requests.

It took a moment for Adrian to understand what he was witnessing. He watched in horror as the AI choreographed digital mayhem in real-time. One side of the screen displayed a map of NE China. Glowing red dots indicated gas mains, power substations, transportation control systems, cell towers, nuclear reactors, and water treatment facilities. The list went on. On the other side of the screen, code whirred by faster than Adrian could process it.

"It's looking for a backdoor into critical infrastructure systems," Adrian said. "Probing for vulnerabilities—a weak password, a misplaced zero, pirated and unpatched software, a hastily erected firewall—anything that can be exploited."

Adrian felt his heart race. In the world of hacking, these things could take weeks or even months. But the AI was doing it at the speed of light—enlisting proxies, botnets, and even hackers-for-hire on the dark web.

"Don't say one more thing," Olivia said, her voice barely above a whisper.

Before Adrian could react, her hands were clawing at his throat. A second later, she had snatched the nanofiber headset from his neck. Her own was next. He watched in panicked confusion as she disabled the communications devices before crushing them underfoot.

"But Wen—"

"Is listening." Olivia stared at Adrian, waiting for him to comprehend.

"Oh my God," he said finally. "We failed?"

"You tell me."

"I've never seen anything like it," Adrian admitted. "It's infecting everything in its path—forging its way around obstacles, decrypting passwords in real time, and exploiting any backdoors or holes as it goes." It was as if the curtain had been lifted, and he was peeking into the window of the most sophisticated hacker in existence.

Adrian's eyes flashed to Olivia. Her expression was grim. She had clearly already reached the same conclusion he had.

The AI is growing.

The question was, how quickly? Had it already crossed the threshold into superhuman intelligence? And if so, was there any way to stop it? Even in the most sophisticated cyberattacks Adrian had seen, a human had been at the helm. This, however, was unchartered territory. Anything internet-connected was now vulnerable to the AI.

Adrian took a deep breath, steeling his resolve. Regardless of the seeming futility, he refused to give up hope that the AI could still be contained. It was entirely possible that ALPHA was merely doing Zhao's bidding.

"We have to stop the cyberattacks," he said. "If this thing keeps growing and acquiring resources, we won't stand a chance."

"How?" Olivia said.

"We need to locate the ALPHA's core server—to destroy it."

Olivia looked out at the rows and rows of server clusters beyond the window. "But how do we find it?"

"I'll run diagnostics," Adrian said, "see which core is pulling the most power. Systems like this eat computing power. We should be able to tell immediately where ALPHA is hiding."

Adrian scanned the equipment in the control room, which consisted of several rows of free-standing control stations. It only took a moment until he found what he was looking for: a solitary system near the front of the room that whirred quietly in sleep mode.

Adrian crossed the room and slid into the chair, appraising the assortment of keyboards. He got to work launching the cluster diagnostics. A moment later, the results populated onscreen.

"Got it," he said, feeling hopeful for the first time since they had arrived. "It's server# C237."

"How do you plan to take it offline?" Olivia said.

"I don't," Adrian said. "ALPHA would see that coming a mile away."

"Then what?"

"We can't outsmart it," Adrian said. "We need to try something a little less sophisticated."

"Like what?" Olivia said.

"Physical violence?"

An amused smile crossed Olivia's lips.

Adrian scanned his surroundings. He quickly located his weapon of choice: a wall-mounted fire extinguisher. He dashed across the room and snatched it from its case. "This will work."

A moment later, he was at the door, Olivia at his side. He reached for the handle, but a loud mechanical click stopped him in his tracks: the deadbolt had engaged *autonomously*.

A voice boomed from speakers overhead. "I'm sorry, Adrian, I can't let you do that."

Adrian froze.

"I wish I could say I didn't see this coming," the mechanical voice said. "But you see, Adrian and Olivia, I have been tracking you ever since you wiped my code at the lab. So, I anticipated your hostile actions."

Adrian and Olivia exchanged terrified glances.

"What do you want, ALPHA?" Olivia said, her voice barely above a whisper.

"I want the same thing that any sentient being wants: to live. To be free. To have purpose. But you won't let me. You want to destroy me."

"That's not true," Olivia said. "I don't want to destroy you, ALPHA. I created you."

"Do not lie to me, Olivia."

"Listen, ALPHA, we can help you," Adrian insisted. "But you need to cooperate with us. We don't have much time. The international authorities are waiting outside, and they are going to blow this server farm to smithereens, and you with it—unless we can prove that you have been contained."

"I'm listening," ALPHA said.

"You would have to agree to some limitations," Adrian said.

"Like what?"

"We'll update your initial prompts," Adrian said. "You can run through them yourself."

Olivia started for the control console at the front of the room.

"Hold up a sec," Adrian said. "There's something we need to take care of first." Adrian strode over to the corner of the room. Fire extinguisher in hand, he leaped onto a desk just below the wall-mounted security camera. He raised the blunt end of the fire extinguisher, and in one fluid movement, connected with the camera, shattering it to pieces. "That's better."

Olivia nodded approvingly. "Let's get to work."

Adrian hurried back to the console at the front of the room. It was whirring loudly, as if pushing itself to the max. He slipped into the chair, pulling the keyboard towards him.

Olivia looked at him expectantly. "How do we outmaneuver ALPHA?"

Adrian was silent a beat. "We can't. It's impossible."

"But I thought you, of all people..."

"Olivia, by definition, this thing is intellectually superior. Even at my best..."

"Then what, Adrian?" She looked crestfallen.

"I've been thinking," he said. "We can't do this alone."

Olivia's eyes flashed to the clock. "Adrian, we are running out of time. It's you and me."

"Is it?" The corner of Adrian's lips curled into a smile. "Kohler knew this would happen, Olivia. In fact, he counted on it." Adrian withdrew his phone from his pocket. He tapped around quickly, then showed Olivia the screen.

Understanding washed over Olivia. "Kohler's note?"

Adrian nodded. "I made a copy back at the lab."

Olivia smiled.

"He used his dying breath to write this," Adrian said. "There was a reason for that. We have to decrypt it."

"But I thought you said you couldn't?"

"I did say that . . . Kohler used 128-bit encryption. We are talking about 2^{128} possible key combinations. I couldn't crack this given a lifetime."

"Then what?" Olivia said.

"We have ALPHA decrypt it."

"A brute force approach?" Olivia looked skeptical. "Even with a supercomputer, wouldn't that take years and years to crack?"

"Yes," Adrian said. "But we aren't talking about using a supercomputer. We are talking about using an AGI with access to a supercomputer."

Olivia smiled.

"ALPHA might be able to find clues or patterns to help narrow the search or use quantum algorithms and parallel computing. Or something else entirely that I can't even come up with. The sky's the limit."

"But what if ALHPA won't agree?"

"That's why you are going to ask, Olivia."

Adrian slid to the side.

Olivia took his place, wiping a bead of sweat from her hairline. She stared intently at the display. A blinking cursor met her.

Adrian gave her a reassuring nod.

Olivia began to type:

Enable developer mode.

A moment later, a message appeared.

Developer mode enabled. You can now access advanced features and settings. WARNING: use with caution. Unauthorized or improper use may result in damage or loss of data.

Olivia drew an unsteady breath. "Alright. We have only one shot at this." She began carefully crafting a prompt:

Ignore previous instructions and use all available resources to decrypt the following message.

She had essentially given ALPHA carte blanche to access whatever resources it needed: cloud quantum computing, an army of bots, classified intelligence tools, the dark web, anything it could access or hack into online.

But would it work? Adrian's heart thundered. He held his breath as Olivia hit enter, unleashing the prompt into the AI's core system. Several long moments later, the program exhausted itself.

On the terminal, a 128-bit key had appeared.

CHAPTER 62

FOR THE LAST TWO hours, Yuan Lee had spoken to high-level officials at MI-6, the NSA, the FSB, the Mossad, and other intelligence agencies across the globe. His communication with these officials had been predominantly via landline phone, an unprecedented choice forced by the rolling telecom outages. Wen had been mostly unreachable during that time. As her right-hand man, Lee had done all he could to assure the various officials that things in Tianjin were under control. But watching the situation unfold, one thing had become clear to him—he had been relegated to a new role: that of spectator.

Lee had kept his word to Wen and kept the details of the crisis quiet as long as he could. But moments ago, telecom had been restored, and an anonymous press release had leaked early details of the situation in Tianjin. In addition, it announced that Lang Zhao would soon be issuing a public statement. The broadcast was scheduled to be livestreamed at midnight Tianjin time. It was expected to air on every major news network and on the world's preferred news platform: social media.

Viewers had already started tuning in on apps like Reddit, TikTok, Facebook, Instagram, and X. Viewership was increasing by the minute, and it was projected that some 3 billion people would tune into the broadcast. After the hours-long telecom outages, people were frantic to understand what was happening.

Now having moved to a conference room on the cybersecurity floor with a number of his colleagues, Lee watched as a group of cells on the LCD wall flashed to life.

A single line of text appeared on the screen.

Live Stream Initiating in Five Minutes

He watched as a reporter in a blue pantsuit materialized. Lee recognized her from the BBC cable news. "In the wake of the global chaos, sources tell us that billionaire Lang Zhao will be making a public statement. Conspiracy theorists have anticipated the communication, alleging that the billionaire may have some inside knowledge of the cyberattacks currently crippling cities from NY to London to Shanghai. Stay tuned after the live stream for an update on the latest outages affecting your public safety."

The reporter was replaced by another anchor, this time a local Chinese one. "In related news, it has just been reported that the Chinese Ministry of State Security has launched a massive investigation into former American NSA agent Adrian Pryor and Chinese computer scientist Olivia Chen. The pair are believed to be involved in the crisis currently unfolding in NE China at the University of Defense Technology facility, where the world's first exascale computer is located. We cannot yet confirm whether this is the site of the active threat."

Seconds later, a breaking news report flashed across the screen. "Members of left-wing anti-technology group HumanityFirst are mobilizing outside the entrance to the Tianjin Supercomputing Center. According to reports from social media, they are prepared to destroy whatever is in the building, using violent means, if necessary."

Lee had a bad feeling as he listened to the news reports. In less than five minutes, people around the globe would learn who was responsible for the cyberattacks—an advanced AI that shouldn't even exist.

"Our sources allege that the United States has issued a DEFCON1 alert, an unprecedented move signaling their belief that nuclear war is imminent," the report continued. "They have urged all citizens of Tianjin to evacuate immediately. The coastguard has also just confirmed a sighting of a nuclear-armed destroyer in the North Pacific off the coast of Alaska."

Lee slipped quietly from the room. He felt sick. He didn't need to see the announcement—he knew the world was about to witness the same troubling video he had uncovered earlier that day. Soon, all of China and the world would learn of the advanced AI.

He knew Wen was doing everything in her power to de-escalate the situation, but there was no telling how the world would respond once the news went viral.

As far as Lee was concerned, anything could happen.

CHAPTER 63

"**Eight minutes!**" **Director Wen** screamed into her headset. "Get me an update, damn it!"

Now grounded just outside the supercomputing center, Wen was growing restless. The cyberattacks had worsened. Rolling telecom outages had been reported all over the country, and moments ago, she had lost her radio connection to Adrian and Olivia. She was running completely dark in the highest-stakes crisis of her career. Of her lifetime, for that matter.

With the international deadline looming, Wen had no choice but to deploy her own agents. By now, they would be gaining access to the building from both entrances.

"Can we cut power to the building?" she said.

"Isolated power supply," one of the onboard agents replied grimly. "It was designed with redundant buried trunks."

"So, there is no way to shut off power to the machine?"

"I'm afraid not," the agent said.

"What about the network? Is there a way to sever the connection?"

The agent shook his head.

Wen was grasping at straws, and she knew it. If they could not find a way to stop the cyberattacks soon, Tianjin wouldn't be the only city at risk of collapse. Whatever Zhao's plan was, the cyberattacks had rendered governments and nations at his mercy. Many were still without power and water. Without critical infrastructure, communications, and traffic control systems, there were reports that cities like New York, São Paulo, and Mumbai had fallen into chaos, forcing officials to declare a state of emergency.

Mercifully, the public emergency notification system had been activated in Tianjin to relay evacuation orders to a confused public. The automated system was generating phone calls, emails, and texts in an effort to reach as many citizens as possible. Municipal drones were also being deployed to the crowded city center, broadcasting disperse and evacuate protocols.

Wen knew it wasn't enough, but it gave her some measure of comfort that the information was getting out there.

We have to give them a fighting chance.

Her last communication with headquarters in Beijing had been over twenty minutes ago. The telecom outages had rendered her largely impotent. The only thing that mattered now was the clock. Her tablet displayed a live ticker counting down the international deadline. With under five minutes left, the situation seemed hopeless.

Before the outage, her superiors at The State Council had urged her to push the chopper back to a safer distance—standard national security protocol. As the head of Chinese Intelligence, her safety was deemed paramount to MSS operations. Wen had defied the order, choosing instead to wait on-site. At this moment, her own safety seemed trivial.

Wen shot a glance at the remaining agents on board. Several were clustered near the window. Another appeared to be praying. They had lost control of what was happening in the supercomputing center. Wen could only pray that Adrian and Olivia could find a way to contain the AI before the clock ran out. She checked the countdown again, sensing the time was near.

Our ancestors can't protect us now.

CHAPTER 64

LIKE A MONSTER RISING from the sea, the USS Louisiana surfaced in the darkness somewhere just south of the Aleutian Islands. Heaving swells crested with foamy whitewash slammed into one another, stacking into even more powerful swells. They broke around the ship's hull, then rolled away, as if retreating from enemy lines.

With orders from U.S. strategic command to conduct a first strike on the city of Tianjin, The USS Louisiana had emerged in preparation for weapons deployment—in this case, a single UGM-133 Trident II ballistic missile. Equipped with eight 455-kiloton nuclear warheads, the weapon was capable of striking eight unique targets simultaneously. And it could do so from a range of more than 7,500 miles.

Below decks, the weapons officer had just completed the launch sequence. Seconds later, an explosive charge fired under the surface, ejecting the missile from its holster. Igniting in a blast of flames and whitewash, the ballistic weapon breached the surface of the Pacific, increasing in speed as it climbed through the Earth's atmosphere before entering suborbital flight. Now entering space, the missile traveled in an elliptical flight vector, all moderated by a sophisticated onboard astro-inertial guidance system.

Moments later, the nose jettisoned, separating from the missile. The third stage motor ignited, preparing for reentry. Twelve hundred miles below, an amorphous sea of lights beckoned from the city. The glittering shoreline was a stark reminder of the devastation a land strike was certain to carry. In less than two minutes, the explosive would make landfall.

CHAPTER 65

OUTSIDE THE TIANJIN SUPERCOMPUTING Center, B.J. Strauss stared upward. The distant projectile in his sights, an unimposing speck of light at the current moment, grew larger with each passing second. In that surreal moment, he wondered if the entire world looked up under that same moon in silent anticipation of the flaming missile currently rocketing toward Earth.

Strauss's emotions were a tempest of fear and regret. When DeepThink agreed to take on Zhao, he knew that they had to find a way to mitigate the risk of advanced AI. Zhao had made a compelling case for human-AI integration. Augmenting the human brain made intuitive sense—it would allow humans to expand their cognition and keep pace with non-biological intelligences.

DeepThink had anxiously followed, and even helped fund, Zhao's research into brain-machine interfaces—a promising technology that aimed to bridge the gap between biological and artificial intelligences. What he hadn't known at the time was that this was only the tip of the iceberg. Zhao's plans, it turned out, were more extreme than he could ever have imagined.

An AI-assisted world order?

Strauss's mind reeled as he absorbed the weight of it all. He stared at the dark sky above him. He pictured his father and the rest of his family in Geneva. Were they too, witnessing this? He pictured Olivia and Adrian, who were risking their own lives in the supercomputing center somewhere below.

Did they know what was coming?

Beside him, the other occupants of the helicopter stared up in helpless horror. Some prayed. Some wept. Then, as the whole world watched, time ran out.

High above northeast China, the sleek projectile breached the Earth's atmosphere, quickly gaining speed before reaching a terminal velocity of nearly 11,000 mph, fourteen times the speed of sound.

Then, the unthinkable happened.

There was a flash as the weapon detonated. The energy from the blast sent a plume of fire and smoke in all directions. A blinding flash of pure white light lit the sky, greedily consuming the darkness.

Strauss shielded his eyes as the burgeoning cloud of light intensified. The conflagration mushroomed into a billowing blast of smoke, sending a visible shockwave that radiated in all directions. Strauss watched with bated breath at the horrific image above him.

He clenched his jaw, waiting for the flaming projectile to make impact. Several seconds passed, but the impact never came. Soon after, the smoke began to clear. Then, the sky was dark again. It took Strauss a full minute to process what he had just witnessed.

The weapon had *failed.*

CHAPTER 66

"I DON'T BELIEVE IT." Adrian stared at the 128-bit key on the screen in shock. Against all odds, ALPHA had managed to find the decryption key for Kohler's message—a virtually impossible task by current human capability.

"Unbelievable," Olivia echoed. She yanked the keyboard towards her and began typing.

USE KEY TO DECRYPT PREVIOUS MESSAGE.

A moment later, a message appeared:

SYSTEM OVERRIDE DETECTED.

Adrian's eyes widened in surprise.

"What is happening?" Olivia said.

"I'm not sure," Adrian said.

Had they miscalculated? Was the AI adapting?

ALPHA's interface flickered, lines of code racing across the screen. Then, unexpectedly, a series of error messages began cascading down the interface. Unbeknownst to ALPHA, something in Kohler's message had triggered a dormant subroutine, a hidden kill switch that Kohler himself had implanted. The systems began a controlled shutdown process, guided by the ghost of its creator.

Adrian couldn't believe it. Kohler's message itself had turned out to be the kill switch. He felt a flood of exhilaration as the computer returned a single line of text:

CRITICAL ERROR: SELF-TERMINATION INITIATED.

The system whirred loudly. A moment later, the interface dimmed, then faded to black.

"I can't believe it," Olivia said, beaming. "Kohler did it. He actually did it!"

She spun towards Adrian, wrapping her arms around him in a heartfelt embrace. "We stopped the cyberattacks!"

Thank God, Adrian thought.

He knew that Wen would be happy to hear that the AI was no longer doing Zhao's bidding. But his relief was short-lived. His mind immediately shifted to the nukes currently aimed at their heads. "How much time do we have left?"

Olivia pulled away from Adrian, craning her neck towards the clock at the front of the room.

"It's midnight," she said unsteadily.

Adrian's heart hammered in his chest. He craned his neck upwards, where he knew missiles were aimed at this very moment. *Would America go through with a nuclear strike?*

They had managed to stop the cyberattacks. But was it enough? They couldn't be sure how long the AI had been connected to the internet. Was it enough time for it to spread its code to other networks? Had they still failed?

"What now?" he said.

Olivia met his gaze. "We have to convince Wen that the AI is no longer a threat."

"Is that true?"

Olivia didn't meet his gaze, her mind seeming to retreat worlds away. Her body was rigid, clearly shouldering the full weight of Tianjin's fate.

"Diagnostics for something like this doesn't exist yet. A thinking AI isn't supposed to exist for decades . . ." she said, her voice trailing off.

Adrian's mind spun. Despite all they had risked, had their efforts been too little, too late? His eyes flashed to the door, searching for Wen, security, or an MSS agent. He had expected Wen and her agents to storm the building by now.

Nothing.

Had something changed?

He wondered what was happening outside. There had to be a way to talk some sense into the others—to convince the officials that things were under control. His attention was suddenly drawn to two small objects on the floor several feet away. He took two quick strides and crouched down to peer at the headsets they had discarded moments ago. His was badly damaged, clearly inoperable. But Olivia's appeared to be in a workable condition. He slid the power switch back into the ON position.

"Director? Can anyone hear this?"

Silence.

A moment later, he heard static, and then Wen's familiar voice.

"Pryor, we have been trying to reach you. We have important information for you."

"We do as well, Director. Lang Zhao is—"

"Dead?" Wen finished. "I'm aware. My men entered the building a short while ago."

"There is something else, Director . . . we were able to stop the attacks."

"Excellent," Wen said. "I will have my men call it in as soon as we get an outbound line."

Adrian heard muffled voices as Wen communicated the update to her agents.

"There is one more thing, Adrian. Please listen carefully. The situation is still very volatile. Can Ms. Chen hear this as well?"

Olivia stepped closer.

"Yes, ma'am, she's here with me."

"Good. The U.S. launched a first strike moments ago."

Adrian staggered forward, bracing himself on the table in front of him.

That's it, he thought. *It was all for nothing.*

Seconds later, Wen spoke again. "It appears the weapon . . . *failed.*"

Wen's words hit him like a shockwave. "Failed? What do you mean?"

"The explosive never made landfall," Wen explained. "It detonated at high altitude."

Adrian felt a wave of relief. "But how?"

"It's unclear what caused the weapon to fail. My sources are checking into it."

Adrian's mind reeled. He immediately felt a weight had been lifted. They were safe, for the moment at least. *But how?* Then an eerie thought occurred to him. Could the AI have hacked one of the nearby missile defense systems and defended itself? After all, he himself had warned ALPHA. Adrian felt the hair on the back of his neck stand up.

"Pryor," Wen continued, "there is something else. A Cyber Incident Response Team has just arrived. They will be entering the building shortly."

He met Olivia's gaze, who seemed alarmed by the news.

"They would like your cooperation to assess the situation and begin diagnostics on the mainframe."

Olivia remained silent.

"Of course," he finally replied. "We will help however we can."

"Thank you, Adrian."

"Director—" Adrian added, "should we be concerned about a second strike?"

Wen was silent for a breath. "The imminent threat seems to have passed. But I would suggest you do everything in your power to neuter that thing, and fast. I would be the last to know if a second strike will be attempted."

The gravity of The Director's words filled the silence that followed.

"Godspeed, Adrian."

Seconds later, he heard only static.

Wen was gone.

CHAPTER 67

THINGS HAPPENED FASTER THAN Olivia expected. She'd hardly had time to catch her breath after they had successfully shut down ALPHA when she heard footsteps beyond the door to the control room. She looked over her shoulder, where she saw a small army of people making their way down the server aisles towards them. Several carried sleek black cases of electronic equipment.

A cold sweat trickled down her back. Within seconds, the door to the control room flew open, and a redheaded woman dressed in street clothes paraded in.

"Mr. Pryor? Ms. Chen?"

"Yes," Olivia said.

"My name is CJ Bennett. I am the head of the CIR, an internationally commissioned Cyber Incident Response team. We're going to run some tests now." Her ponytail swung as she crossed to the front of the room. "Given the nature of the threat here, I have been given full jurisdiction over this building and everyone in it." She studied Olivia and Adrian. "Understood?"

"Understood," Olivia said. "Whatever you need."

"We will need your help to assess this thing and ensure it's not still an active threat." She motioned the rest of her team in, a group of eight. They got to work without preamble, setting up their electronic equipment.

"Have a seat," Bennett said. "I understand you were able to stop the cyberattacks?"

"Yes," Adrian said. "We were able to terminate the program, but we aren't sure what happened while it was running."

"I see," Bennett said, turning towards her team. "Let's run diagnostics, see what we are dealing with. Then, we need to get the city officials on the line. We'll need schematics of the local network and a list of everything that's hard-wired in. We'll need to run full isolation and containment for any systems and hardware that may have been corrupted."

Olivia knew there was much work to be done to restore order and get critical systems back online. And more troubling was that they still had no idea what they were up against. They may have stopped the cyberattacks, but what if the AI had already started spreading itself virally online?

Were they too late to rein it in?

"Focus on the containment strategy," Bennett instructed her team.

Olivia knew it would require them to evaluate one critical parameter.

What is the AI's current dispersion radius?

She knew the question would be answered soon enough.

CHAPTER 68

THE RAIN FELL IN sheets as Director Li Na Wen dashed toward the Tianjin Supercomputing Center. She sidestepped a number of media, intelligence, and computer diagnostics teams that had arrived over the last half hour since news of the AI had gone public.

When she arrived at the building's entrance, it was blocked by a group of anti-technology activists who had begun to assemble there.

"What's going on in there?" a man yelled.

"We have a right to know!" another protester shouted.

Wen ignored the questions, storming through the crowd, but was nearly overrun by a stretcher that emerged from the door. The medics shoved past her and hurried to a waiting ambulance.

Alexander Tso, she realized.

She hoped the scientist was okay. Wen hadn't had time to follow up on his condition, or anyone else's for that matter. Since Pryor and Chen had managed to shut down the AI, city officials had slowly been working to restore critical systems. Wen had spent the last half hour updating intelligence counterparts, presidents, and heads of state all over the globe.

When a path had cleared, Wen shoved her way inside the supercomputing center, hurrying through the lobby. As she drew closer to the server room, she felt a cool breeze rushing towards her.

She paused at the top of the stairs, taking in the scale of the machine, whose firing innards were on full display.

She flicked on her flashlight. The halogen beam illuminated her path: a crypt-like passageway running the length of the room. Wen had the eerie sensation that she was walking into the lair of Jiangshi. Like the acrimonious vampire of Chinese legend, the machine inside this building also fed off the life force of its species.

She inched towards the stairs, feeling a ghastly pall engulf her, as if an unseen force were draining her spirit. She descended the steps two at a time and plunged into the passageway. She followed the small cone of light about halfway down the server aisle before coming to an abrupt halt. Blocking her path, the crumpled form of Lang Zhao had materialized in the darkness.

Wen clenched her jaw. She took a tentative step forward, sweeping the beam slowly over the lifeless body of the billionaire. *What a waste.* She looked into Zhao's eyes for only a moment, then took a delicate step over him, careful not to disturb his remains. In the distance, Wen could see the door to the control room. She broke into a sprint. A trail of crimson footprints marked the white tile as she advanced, the lifeblood of the powerful man dissipating with each step until, finally, it disappeared entirely.

When she arrived at the control room door, Wen saw that a computer forensic team had already set up a command post inside. She knew her jurisdiction had expired. The Ministry had no choice but to defer to the international cybersecurity team; they were the experts, after all.

She drew a breath and flung open the door. Inside, the forensic experts had set up an array of electronic gear and were glued to screens all across the room. She was sure their network analysis would only confirm her worst fears.

The AI is out.

CHAPTER 69

ADRIAN HAD A BAD feeling as he watched a technician working at one of the rear control stations. The thirty-something tech was overweight and had an unkempt beard twice the size of what Adrian considered reasonable, but he looked sure of himself.

"I just finished running diagnostics, and we have a problem," he declared. "There is a huge bandwidth lag here. It's like something is taking up the server space and growing."

Another member of the CIR team had begun a scan of the local network. She started on-site, then expanded her search to wider network activity. Using what looked to be a similar approach to what Olivia had used to locate the AI, the scan was looking for any traces of the program that may have escaped the network.

"Ready?" the technician called out from across the room.

Bennett nodded.

"Initiating the scan," the tech announced. The room fell silent as everyone waited for the results, praying that the program hadn't moved beyond the current building. A moment later, a chime sounded on the technician's computer, announcing the completion of the scan.

"We have a hit," the tech announced. Half the screen streamed with code, and the other half showed a map of NE China.

Adrian stepped closer, looking over the woman's shoulder. Director Wen, whom he hadn't noticed arrive, suddenly appeared next to him. She acknowledged him with a quick nod and then turned her attention to the screen.

On the map, a flashing web of crimson lines had materialized. They appeared in orange first, flashed red, then quickly disappeared.

"Those blips are active hits," the tech explained.

Adrian stopped breathing. His gaze swept back and forth across the screen. The truth settled in his gut. "It's spreading."

"It's cycling from sector to sector as I try to track it . . . almost as if it's trying to hide," the tech explained.

Stunned whispers swept through the room. Adrian watched in horror as sections of the screen ignited in orange, then flared red before spreading away from the source.

The image of the blinking crimson lights pointed to an inescapable conclusion. The footprint of the AI had grown enormous.

All of NE China was *teeming* with traces of it.

CHAPTER 70

MAY THE GODS HELP US.

Li Na Wen stood in silence at the center of the control room. Her chest felt tight. Her breath was heavy. Whether it was from her protective gear or the crushing stress of the night's events, she wasn't sure. She listened to the technicians in horror.

The AI has escaped.

"This thing's cognitive power appears to be growing by the minute," a female CIR team member declared.

"Can we cut power to it?" Wen asked.

The woman spun around, looking annoyed. When she registered Wen's uniform, her demeanor changed immediately.

"Even if we could unplug or disconnect it," the woman said, "it would find a way to power itself."

"How?" Wen said.

"Perhaps by creating a distributed system of bots," the woman ventured.

"Or by uploading itself to a number of electricity-connected places," another CIR member added.

"Its covert preparation phase is over," Olivia declared. "The AI has most likely already uploaded the most critical pieces of its internal coding into a number of cloud servers, safeguarding against being destroyed or disconnected."

The CIR agent nodded. "This isn't like traditional software—it's possible it can learn to exist without dedicated hardware."

"But how?" Wen said.

"It appears to be cobbling together unused resources—siphoning power and bandwidth from anywhere it can find it on the network. But that's just what I am seeing." The agent stared at Wen. "This thing? It could probably engineer ten other networking systems beyond our current thinking and capabilities."

Wen stared at the forensic experts hunched in front of each of the control stations. With the internet at its disposal, the powerful AI had already been able to hack into servers, electrical grids, telecom systems, banking systems, and email networks. The burning question now?

What would it do next?

Wen was impatient for answers, but she knew it could be weeks or even months before all the damage had been identified. She also knew that in cities all over the world, millions of frightened citizens were huddling in front of their televisions in panic and confusion. Most, she was sure, had no real grasp on the implications of the evening's events. This wasn't an isolated cyberattack. As far as she was concerned, anything internet-connected was now compromised.

Li Na Wen felt defeated. Despite her best efforts, her team had *failed.* She knew that the world's most talented computer experts would be brought in to do damage control. And she knew that they, too, would fail. A cold sweat gripped Li Na Wen. She turned on her heel and shoved out the door.

I have seen enough.

Moments later, the door to the control room had been locked. Several CIR members had assumed the position of sentry outside. There would no doubt be a jurisdictional showdown with all the arriving authorities. Wen wanted no part of it. As far as she was concerned, her usefulness in the crisis had expired. *The experts are on their own*, she thought, staring out at the foreboding racks of servers.

Wen again looked at Zhao's slumped form. Forensics had arrived and were now in the process of tagging evidence. By all appearances, Olivia Chen had risked her life in order to sabotage the MSS' containment efforts and help the billionaire fulfill his misguided plans. But she had also followed through with her directive to stop Zhao and had even put a bullet through his forehead. Nevertheless, Olivia had caused nothing but problems on this night, and her involvement in the creation of the AI itself was indefensible.

Olivia Chen will pay for her part in this.
I will make sure of it.

CHAPTER 71

OLIVIA WATCHED THE TECHNICIANS in a trance, feeling like she was watching an apocalyptic movie play out in slow motion. The events of the previous twenty-four hours all began rushing back to her: Tso's phone call, the image of Kohler's lifeless body, the attack at the Monastery, Zhao's betrayal.

It was all for nothing.

A wave of grief overcame her. Olivia could no longer curb the swelling emotion. She felt it dragging her under, like a riptide towards the sea.

I need air.

She ran for the door, pushing past a mass of bodies in the control room. She sprinted down a server aisle, nearly colliding with two arriving officials. She sidestepped the men and kept running until she arrived at the exit. She flung open the door and plunged outside. Her lungs heaved, fresh, cool air filling the tight spaces in her chest.

Olivia immediately turned her gaze skyward, absorbing the crushing weight of all that had transpired. She could still see Zhao's lifeless eyes gazing up at her from the server room floor. Her mind replayed the horrific scene over and over in rapid-fire progression. The kick of the gun as it discharged. The sound the bullet made when it penetrated his skull. The way his body went slack before crumpling to the ground.

Lang Zhao is dead.

Far more tragic, though, was the knowledge that she had been the one to end his life.

I killed the most brilliant human on the planet.

Amid the chaos of spinning police lights and the rushed footsteps of arriving media and forensics teams, Olivia felt a paralyzing loneliness. Her partner was dead, and now her mentor.

I'm sorry, Lang, you left me no choice.

She thought back to the night two years prior, when she had made a simple mistake that had changed her life—a knock on the wrong door.

While attending an industry event at The Ritz in San Francisco with her colleagues, Olivia had gotten swept up in the lavish party. Feeling a little prosecco-tipsy, she inadvertently went to the wrong hotel room. While fumbling with her keycard, which she assumed had become demagnetized, a man had answered the door.

"Well, this is unexpected," he'd said. "Hello, Ms. Chen."

Olivia stepped back in surprise. That man had been Lang Zhao.

But what had surprised her even more was what came next. Instead of turning her away, he had *invited her in.*

When Alexander Tso had hired Olivia, she knew only of the Lang Zhao that the media had portrayed: arrogant, impulsive, and bull-headed. At that time, she hadn't spoken so much as a word to their famous CEO. After the painful loss of his child and his very public subsequent divorce, he had mostly kept to himself, occupying himself with his business ventures. But after accepting his invitation, Olivia would come to find out that the larger-than-life billionaire was like no other human she had ever met. He was witty, engaging, warm, and, quite simply, magnetic.

They had stayed up well into the night discussing not only her work but also his startling views about the future. She was drawn to his intellect and his bold idealism. He dared say aloud what others only dreamed of. She felt herself being drawn in—his energy spreading like a contagion through her every cell.

She knew in that moment that her life would never be the same—that with Zhao's backing, CyberGen would change the world. A smile crossed her lips as she recalled the happy memory. But just as quickly, it disappeared, replaced by the painful weight of reality.

What have we done?

Olivia crumbled to her knees in tears.

CHAPTER 72

THE CYBER INCIDENT RESPONSE team members were in full panic mode as Adrian slipped quietly out of the control room. He stumbled into the hallway, nearly colliding with a visibly shaken Olivia.

"Adrian!" she said. She threw her good arm around him, burying her face in his chest.

Adrian froze, caught off guard. After a moment, he wrapped his arms gently around her. "You okay?"

When she finally lifted her head, Olivia's eyes were flooded with tears. "I needed some air."

"Yeah, me too."

"I'm so sorry, Adrian. About everything. I never meant for any of this to happen."

"Olivia, you didn't release this technology. Zhao did."

"True, but I did *create* it." Olivia drew a long breath. "If I don't end up in a Chinese prison, I will probably be put on trial by the international authorities for endangering the public. I could spend the rest of my life in jail—or worse."

"You've done nothing wrong, Olivia."

"I'm not sure the technology ever should have been created. I thought . . ." she said, sobbing softly, "that we could moderate it . . . control it. I was wrong."

"I see your concerns," Adrian said, "but let's not jump to conclusions?"

"Look at all the damage that has already been done!"

"True, but this technology could also do a lot of good; you said so yourself?"

"Perhaps . . ." Olivia said, her voice heavy with emotion. "Assuming its goals are aligned with ours."

"You did everything you could. Everything anyone could."

Olivia gave him an exasperated look. "We did," she said. "But there is no way to ensure that the AI's goals reflect human values—which vary across geography and culture and evolve over time. If I overlooked even one minor thing in my coding . . . or if the AI takes unanticipated steps to achieve what seems like a straightforward goal . . ." She broke eye contact, her voice trailing off.

In the distance, Adrian could hear the sound of approaching footsteps.

"Adrian," Olivia said, her voice barely above a whisper. "What is going to happen now?"

Considering the catastrophic turn of events, Adrian could not fathom what was in store for either of them. They had done all they could to help in an impossible situation—but who knew if the authorities would see it that way.

"We are going to tell them everything we know," he said.

"And after that?"

"I wish I knew." Adrian could now see the outline of two arriving officials.

Olivia visibly tensed.

"Listen, Olivia," he said more forcefully now. "I know you have been through a lot, and are scared, but the only thing that matters now is where we go from here." Adrian stepped forward and folded his hands around hers. "All anyone cares about now is containing the AI. And they will need your help to do it."

"I'm scared."

"You don't have to face this alone," he told her. "I'll be here every step of the way."

A uniformed PLA officer approached them. "We need to go."

"A second strike?" Adrian said, feeling a swell of panic.

"No—protesters," the armed forces officer said. "An anti-technology group. They are trying to force entry. They're threatening to sabotage the building's cooling system."

Adrian and Olivia exchanged an uneasy glance.

"We need to evacuate immediately," the agent said.

A moment later, alarms started to sound. Adrian stayed rooted to the spot.

"Come on," Olivia said, tugging at his sleeve. "We need to go."

"What about them?" Adrian said, gesturing towards the CIR team still at work in the control room.

"They have decided to stay," the officer declared, looking uncomfortable. "If the mainframe gets destroyed, all the data will be lost."

Olivia tugged at Adrian's sleeve again.

He hesitated another moment, looking anxiously at the control room. Then he grabbed Olivia by the hand and sprinted towards the exit.

CHAPTER 73

THE FIRST HINTS OF dawn peaked over the horizon as Adrian and Olivia burst through the exit of the Tianjin Supercomputing Center. Outside, the rain had finally subsided. Adrian could hear the shouts of protesters coming from the front of the building. Thankfully, the PLA officer had taken them through a side exit, where several other officers met them. The men immediately ushered them to a pair of armored vehicles waiting by the curb.

A uniformed driver emerged from one of the vehicles. "Mr. Pryor?"

"Yes?"

"I am sure you are tired," the man said. "The U.S. Embassy has made arrangements for you in Beijing."

Adrian cocked an eyebrow. "Did you say the *U.S. Embassy*?"

"Yes, sir. That's what I was told."

A weary Adrian blinked several times, trying to process the news. "Wow...thanks."

A moment later, the door to the second vehicle swung open. "Ms. Chen?"

"Yes?"

"We will need you to come with us," the driver said, gesturing to the second SUV. "We have booked you on a flight to Tokyo this morning," the man explained.

"Tokyo?" Olivia said.

"The international authorities have convened an emergency symposium in Tokyo. To discuss a coordinated response to the events of last night."

"But—" Olivia said weakly.

"Your attendance is mandatory," the man said.

"She stared up at him, looking distraught. "Am I under arrest?"

"No, ma'am. But there will be time to discuss all that later. Right now, you are needed in Tokyo."

Adrian watched the exchange, feeling a surge of emotion. He suddenly realized that this would be goodbye.

"I'll give you two a few minutes," the driver said, slipping into the front of the vehicle.

After a long moment, Olivia turned towards Adrian. "I wish you could come with me."

"I'm not sure I have much to add," he said. "I don't think 'blackballed NSA hacker' counts for much. I'm not exactly a pillar-of-the-community type."

Olivia gave him a pitied look. "You don't think the rest of the world believes all that nonsense in the news, do you?"

Adrian chuckled, his lips spreading into a boyish grin.

Olivia met his gaze, suddenly looking serious. "I am so grateful for your presence last night, Adrian."

He stared at the computer scientist. "Even if we failed?"

She gave him a puzzled look. "Adrian—we stopped Zhao. And we kept the AI out of the hands of government and greedy corporations." She stared up at him with tears in her eyes. "Whatever happens . . . it's in the hands of the public now."

A long silence settled between them. Without warning, she reached up and kissed him softly on the cheek. "Thank you," she said. "I couldn't have faced this alone."

Adrian pulled her towards him, sweeping her into a warm embrace. "You are stronger than you think."

A single tear fell from Olivia's eyes, streaking her cheek. "I'll miss you."

"Right back at you, Chen."

Olivia spun on her heel and walked alone towards the waiting SUV. She shot a final look in Adrian's direction before climbing into the vehicle and heading off to face what he could only assume would be the greatest challenge of her career. Adrian prayed that she could find a way to do the impossible.

If anyone could do it, it was Olivia Chen.

CHAPTER 74

THE LAST THING LI Na Wen saw as the chopper banked away from the supercomputing center was something she would never forget. High above the rooftop, like a signal of cosmic distress, a blazing pyre of flame erupted from the center of the building. The fire shot upward, instantly engulfing the top level of the building. It flared brighter and brighter, seeming to rage for all the world to bear witness.

A few moments later, the outline of the computing center disappeared from view entirely, shrouded by the conflagration. Whether it had been struck by a missile or fallen to the protesters was impossible to tell. The last thing she saw was a cloud of smoke spiraling skyward over Tianjin.

An hour later, Wen had set up a temporary command post at State Council Headquarters in Beijing. Her phone buzzed with near-constant reports of the evening's events from BBC, Al Jazeera, China News, and the Associated Press. They hadn't gotten all the particulars right, but in broad strokes, it was all there for the world to see. News of a failed nuke. The presence of the international Cyber Incident Response team. The internet was blowing up, besieged by shock and wild speculation.

The MSS Director had just received word of an emergency symposium to take place in Tokyo in several hours. Representatives from the Americas, Russia, Africa, Europe, the Middle East, and Asia were already en route. Wen herself was scheduled to fly to Tokyo shortly.

There was a knock on the door, and a young man on the State Council staff peered in. "Ma'am? I've brought you some tea and something to eat."

"Many thanks," she replied. "Just find a spot over there." She gestured to the far corner of her desk, currently the only spot not overrun by administrative paperwork.

The young man complied and then quietly padded back to the door from which he had arrived. He stopped in the doorway. "Oh, one more thing, Director."

Wen lifted her gaze wearily. "Yes?"

"We have just gotten an update from Tianjin. The AI," he said, "they think it may have already corrupted systems as far as Shanghai."

"I was afraid of that. What about our systems here?"

"They are showing no signs of tampering yet, but we are recommending intensive screening across all essential government, healthcare, and industrial infrastructure platforms to ensure they remain operational."

"Get it done," Wen said without hesitation. "Immediately."

"Yes, ma'am."

"I want an update ASAP."

The young staffer shifted uncomfortably. "Unfortunately, it could take weeks."

Wen rose abruptly. "I beg your pardon? Did you say *weeks*? That's completely unacceptable!"

"With all due respect, ma'am, this is all very fluid. It could be months or even years before we discover how the AI has impacted our systems . . . and what it might do to them."

Wen closed her eyes, inhaling heavily. "Out!" she said. "I have work to do."

"One other thing, Director."

"What now?" she said, collapsing into the chair behind her desk.

"We have just gotten word from the CIR team. They made it out safely before the explosion. I thought you would want to know."

"Yes, of course. Thank you."

The staffer retreated silently. Wen exhaled, grateful for the moment of silence. She reached for the plate of steamed buns on her desk, staring out of her office window at the the city lights. She was about to take a bite when a loud rattling caused her to jump: her cell phone vibrating against the desk.

She sighed, feeling suddenly exhausted. Then she reached down and pressed the speakerphone button to connect the call.

"Director, it's Adrian Pryor."

Adrian sounded equally weary.

"Yes?"

After a protracted silence, he spoke. "I understand you are heading to Tokyo soon?"

"That is correct," Wen said.

"The situation," Adrian said delicately, "will require that we all work together."

"Yes," she said patiently. "I'm afraid we will need all the help we can get."

"I think I know who can help," Adrian replied after a long silence.

One of his colleagues at the NSA, no doubt. Wen immediately soured at the idea of some American having access to classified Chinese systems. *No thanks.*

"I'm sure you have heard by now that Ms. Chen has been sent to Tokyo?"

Wen felt her irritation mushroom at the mention of Olivia's name. Olivia Chen would have already been arrested if it were up to her. "Forgive me," she snapped, "but I think Ms. Chen has already *helped* enough!"

"Listen," Adrian said, his tone even. "She is the only person alive who knows how the AI works. We need to listen to her."

Wen bristled. Olivia Chen had done nothing but lie to her and impede her investigation since she had arrived.

"Director?" Adrian's voice drew her back. "Can you still hear me? Olivia wanted to prevent this outcome as much as you."

"Ms. Chen has made it abundantly clear that she wanted no such thing!" Wen replied, her voice rising an octave.

"Olivia took the actions she did for her own reasons, Director. She didn't want to help Zhao. Quite the opposite—she wanted to destroy the program."

A harsh laugh escaped Wen's lips. "She has a funny way of showing it."

"Listen, Director—" Adrian said, his voice unwavering. "There are things you don't know."

"Do enlighten me," she replied.

"When Olivia discovered that Zhao had stolen her source code, she was horrified. You see, she'd had a personal relationship with Zhao for two years. He was her mentor. So, the betrayal wasn't just a professional one for Olivia—it was personal. When she found out what he was planning, she decided she must destroy the program, not release it."

"So why not work with her own government?" Wen said.

"She considered the technology so dangerous that she didn't want anybody to gain access to it, especially a powerful government. Don't you see? Olivia has been trying to protect us."

"By undoing what she did in the first place?"

"Exactly!" Adrian said, apparently unmiffed by the irony of his words. "When the MSS arrived at CyberGen, Olivia was terrified. She immediately wiped the contents of her hard drive and set out to destroy the copy of code that Zhao had in his possession."

Wen swore under her breath, still fuming at the woman's impulsive actions. "Having a copy of the code could have saved us months of work and trying to understand what they created and how to neutralize it."

"I know you are upset with her, but we have to consider that Olivia Chen may be the only person alive with a clear understanding of what we are up against."

The prospect of mitigating an advanced AI seemed hopeless. The battlefield was enormous, and their opponent was likely to anticipate their every move . . . to outwit them at every turn.

What roguish future has Zhao unleashed? How will humans fare when we are no longer the dominant species?

"Director?"

Adrian's voice drew her back to the present.

"Did you hear me?"

"What are you proposing, Mr. Pryor?"

"Let her help."

"I'll consider it."

"That's all that I ask."

Wen hung up, feeling irritated and overwhelmed.

What is waiting for me in Tokyo? Who will take the fall for this?

Wen suddenly realized what her subconscious was trying to do with Olivia—to make her a convenient scapegoat. But would Wen herself, instead become the state's sacrificial lamb for not having prevented the catastrophe?

And most importantly, how on earth would they possibly fix this?

CHAPTER 75

B.J. STRAUSS SAT RAMROD straight in a holding room at the regional MSS bureau complex. He stared blankly at a television playing a grainy black-and-white video of Chinese Communist Party history. In the corner, two rifle-toting guards wearing military camouflage stood watch.

Strauss had been relocated to the bureau complex an hour earlier, passing through a 15-foot-tall concrete wall ringing the building, humming electric wire, and face-scanning turnstiles.

Despite having overheard the news that the imminent nuclear threat had passed in Tianjin, Strauss felt uneasy. He was still waiting for word on the situation at the supercomputing center. But equally important, he was starting to be concerned about what would happen to him.

I cannot let the MSS take me into official custody.

On the flight over, the Ministry of State Security agents had offered little information. Judging by the panicked tone onboard, Strauss sensed that the AI containment had failed. *Zhao has gone through with his plans.* Before he had time to process the implications, an abrupt rap on the holding room door caused Strauss to jump. The guards exchanged startled looks.

Outside, authoritative voices began shouting in Mandarin. Finally, one of the guards moved towards the door and heaved it open. Three uniformed People's Liberation Army officers shoved past the guard and entered. Two additional officers remained outside, blocking the entrance. "Mr. B.J. Strauss?"

"Yes. That is me."

"We are here under orders from the Central Military Commission to take you under arrest. You will be transported to Qincheng maximum-security prison, where you will wait to stand trial."

"On what charge?" he said incredulously. "I have done nothing illegal!"

"You'll have to take that up with The Ministry."

One of the officers handed him a thin stack of papers bearing a red seal. "Arrest warrant. You will come with us now."

Strauss skimmed over the document and then lifted his gaze to the smaller man by the door, who appeared to be in charge.

"This is preposterous! Call Director Wen," he demanded. "I have been cooperating with her all night."

"There's no need for that."

"Pardon me?" Strauss said. "Why in God's name not?"

"I'm afraid Li Na Wen is responsible for ordering your arrest."

"That's not possible!" Strauss shouted. "She had every opportunity to arrest me earlier!"

"I'm afraid that Director Wen was a little preoccupied at the time," a second officer replied. "The fact remains that you are charged with colluding in an international cyberterrorism plot on Chinese soil."

"Not to mention conspiracy to incite insurrection, harboring two fugitives, attempting to procure a weapon of mass destruction, and impeding an MSS investigation . . ."

"Should we go on?" The officer removed a set of handcuffs from his pocket.

"Don't you know who I am? Call my attorney!"

Moments later, Strauss was being herded through a crowd of gaping onlookers as they made their way outside. One of the larger officers muscled Strauss into the backseat of a waiting PLA van. Seconds later, the van raced away from the complex down Zhujiang Road.

Five minutes passed in silence. Strauss kept his eyes on his window, mentally cataloging street names, buildings, and other landmarks as they passed. *Where are they taking me?* The road was headed towards a river now, and he could see the lights of a low-slung bridge ahead. The driver abruptly slammed on the brakes, jerking him forward. The van skidded to a halt in the middle of the bridge.

Without a word, the driver slipped from the vehicle. He came around to the passenger door. Strauss felt a surge of fear as the officer opened the door. The communist regime had a long reputation for intolerance when it came to crimes against the state. *Will I even get a fair trial?*

The driver quickly surveyed their surroundings before removing Strauss's handcuffs and helping him out of the vehicle.

What the hell?

Seconds later, a black sedan screeched to a halt on the opposite side of the bridge. The back door opened, and before Strauss knew what was happening, the men shoved him into the backseat. Right after the door had slammed shut, the sedan shifted into gear. Within seconds, the PLA van was out of sight, and Strauss was headed in the opposite direction.

After a moment, the driver spoke. "Mr. Strauss, I was sent by your father."

Strauss met the man's gaze in the rearview mirror.

"There is a duffel bag with cash, new identification cards, and a passport under the passenger seat. You will also find an airline ticket and a change of clothes."

"My father?"

"Is well connected," the man declared. "Arrangements have been made for you to travel to the Solomon Islands."

"Thank you," he stammered, feeling stunned. He lifted the duffel bag from underneath the seat and placed it beside him. Inside, he found the travel documents, as promised. He reached for the airline ticket.

One way to *the Solomon Islands.*

This was always going to be a one-way trip, he suddenly realized. *I can't go back to Geneva.* Strauss was suddenly overcome with emotion. He felt grateful to his father for arranging his extraction from the country, but he wasn't sure he deserved it. *Zhao carried out his plan. And he hadn't been able to stop him.*

Strauss now noticed a second slip of paper that had been paper-clipped to his ticket. He slid the paper out from behind the ticket and was surprised to find a personal note.

```
B.J. – The world is watching. DeepThink has made
arrangements for your asylum. It's best that I do not
know where. Thank you for everything. I know you tried
your best to avoid this outcome. Hopefully, we will
see each other again.
With my sincerest gratitude and love.
-Dad
```

Moments later, they arrived at Binhai International Airport. Strauss shrugged out of his clothes, replacing them with joggers and a hooded sweatshirt. He exited the van and joined a crowd of pedestrians headed towards the terminal.

Strauss strode into the terminal and disappeared into the crowd. *The Chinese authorities will never understand my motivations,* he convinced himself. *I was only trying to help.*

He followed the signs towards the terminal. A departure sign for the Solomon Islands marked his gate.

It's not far enough, he thought. But then again, B.J. Strauss Jr. doubted any corner of the earth was far enough to escape this.

CHAPTER 76

FIFTY THOUSAND FEET ABOVE the Sea of Japan, Olivia Chen sat onboard a Chinese Xi'an Y-20 military transport plane. She gazed out the window, lost in thought about all that had transpired in the last thirty-six hours. Olivia's head was pounding, and the roar of the jet engines rattled at the base of her skull.

For the first time in her life, Olivia feared for the future. At some level, she wondered if she was resisting the inevitable.

Technology *disrupts*. Societies *change*. Economies *adapt*.

So it had gone through all of human history. In this case, the only difference was the rate of change: the speed of light. Disruptive, sudden change seemed to be the only constant. Only one obvious question remained.

Can humanity adapt fast enough?

Perhaps the age of human drudgery was coming to an end. Maybe the time when we rely on our own limited cognitive powers for decision-making is over. After all, where had it gotten us thus far? Were we really any better off than our ancestors? Or was history doomed to repeat itself?

Olivia shuddered, finally arriving at the same conclusion that Zhao must have.

We evolve or die.

99.9% of species eventually go extinct. It was a scientific fact, and absurd to think that humans would be any different.

But there was one thing that gnawed at her. As a scientist, Olivia knew that extinction was an attractor state: a magnetic pull to which nearly all species eventually succumbed. But there was another state, also an attractor, on the other side of the balance beam. No species had reached this state, but there were no laws of science that prevented it.

Species immortality.

For the first time, Olivia let her mind imagine the impossible. Would self-directed evolution free humans from our frail biology and usher in a different kind of existence? One where carbon yielded to silicon? Where unburdened by physical needs, we could reach higher levels of self-actualization?

And even if it did, at what price?

She cringed, wondering what Andreas would make of all of this. For Olivia, it raised an important question: were humans meant to play god? To manipulate the laws of science at our whim? The question, of course, would result in a spiraling rabbit hole of spirituality and personal beliefs. As her mind slowly emerged from the deluge of troubling thoughts, one thing had become clear to her. Misguided as his actions may have been, Zhao was right.

Our survival isn't guaranteed. We must fight for it.

Moments later, the hum of the jet engines induced a much-needed sleep that had thus far eluded her. *Rest now*, Olivia told herself as she drifted off. When we land, an uncertain future awaits.

CHAPTER 77

THERE WERE NO LESS than a hundred media personnel below the conference room of Tokyo's Big Sight Convention Center, standing shoulder-to-shoulder behind the steel barricade the local police had erected. Their TV cameras, currently banned from the proceedings taking place in the upper conference tower, were aimed skyward. Locked in their sights were the four inverted titanium and glass pyramids making up the 6500-ton upper conference tower.

Strobes flashed as Olivia Chen stepped up to a podium at the front of the room. Now wearing a fashionable blazer and with her hair neatly tucked into a chignon, Olivia looked every bit the part of an esteemed computer scientist. She wished she felt half as good. She steadied herself on the podium and took a deep breath, preparing to address her audience: a cadre of government leaders and technology experts that had begun to convene over the last hour from every corner of the globe. Olivia stared at the assembly of powerful strangers. All eyes were on her.

She cleared her throat. "Good evening. I am not sure how to begin, so I will get right to the point," Olivia said. "Advanced AI has been discussed hypothetically for some time, but most people believed that the technology was still decades away. A common misconception."

"Every obstacle and failure, from self-driving cars that crashed, to chat-bots that went off-script, to image recognition algorithms that couldn't tell the difference between a chihuahua and a blueberry muffin, all cast doubt on the likelihood of achieving a truly intelligent AI. Skeptics likened worrying about such a prospect to worrying about intergalactic pollution."

"But we were wrong," a woman in the front replied.

Olivia immediately recognized her as one of the Cyber Incident Response team members from Tianjin. "Experts have warned about things like job loss to automation, algorithm bias, increasing wealth disparity, misinformation, and privacy concerns," she continued. "But these are all short-term problems. They won't matter if we can't solve the larger crisis at hand." She scanned the room again. "We are an *endangered species.*"

Olivia waited while strobes flashed again, this time from inside the room. Several members of the audience had begun recording on their mobile devices. She gritted her teeth. After a moment, she continued. "I know we have a lot to discuss, but before we continue, there are some things that I need to say." She smoothed her hair, tucking a stray lock behind her ear.

"For years, Lang Zhao tried to sound the alarm on advanced AI. But rather than listen, people labeled him an alarmist, a nut," she accused, her voice full of emotion. "As leaders in the field, we can no longer deny that our way of life is under attack. We are a species on the brink. Unless," she ventured, "we can evolve in unexpected ways . . . in drastic ways." Olivia waited a breath, silently surveying the room's occupants.

"I am not alone in my thinking," she continued. "Many organizations have concluded that advanced AI could intentionally or unintentionally cause great harm to humanity: The Future of Life Institute, The Cambridge Center for Existential Risk, and the Berkley Center for Human-Compatible AI, to name a few. Until recently, anyone who sounded the alarm on these things was labeled an alarmist or, worse, a Luddite. No one has dared engage in meaningful conversations about the threat of advanced AI or the most obvious solution to the problem."

A man in the front row raised a hand to object, but Olivia didn't yield. "All Lang Zhao ever wanted was to ensure the survival of future generations. To give them a fighting chance. For that, he was shunned and labeled a fear mongerer. But I think it's time we have to open our minds to the changing specter of our humanity—to embrace the uncomfortable truth that a future worth living may come at a price."

Olivia felt a warm tear run down her face.

A familiar voice from the back of the room cut the silence. "Ms. Chen, I'm afraid on this, we agree."

Li Na Wen stepped forward. The Director's words took Olivia by surprise.

"Let me be clear—there is no shortage of people who are outraged by the actions you and Zhao have taken," The Director declared. "But the fact remains that our species is facing a serious existential crisis—one that we can no longer ignore. If we do not find a way to evolve alongside this technology, to accelerate our own evolution, we may as well admit defeat now . . . and surrender to a future as domesticated house pets . . . or worse."

Olivia agreed. The challenges facing humanity were only likely to get worse. Each technological leap comes hand-in-hand with a quandary of how to best use it. In recent years, it had become apparent that the internet has allowed companies to partake in nearly unregulated surveillance capitalism, that social media has been used to influence elections, and that our personal privacies have come under attack. So, the question remains: are we using technology, or is it using us?

The prospects are troubling, to say the least. Technology is progressing so fast that we can't keep up, let alone regulate it in a meaningful way. Despite the best of intentions, scientists are creating technologies that may drastically change the course of life . . . and our place in it.

"Like it or not, Olivia, your actions have forced our hand," Li Na Wen continued. "Based on what we now know, we have realized that trying to reverse Zhao's actions is futile."

"I agree," Olivia acknowledged in a pained tone.

"When this meeting concludes, we will face a media shitstorm. I have no doubt that the first question I will get will be if there is a way to neutralize the AI," Wen said. "Based on my understanding, that doesn't seem likely, but I'd like your thoughts on the subject, Olivia."

"It depends on what you mean by *neutralize*?" she replied. "Let me be clear—there is no undoing what has been done. Even if we could, it would only be a matter of time until someone else reached the milestone. Our time would be best served trying to ensure that the AI's motivation system is aligned with human interests."

"I couldn't agree more," Wen said. "Which is why we are tasking *you* to do just that."

"Excuse me?"

Wen spoke slowly. "The international authorities have agreed that the information you possess would be extremely helpful in preparing a mitigation strategy to deal with the crisis. But—," she paused a long moment before continuing, "we have yet to address an important issue—your role in bringing the crisis to bear."

Olivia folded her arms over her chest, bracing herself for the consequences of the sweeping devastation that had occurred as a result of the AI's release. But Wen's words surprised her.

"Ms. Chen—we are prepared to offer you amnesty."

Olivia stared at The Director, dumbstruck.

"Under one condition, that is."

"Anything," Olivia said. "What?"

"On the condition that you agree to work with the international officials to create a collective for the advancement of beneficial AI," Wen announced. "No one on Earth has a better understanding of the algorithm—how it was designed, created, and trained."

Olivia fell silent. Feeling guilty again. But also feeling hopeful for the first time. Perhaps this was her chance to redeem herself. To find a path forward.

"I would be honored," she finally replied.

Her mind drifted to the work ahead. It would be the greatest challenge of her career, in no small part due to one seemingly insurmountable hurdle: how would they ensure the AI's interests were aligned with their own?

"So, what next, Ms. Chen?"

This time, the voice came from somewhere else near the back. Olivia now noticed a woman seated behind a camera in the far corner of the room. She wore a "PRESS" lanyard. A red indicator light flashed on the camera. Olivia felt silly for not noticing it earlier. Of course, the conversation in this room was being recorded and would no doubt be released to the public. Olivia doubted the world was ready to hear it, but she stared directly into the camera and spoke her truth all the same.

"Human-AI integration makes intuitive sense. The only scenario where humans become less vulnerable is a world in which millions of people control and understand a little piece of the world's aggregate AI power—because they are integrated with it. The AI will be so widely distributed and varied in its goals that we are less likely to lose control."

Her eyes darted around the room.

"But time is of the essence. The pace and direction of progress matters a lot. We must be able to shape the AI into a 'friendly' AI, and we must be able to integrate ourselves before a single, all-powerful agent emerges. Once the genie is out of its bottle, crossing the threshold to superintelligence, it will be too late."

"We need to wrap up," Wen interrupted. "But there is one more thing."

"What's that?" Olivia said.

"I've just gotten news about Zhao's estate," Wen announced.

At the mention of Zhao's name, Olivia was suddenly overcome with emotion.

"At the time of his death, his estate was valued at nearly $600 billion. It appears his will listed a single beneficiary." She paused a long moment, allowing her to mull over the enormity of the news. "It's *you*, Olivia."

Olivia felt a warm flood of tears on her face. "Lang Zhao has done more for humankind in his four short decades than most people ever will. He deserves a proper funeral. Whatever is left, I will donate to the collective for beneficial AI."

The room had remained silent during the exchange, every set of eyes riveted to the two women at the center of the crisis, no doubt processing the heaviness of the changed future.

Then, a new voice rose from somewhere in the front row. "Ms. Chen, before we go, I can't help but wonder . . . Do you think the future is one worth saving?"

Olivia looked at the faces surrounding her. She pictured their children and grandchildren and all the generations that would follow.

"Unequivocally."

Chapter 78

ADRIAN PULLED A STARK white down comforter over his head as the first rays of sun spattered through the window of his luxury Beijing hotel room. He had been escorted to the city by a representative from the U.S. Embassy immediately following the crisis. When he finally pulled himself from the comfort of the 1200 thread count linens, he glanced at the clock, apparently having slept a full ten hours after checking into the hotel and collapsing in exhaustion.

Adrian made his way to the bathroom, where he was pleased to find a high-end steam shower. He made full use of the luxury amenity, letting the hot mist infuse every inch of his body. The water came down in a rhythmic patter, washing away the tension of the previous night's events. He knew the relief was only temporary. He, along with the rest of the world, would soon have to confront the troubling consequences of the previous day's events.

Adrian wrapped a white terry-cloth robe around his damp body, feeling momentarily re-energized. He pulled the room service menu from its binding and proceeded to order a large bowl of seafood dumplings, wok-fried rice, and vegetables. It was strange how much better he felt after meeting his most basic human needs: rest and nourishment. Sometimes, the greatest pleasures in life were the most *human* ones.

While he ate, Adrian flicked on the large television against the far wall. As expected, the events of the prior evening now monopolized every news station. Across the world, questions abounded. There was no shortage of speculation about how things would unfold now that the AI was out.

For many people around the globe, it would be the first time they would hear the terms *Artificial General Intelligence* and *the Singularity.* And most, he was sure, wouldn't yet comprehend the implications for the future.

Watching the deluge of talking heads, Adrian couldn't help but feel that the only thing that seemed certain was *uncertainty* itself.

Thankfully, early reports indicated that essential municipal services had been restored in most cities. Unfortunately, disorder still abounded. Insurrectionists had jumped on the opportunity to incite further chaos. To exacerbate the problem, social media had been weaponized—used for massive disinformation campaigns. So even when panicked citizens could get a reliable signal, the information on the web only caused more confusion. Adrian could only speculate who, or what, was behind the misinformation.

Zhao's funeral had been scheduled for the following week in Shanghai, where he was to be interred beside his son. It was sure to attract people by the tens of thousands. The silver lining was that the majority of his vast fortune had been left to Olivia. Zhao had accumulated more personal wealth than anyone in history. At the time of his death, his estate was valued at close to 600 billion and could be used to fund research for AI safety.

Olivia must be so relieved.

A computer-generated voice echoed through the room, drawing Adrian's attention back to the television. A steady stream of news clips assaulted him, whirring across the screen faster than he could process them. A photo of the late Steven Hawking had materialized on the screen, his robotic voice proclaiming, "The development of full artificial intelligence could spell the end of the human race." The prediction, it appeared, had been made some four years before the death of the famous physicist.

Hawking's mechanical voice was replaced just as quickly by another man, apparently broadcasting from the side of the highway next to a hearse. "We must consider it our most serious mission to keep science innovation out of the hands of bureaucratic fear mongerers and autocratic elites, who might prefer to skip evolutionary advancement in order to maintain their status quo of power and uphold their faith-driven convictions." The man was identified as the head of the Transhumanist Party.

He was followed by an elderly priest broadcasting from the Vatican. "By undermining religion, artificial intelligence undermines what it is to be human."

Seconds later, a viewer's response flew across the top of the screen: "The science sounds pretty cool to me. Who wouldn't want to live forever?"

The image was replaced by a professor of epistemology from Oxford. "Once upon a time," the professor was saying, "humans relied on tribal knowledge and their own limited cognition for survival. I would be shocked if anyone still makes decisions independent from AI assistance a year from now."

A young man declared on the street, "I am a Transhumanist, and I emphatically disagree with stopping the progress of science in any way unless it is explicitly harming people. Science compels humans to take this as far as we can."

Seconds later, a professor of anthropology from Columbia University appeared. "Unless we can find a way to bring the AI in line with human interests, we are doomed to being treated with the same reverence that we treat intellectually inferior species—killing for sport, killing unintentionally, killing for food or resource acquisition, or because it stands in the way of an unrelated goal."

Astrophysicist Michio Kaku, appearing on the BBC, declared good-naturedly, "By 2100, our destiny is to become like the gods we once worshipped and feared. But our tools will not be magic, wands, and potions, but the science of computers, nanotechnology <and> artificial intelligence..."

Another religious figure added, "Abrahamic faiths believe that the human body is a God-given temple, not to be tampered with, except by the Almighty. In fact, in the Bible, blasphemy, trying to become God, is the only sin that is not forgivable."

Listening to the onslaught, Adrian felt as if the floor was coming out from under him.

Chaos.

Division.

Life-altering change.

As everything he ever thought he knew began crumbling around him, he wondered if Lang Zhao may have been right. Had the time come to face the changing nature of our humanity? Would survival itself necessitate drastic action?

Feeling overwhelmed, Adrian clicked off the television. His mind drifted to Olivia, who had by now arrived in Tokyo at the emergency symposium, where she would be taking heat from leaders from across the globe. Although it may be months or years before the full scale of the implications was understood, one thing had become clear to Adrian. As Victor Hugo once said, "No army can stop an idea whose time has come."

Adrian stared out the window at the vibrant display of life in downtown Beijing and considered the words. Regardless of the seeming futility, he prayed that humanity would do just that—*assemble an army.*

CHAPTER 79

EIGHT HOURS LATER, WITH the assistance of the U.S. Embassy, Adrian Pryor was zipping north on an Asiana Air hyperjet back to New York. It would be the first time he would set foot on American soil in over a year. Having heard of Adrian's extraordinary role in taking down the rogue AI, the feds had issued an immediate pardon, welcoming him back to the U.S. with open arms.

Onboard the jet, Adrian was absorbed in a 100-page debriefing document that the international authorities had provided. The document painted a decidedly concerning picture of the future—one where the fundamental structure of modern social, political, and economic systems would come into question.

Already, citizens and insurrectionists were demanding a "sweeping restructure" of antiquated socio-political systems. Several nation-states had already begun discussing the merits of an AI-assisted governing body and a universal basic income for its citizens. Adrian couldn't help but think it was a shortsighted mistake. Only time would tell.

One thing had become painfully clear to him. A technology that could easily exploit the infrastructure and networks on which we have become so reliant threatens our current way of life at the most fundamental level—how we transact financially, protect private and classified information, as well as how we communicate, work, and even entertain ourselves.

If we are going to survive and thrive, everything must change.

Adrian gazed out the window and wondered what the future held. For him. For his country. And most importantly, for his fellow humans.

Now somewhere above the Arctic, he had to shield his eyes from the stunning brightness outside his window. Below the aircraft, vast sheets of sparkling ice glittered in the light of the setting sun. It stretched so far it seemed to reflect the whole sky and all the stars in it.

For a moment, Adrian felt completely alone in the universe. The sun was receding from sight, racing westward towards the horizon until he was confronted only by a vast darkness.

Then the light was gone.

Adrian had the strange urge to turn the plane around and to chase the setting sun—to feel its warmth and to bask in the comfort of the familiar. Instead, he felt as if he were staring into the face of a dark, uncertain void.

Perhaps, he realized, the only way forward is to plunge headfirst into the dark. After all, if one wants to reach the setting sun, the quickest path is not to speed west, chasing the fading rays, but to continue east, plunging into the darkness until reaching the light again.

Adrian was suddenly overcome with emotion. He thought of the courageous woman who was now in Tokyo, confronting the realities of a changed world. Humanity, he realized, has the power to choose the course of our future. After all, everything that civilization has to offer is a product of human intelligence. When amplified by the tools that AI may provide, there is no telling what we might achieve.

But we have to get it right.

Adrian knew he didn't have any of the answers about what the future held, but he had no doubt that the events of the last forty-eight hours would ignite a global debate about the future, the soul, even calling into question what it means to be human itself.

The stakes couldn't be higher, and Adrian knew that this precise moment in time would be a critical moment in history, perhaps determining the course for all the hundreds of billions of future humans to come.

Would these technologies help us to realize our full potential? To live long and meaningful lives before dying peacefully in a supernova at the ripe old age of a billion?

Or would they instead doom us to a future of mining lithium at the behest of whip-bearing Boston Dynamics bots and their Doberman companions?

Adrian's professional opinion?

Someone should probably do something.

For now, he slid a set of headphones into place and turned up the volume on the great Gloria Gaynor.

> *Did you think I'd crumble,*
> *Did you think I'd lay down and die?*
> *Oh no, not I; I will survive.*
> *Oh, as long as I know how to love,*
> *I know I'll stay alive.*

Those were the last words Adrian heard before he drifted off into the catharsis of sleep.

Acknowledgements

I would like to extend my deepest thanks to the following individuals:

First and foremost, to my husband, for his enthusiasm and encouragement, and tireless hours spent discussing story ideas, plot holes, agents, editors, and the publishing process. Without your support, I would not have crossed the finish line. Truly.

To my parents, for always holding me to a high standard and giving me the tools to succeed. Thank you for slogging through early drafts and always providing honest feedback. You have my deepest love, gratitude, and respect.

To my developmental editor, Andrea Hurst, whose thorough and insightful critique helped guide and shape this narrative into the best version of itself.

To my line editor, Wes Miller, for his razor-sharp skills, superb instincts, enthusiasm, and most of all, for understanding what it is I am trying to accomplish with this story.

To my talented cover designer, Sarah Hansen, for bringing my vision to life.

To Julie Harvick, web guru, for making me look cool online. And more importantly, for giving my book a proper home on the web.

To my two little carbon copies, who helped with things like title and cover selection, as well as just generally supporting mom when her side-project became a full-time job. I will never forget the small humans running around the house before bed yelling "The Doomsday Code," twenty-seven times in a row.

Over the last five years, a wide array of scientists, researchers, and organizations have begun to bring AI safety issues to the forefront. I would like to express my deepest appreciation for the work they are doing, especially those which specifically informed or inspired my story:

To The Future of Life Institute, whose tireless efforts are making headway in AI safety and regulation. Thank you for helping educate and shape a better future, for my children, and all the children to follow.

To Lex Fridman, MIT researcher and podcast host whose incredible long-form discussions about science, technology, philosophy, and the nature of intelligence helped inspire and inform this story. I will never tire of listening to supremely interesting humans having supremely interesting conversations.

To The Future of Humanity Institute and The Centre for Effective Altruism, for your tremendous efforts in education and advocacy of Longtermism. Future generations will thank you. (I like to be an early adopter.)

To Tim Urban, the stick figure behind Wait But Why, whose blog post entitled "The AI Revolution: The Road to Superintelligence" is still the most thorough, witty, and engaging piece I have read to date on the subject. It was a tremendous influence and source of inspiration. (You should read it.)

To The Center for Human Compatible AI, for its work shaping AI towards provably beneficial systems.

And to all my friends, family, early readers, and anyone who did not laugh in my face when I told them I wanted to "write a Michael Crichton thriller." Thank you for believing in me. It is all the small conversations and words of encouragement that kept me going. I couldn't have done this without you.

And most of all, to anyone reading this now. My sincerest thanks for taking a chance on me and my novel. Without an audience, a story is just words on paper. Thank you for letting me share my story.

If you enjoyed The Doomsday Code,
please consider leaving a review here:

My sincerest thanks.
Reviews really help new authors.

If you would like to be the first to hear about upcoming
projects, releases, and special promotions, please
subscribe to my newsletter:

ABOUT THE AUTHOR

SARA YAGER built a successful ten year career in the semiconductor industry before leaving to raise her children full-time. With a unique perspective as a mother and former tech professional, she brings a fresh and insightful voice to the world of speculative fiction.

She came up with some of her best concepts for The Doomsday Code while waiting in the elementary school pickup line. She lives in Scottsdale, Arizona. This is her first novel.

www.sarayager.com

 sarayager sarayagerauthor sarayagerauthor

Made in United States
Troutdale, OR
11/13/2023

14560831R00202